"Why are you here? Is everything okay?"

Taylor stared at Rayne in astonishment. *Did she really just ask me that? After all these months without a word?*

Looping her arm through his, Rayne wore a tight smile. "Where are my manners? Misty, this is my husband, Taylor Carrington." Giving him a sidelong glance, she asked, "Why didn't you tell me you were coming, honey?"

Honey. What was she up to? He decided to play along. "It wouldn't be a surprise if I'd told you."

"I'm glad you could," Misty said. "Rayne told us you're thinking of moving to the island."

Rayne shuddered.

"Really?" He looked at her. "I thought you were going to hold off on saying anything."

"I saw my family and couldn't wait to spill the beans. Sorry."

Misty adjusted her apron. "I need to get back to work. Taylor, it's wonderful meeting you."

When Misty disappeared through the double doors, Taylor turned to Rayne. "What kind of game are you playing?"

Dear Reader,

Don't you just love Christmas? This is a special holiday in our family because the emphasis is on celebrating the birth of Christ. During the holiday season, we also celebrate family and friends who are important to us. *Twins for the Holidays* is the fifth book in the Polk Island series. It was inspired by my love of secret-baby and marriage-of-convenience tropes.

The Christmas season is always magical on Polk Island, where the residents cherish family, community and traditions. If you've read the previous books in the series, then you've met members of the Rothchild family. In *Twins for the Holidays*, Rayne Rothchild returns to the island after a twenty-year absence. The reunion she had in mind is threatened when Taylor Carrington shows up with divorce papers and no knowledge that he's the father of twins.

I hope you will enjoy Rayne and Taylor's attempts to navigate parenthood and their future as a couple. Put on your favorite Christmas music, grab snacks and prepare to experience a Rothchild Christmas on Polk Island.

Thank you for your support as always.

Jacquelin Thomas

HEARTWARMING

Twins for the Holidays

—

Jacquelin Thomas

HARLEQUIN
HEARTWARMING

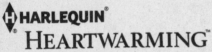

ISBN-13: 978-1-335-47557-2

Twins for the Holidays

Copyright © 2023 by Jacquelin Thomas

Recycling programs
for this product may
not exist in your area.

This is a work of fiction. Names, characters, places and incidents
are either the product of the author's imagination or are used fictitiously.
Any resemblance to actual persons, living or dead, businesses,
companies, events or locales is entirely coincidental.

For questions and comments about the quality of this book,
please contact us at CustomerService@Harlequin.com.

Harlequin Enterprises ULC
22 Adelaide St. West, 41st Floor
Toronto, Ontario M5H 4E3, Canada
www.Harlequin.com

Printed in U.S.A.

Jacquelin Thomas is an award-winning, bestselling author with more than fifty-five books in print. When not writing, she is busy catching up on her reading, attending sporting events and spoiling her grandchildren. Jacquelin and her family live in North Carolina.

Books by Jacquelin Thomas

Harlequin Heartwarming

A Family for the Firefighter
Her Hometown Hero
Her Marine Hero
His Partnership Proposal
Twins for the Holidays

Love Inspired Cold Case

Evidence Uncovered
Cold Case Deceit

Visit the Author Profile page
at Harlequin.com for more titles.

PROLOGUE

"Ooooh…" RAYNE ROTHCHILD moaned softly as she slowly opened her eyes. She felt the subtle stirrings of what would become a throbbing headache; even her attempt to sit up sent a dull twinge spiraling through her brain. A muddled memory of the previous night entered her mind.

The Carrington Luxury Cars team and special guests were on hand to celebrate the opening of their new location in Las Vegas. After the other employees had gone, Rayne stayed behind to direct cleaning staff and pack up left-over gift bags. She and Taylor Carrington, the owner of the company, had finished off a bottle of champagne. Rayne was a complete lightweight when it came to alcohol.

When the fog cleared from her vision, Rayne's first clue that something was amiss was her surroundings. She wasn't in her own room; she could tell that much as her eyes traveled to the floor-to-ceiling windows offering a panoramic view of the Vegas Strip and the opulent furnishings…she was in the penthouse suite.

Rayne's body stiffened as her gaze strayed to the foot sticking out from under the rumpled sheets. It clearly belonged to a man. She eased her own foot out of the bed, placing it on the floor, then turned slightly.

"Noo…" Rayne uttered, biting her lip in dismay while her heart pounded an erratic rhythm.

As if on cue, Taylor opened his eyes, and she found herself staring into his intense gray gaze. He seemed just as surprised to see her.

He shot upward to a sitting position. "W-what…"

"We clearly had too much to drink," she blurted out while pulling the sheet up to cover herself. Rayne couldn't believe that she'd ended up in bed with Taylor. Her boss.

"Rayne, I…I'm sor—"

"Taylor, stop," she said, cutting him off. "You don't need to apologize. You didn't take advantage of me. This is all self-explanatory. We had a lot to drink…one thing led to another."

He nodded in agreement. "I wish I knew what to say to you right now. It's not enough to say that I got caught up in the celebration. I…"

Taylor's voice was filled with what sounded like regret.

"Um…" She had just noticed something even more alarming. "I think we should be a little more concerned about what happened *after* the celebration." Blood pounding in her temples, Rayne held up her left hand, displaying a plain gold wedding band.

Taylor swallowed hard. "Where'd you get t-that?"

"You're wearing a matching one."

He glanced down at his left hand, then looked at her. *"We're married?"*

Rayne retrieved a piece of paper off the night-stand. "According to this document…you're my husband."

"I think it's coming back to me," he uttered, placing a hand to his forehead. "We rode around Las Vegas in the hotel limo. I saw a chapel and asked the driver to stop. We got out and went inside."

Her breath quickened and her cheeks became warm, burning in remembrance. "I remember," she said quietly. "Taylor, we've made a terrible mistake. I'm perfectly happy just being your executive assistant. I think marriage is great, but I've never considered taking the matrimonial route."

Taylor eyed her in surprise. "You've really never dreamed of getting married? I know you've said that before—I just didn't think you really meant it."

"Nope, I've never given it any thought. It was the truth."

"I guess I figured that most women your age want husbands," Taylor stated.

"I'm twenty-eight, but I'm not desperate for a man," Rayne responded. "I've been perfectly happy in my singleness. Especially after I realized that I have terrible taste in men. I'm a magnet for all the bad ones."

"I don't agree with you on that. Especially since you're my wife… Wow, I can just imagine the office grapevine spreading all kinds of rumors about us."

"No one has to know about this," she said. "We can quietly dissolve this marriage, then move on as if nothing ever happened. I'll find out what we need to do to get out of this mess."

"I feel like I should be offended that you're in such a hurry to divorce me."

"Why?" Rayne inquired. "You know that you're just as relieved that we're on the same page. The last thing you want is a wife."

"You're right," Taylor stated, relief evident in his tone.

Ignoring the headache, Rayne slipped out of bed, wrapping the sheet around her body. "I'm going to get dressed and get out of here."

"We're both mature adults. There's no need to be embarrassed. You don't have to rush off. We need to come up with a plan to fix this."

Rayne walked briskly into the bathroom, closing the door behind her.

Her embarrassment turned to raw fury. "Another mistake in a long line of mistakes... When are you going to stop this?" she asked herself. "I thought you'd learned your lesson by now." Rayne found her purse beside the sink and pulled out a bottle of aspirin and a small packet of pills. After tossing a couple aspirin into her mouth, she prayed they would work fast. Her head was beginning to throb from the pain.

Rayne stepped into the shower, too upset to really appreciate the spa-inspired bathroom. It was the reason she had booked this particular suite for Taylor.

Twenty minutes later, she walked out of the bathroom completely dressed. "It's all yours," she said. Her long hair was slightly damp and reverting to its naturally curly state. She removed her phone from her clutch. "I'll be in the living room."

"I ordered breakfast for us." He said the words tentatively as if testing the idea. "Better to figure this out on a full stomach. If it comes before I'm out, just have them add it to the room."

"Will do," she responded, although eating was the last thing on Rayne's mind. The dull headache refused to dissipate despite the pain medication, which only added to her frustration. How could they have allowed this situation to happen? She began to look up legal options for them.

"One of us will have to stay in Vegas for six weeks before we can get the divorce," Rayne announced when a fully dressed Taylor exited the bathroom fifteen minutes later.

"Okay," he responded, rolling with her plan as he often did. He always trusted her opinion. "I think it's best that you stay here in Vegas. You can work remotely and check in periodically with the new dealership to make sure they have everything they need," Taylor stated. "I'll rent an apartment for you, then come back in a couple of months, and we'll dissolve the marriage. After that, our lives will be back to normal, and we can forget about last night."

Rayne couldn't explain why she felt this way, but the unease in the pit of her stomach indicated that while he might get back to normal, life would never be the same for her.

CHAPTER ONE

Eleven months later...

RAYNE STOOD OUTSIDE the double doors of the Polk Island Bakery & Café. She rubbed her arms, trying to erase the slight chill she felt. It was mid-November, and despite the bright sunshine, the air was a bit nippy. Pulling the folds of her coat together, Rayne swallowed her uneasiness before going inside.

Seventeen years ago, she'd been dragged out of these very doors kicking and screaming by her mother, leaving their family and their home behind. Rayne glanced over her shoulder, taking in her surroundings, hoping to regain a sense of familiarity. Her gaze landed on the clothing boutique beside the restaurant.

A woman leaving the café held the door wide open for Rayne to enter.

"Thank you," she said, pushing the double stroller inside.

Rayne's eyes traveled around the cozy restaurant, noting that a lot had changed since the last time she'd been here. However, some things were familiar, like the rustic holiday theme that incorporated earth tones instead of the traditional red decor. Small lanterns and candles with wonderful Christmassy scents were placed on every table. A huge Douglas fir stood guard in the back of the café, adorned with ornaments made of wood, rattan and clay, all of which had been crafted by local students.

Rayne recalled her aunt Eleanor's annual tradition of inviting the kids to an ornament-making class on the Saturday after Thanksgiving. Kids all over the island used to look forward to the delicious lunch, laughter and fellowship as they designed an ornament for the café and one to take home. She remembered how she looked forward to making holiday ornaments with her friends and family.

Rayne stood near the door, wondering if her aunt had taken the day off. From what she remembered, Eleanor Rothchild Stanley always circulated the dining room, making sure her patrons were happy and enjoying their food. If there was the slightest complaint, she'd personally take the food to the kitchen and come back with a replacement. Her aunt took pride in making sure her patrons left the café satisfied and full.

"Hello," a woman cheerily greeted her as she walked up to the counter.

Rayne noticed the faded jeans she wore were the same brand as the ones she was wearing and felt an instant kinship with her. Her dark mass of curls was held to the nape of her neck with a ponytail holder.

Oblivious to Rayne's intense scrutiny, she asked, "Are you dining in?"

"Actually, I'm looking for someone," Rayne stated. "My aunt Eleanor. She owns this place."

"Aunt Eleanor retired about eight years ago after she was diagnosed with Alzheimer's. I'm Misty Rothchild...Leon's wife."

"Oh, wow. My mom mentioned that he'd gotten married..." She shook her head, then said, "I'm sorry. My name is Rayne. Rayne Rothchild. I left the island a long time ago."

Misty broke into a welcoming grin. "I've heard Leon and Trey talking about you. Your mother is Carol, right? Aunt Eleanor's youngest sister."

Rayne gave a nod at the mention of her mother. "Yeah, that's my mom."

"It's very nice to finally meet you," Misty said as she came from behind the counter to give Rayne a hug. "How long has it been since y'all moved away?"

"About seventeen years." Glancing around,

Rayne said, "I can't believe Aunt Eleanor actually retired. I remember how much she loved this place. I see she expanded to add a bakery."

"She did that a couple of years before she retired," Misty responded. "She and Rusty—do you know Rusty?"

"My mom mentioned that she married him. I'm glad. I could tell that he was in love with her even back when I was younger. Does he still own the appliance store on Walnut Street?"

"He does. I know Leon and Trey are going to be ecstatic that you're in town," Misty said. "Aunt Eleanor, too."

Rayne grinned at the mention of Trey's name. She loved both brothers, but she had been particularly close to Trey growing up. She'd missed both her cousins tremendously. Their childhood had been marked by tragedy—they'd been raised by Aunt Eleanor after their parents died.

Misty glanced over at the sleeping babies bundled under layers of blankets. "Oh, you have twins. May I see them?"

"Sure," Rayne said, pushing the blankets away from their faces.

"Oh, my goodness," Misty murmured. "They're adorable."

"Thank you," Rayne said. "That's Ian in the red cap, and Ivy is in the white."

"A boy and a girl. Congratulations."

Rayne didn't know what Misty had been told, so she decided to be upfront about her position in the family. "In case you haven't heard, my mom and I happen to be the black sheep in the Rothchild clan."

Meeting her gaze, Misty responded, "I don't believe that, Rayne, and I assure you no one in your family thinks of you in that way."

"It's true," she insisted. "That's the way everyone looked at us. It's one of the reasons why I've stayed away for so long. I needed to work on myself…get my head in the right space. I'm hoping we can all sit down and finally come back together as a real family." Rayne hope they would accept her back into the fold.

"Well, I'm thrilled to meet you, and I know everyone is going to be so excited to have you back home. I know that Leon and Trey have truly missed you and your mother."

Rayne wasn't so sure this was true. But she knew that her mother reached out to her oldest sibling from time to time. She and Eleanor had been close, long ago.

"How many children do you and Leon have?" Rayne asked.

"We have two girls and a boy. My oldest girl is not his biological daughter, but he loves her as much as he does our other two."

She smiled. "That's Leon. He's always been about family. Now Trey...he was always a flirt."

"You know he's married and has a child as well, a little boy."

Rayne's eyebrows rose in surprise. "Whaaaat... Trey got married? I had no idea." She never thought he'd ever settle down.

"I'll be leaving here shortly," Misty announced. "Why don't you come home with me? I'll make dinner and invite everyone over."

"Oh, no, you really don't have to go to any trouble for me." She was a little afraid of facing them all at the same time. Rayne didn't want them ganging up on her. She knew they'd have questions, but she wasn't emotionally ready to handle all that just yet.

"You're family, Rayne. We want to celebrate your return to Polk Island." Misty led her over to a table near the window. "In the meantime, would you like something to eat?"

Her gaze traveled to the display case. "I see you still have banana nut muffins—is it Aunt Eleanor's recipe?"

"Yes. Her muffins are addictive and still very much a local favorite."

"When I was little, she would always have one for me before I went to school," Rayne said. "It was the perfect start to my day. I still can't believe she retired. I know how much she loved this place."

"She still does," Misty responded. "She comes in a few times a month. I suspect she's checking on me."

Smiling, Rayne stated, "Now that sounds like the Aunt Eleanor I remember."

"What would you like with your muffin?"

"Hot chocolate."

Misty grinned in approval. "A girl after my own heart. We're going to get along great."

"Thanks for being so welcoming. I have to confess I wasn't sure what to expect when I arrived. Especially after the way we left."

"You're family," she said simply, then headed for the kitchen.

Rayne's eyes bounced around the dining area once more. She was truly glad to be home. Her gaze traveled to the sleeping infants. *My sweet babies. You deserve a family, and I'm going to make sure you have that. You're going to have what I didn't.*

A young girl brought the muffin and hot chocolate to the table.

"Thanks," Rayne said. She took a bite of her muffin and groaned. It was definitely her aunt's recipe. She lathered on more honey butter.

Despite everything, it felt good to be home. When Misty was ready to leave thirty minutes later, she said, "Okay, so everyone is coming to the house around six."

"Did you tell them that I'm here?" Rayne asked.

"They don't know a thing. No, not even Leon," Misty responded. "I think we should surprise them."

"My car is right outside. I'll follow you to your place."

Rayne noticed that Leon and Misty didn't live too far from her aunt's former home. She reduced her speed as she looked out the passenger-side window. Whoever lived there now had clearly done some renovations, but her aunt's signature rosebushes were still in the yard. Rayne always loved that wraparound porch. She recalled the huge Boston ferns that used to hang down on either side of the front door and how she used to try to jump high enough to touch the bottom of the pots.

The entire drive took less than fifteen minutes.

She parked across the street per Misty's instructions.

"Where are you staying?" she asked as she assisted Rayne in taking the sleeping twins out of the car.

"I was thinking of asking Aunt Eleanor if I could stay with her."

"I'm sure she wouldn't mind, but you're more than welcome to stay with us," Misty told her.

Rayne followed her through the garage entrance and into the house.

"I appreciate that. However, we should probably wait and see how Leon feels about all this."

"He'll agree. I'm sure of it." Misty gave her a warm, welcoming smile.

Rayne glanced around. "Your house is beautiful."

"Thank you," she responded. "Leon and I had some renovations done. We enlarged the kitchen and added a screened-in patio complete with ceiling fans, a fire pit and a television."

She led Rayne into the family room, which had been transformed into a whimsical winter wonderland. Crystal decorations and silver and gold orbs dangled from the ceilings. Oddly, an all-white Christmas tree was decorated with lights but no ornaments.

"Decorating the tree is a huge deal in our house," Misty explained. "We make a party out of it. We'll probably do it right before or after the Christmas festival."

"Oh, wow," Rayne exclaimed. "I used to love the festival. I looked forward to it every Christmas."

The wintery theme carried over into the dining room, with snowmen and reindeer napkin rings around white cloth napkins. An elaborate centerpiece featured holly and four lanterns in silver, gray, ivory and tan.

Rayne walked into the family room and pointed to the photographs on the mantle of the fireplace. "Are these my little cousins?"

"Yes. That's Talei," Misty said, pointing to a silver frame. "This is Fawn, my youngest, and that's Leon Jr. We call him Leo."

"They're so beautiful." Rayne picked up another framed photo. "This must be Trey's son."

Misty nodded. "That's Trevon."

"He looks just like the way I remember Trey, although he was older."

"We have a guestroom down here, so I'll put y'all in there," she told Rayne. Her tone was firm and friendly. "You can get settled, because you're staying with us. I know Leon won't have a problem with it."

"Thank you, again."

"I look forward to getting to know you." Misty glanced down at her watch, then said, "I need to run out to pick up my babies from school and day care. Make yourself comfortable."

She left Rayne alone in the guest bedroom.

While Misty went to pick up her children, she sat on the edge of the bed thinking about

Taylor and everything that had transpired since their unplanned marriage.

Rayne left Las Vegas after a pregnancy test confirmed her suspicions. She sent Taylor an email stating that she was resigning effective immediately. Rayne didn't disclose her pregnancy because she knew that he had zero interest in being a father. She was the product of an unmarried mother and wanted a different outcome for her children. Her father had made it clear that he wasn't interested in her. She couldn't keep their existence from Taylor, but if he didn't want to be in their lives—she would rather he never met them.

She glanced out the window when she heard the garage door rolling up. Misty was back.

"Hello." A little girl with two long braids appeared in the doorway a short while later. "My mama said we had a special guest, and I wanted to meet you. Nobody else is supposed to know you're here until dinner."

Rayne smiled. "You must be Talei."

Playing with one of the braids, she nodded. "What's your name?"

"I'm Rayne. Leon...your daddy is my cousin."

"So, you're my cousin, too." Pointing to the infants, she added, "They're my little cousins. Can I see them?"

"You sure can. They should be waking up soon for a bottle."

"I'll be real quiet," she whispered. "I'm happy I have more cousins." Talei tiptoed over to the crib. "Babies sure do sleep a lot."

"I'm told that it helps them grow. Why don't you sit and talk to me for a while?"

"I don't want to wake them."

"How old are you?" Rayne asked.

"I'm ten," Talei responded. "I'm in fifth grade."

"I bet you're one of the smartest in your class?"

"There are some really smart people at my school, but I do my homework and Dad makes me study every day. I guess that makes me kinda smart, too."

Grinning, Rayne said, "I remember those days. Don't forget that learning can be fun, Talei." As the words came out her mouth, she realized that this was something her mother, the assistant principal would say.

She was suddenly reminded of how Carol had been so against her coming back to the island.

They heard a whine.

"Ian's waking up," Rayne said. "I see Ivy's stirring, so she'll be awake soon."

Talei watched as she picked up each baby, placing them in the center of the bed. "I do like learning—I just don't like boring stuff. You know...science and math."

"Yeah. Those weren't my favorite subjects, either. So, what do you do for fun?"

"I dance. I perform at powwows, and I just started taking ballet classes."

"I used to study ballet. How do you like it?"

"It's okay," Talei responded, "but I like pow-wows better than ballet recitals."

"I went to a powwow once," Rayne said thoughtfully. "It was a beautiful and spiritual experience. I had fun, and I learned a lot about Native Americans."

"I'm Native and Black," Talei announced proudly. "Cherokee."

"That's fascinating."

"Can I help you with the babies? I helped my mom with Leo and Fawn." Rayne was capable of handling both babies but didn't want to refuse Talei.

"I would appreciate your help." Rayne pointed to the infant in blue. "This is Ian, and that's my little girl, Ivy."

"They're sooo cute," Talei gushed. "I looove babies."

"Could you take two bottles out of the diaper bag, please?"

"Do they need to be warmed? 'Cause if they do, I can have Mommy help me."

"I have a warmer in the bag. I'll set it up, and you can put the bottles in it."

Talei grinned. *"Wado."*

"What does *wado* mean?"

"Thank you."

Rayne smiled. "I like that. And you're welcome."

"What's your husband's name?"

She swallowed hard. Rayne hadn't expected this question to come from Talei. "His name is Taylor."

"Is he coming here, too?"

"No, he isn't," she responded.

She released a soft sigh of relief when Talei returned her attention to the babies. Rayne hoped the rest of the family would avoid asking too many questions about Taylor. She didn't have many answers.

Together, she and Talei fed the babies while making small talk. After Rayne changed them, Talei cuddled with Ivy until the baby fell asleep. Ian, in Rayne's arms, went down minutes later.

Shortly after six o'clock, Rayne heard the garage door going up and stole a quick peek out the bedroom window.

Her heart pounded faster.

Leon was home. Talei carefully placed Ivy back in the stroller then raced out of the room to meet him.

Minutes behind him, another car pulled into the driveway. Her eyes teared up when she glimpsed her aunt Eleanor with Rusty.

Her mother's flight with her from the island had angered Rayne because she had never wanted to leave her family behind. She'd been witness to her mother's interaction with her father's wife. It had been ugly and embarrassing, but they shouldn't have run away in shame. Carol had since explained how her family had turned against her—against them—and Rayne had a better understanding of her mother's reasons for leaving. Carol refused any contact with her siblings except for Eleanor. But could this loving family really have turned their backs on Rayne as a child? She wasn't so sure now.

Rayne considered calling her mother to tell her about her plans to stay on the island, but quickly tossed out the thought. Maybe another day.

Carol was going to be furious with her, but it was a risk Rayne was willing to take. Their family had been close once—it was long past time for Rayne and Carol to come together with them again. This was one of her Christmas wishes.

She heard another car pull into the driveway.

Rayne broke into a grin when she saw that it was Trey.

She stole a quick glance over her shoulder at the twins. They were unbothered and sleeping peacefully. "You're going to meet your family," she whispered.

Rayne crossed the floor, easing over to the door, and pressed her ear to it, delighting in the sound of her family's laughter and lighthearted banter as they gathered in the living room. She couldn't wait to be reunited with them.

She soon heard Trey say, "Misty, what's up with you? You're walking around here grinning like you're busting with news to share. I bet I know what this dinner is about. I'm getting a new niece or nephew?"

There was a soft knock on the door.

She opened it.

"Mommy told me to come get you," Talei whispered. "They're gonna be so surprised."

Rayne picked up her twins, then followed Talei to the living room, where everyone had gathered.

"Surprise," Rayne said. "I'm back."

The room went silent for a moment. Everyone appeared to be frozen in their shock.

"Rayne..." Leon uttered. "Is that you?"

She nodded. "Yeah... It's me."

Rayne hoped that they were as thrilled to see her as she was to be with them. She desperately desired that this unexpected reunion would be a happy one.

"Chile, when did you come back to the island?" Eleanor asked.

"I arrived earlier today."

"Are those your babies?"

"Yes, ma'am," she responded. Her eyes darted around the room, landing on Leon and then Trey. Rayne was hoping for a sign of some sort that they were happy to see her.

"I don't know why I asked such a silly question. Gurl, bring them over here to me."

Her aunt relieved her of her son while Rusty took Ivy.

Leon walked over briskly and embraced her, holding her close. "Wow...this is a real surprise."

"I hope it's a good one."

"Of course." He gave her another hug, and the warmth of his arms around her reminded Rayne that she was finally home. "You have no idea how much we've missed you and Aunt Carol."

When Trey stood up, Rayne immediately saw something different about him.

He walked with the assistance of a cane.

Blinking back tears, she eyed him as she tried to imagine what could've happened.

As if he could read her mind, Trey said, "I'm fine. We'll talk later, okay?"

She gave a slight nod. "I'm so happy to see you."

"Same here," he responded with a smile. "It's about time you came home."

They embraced.

He introduced her to his wife and son.

"Gia, I think I remember you," Rayne said studying her face. She remembered a little girl with honey brown hair and hazel eyes. "Didn't you grow up here?"

"I did."

"You used to hang out with Leon. Back then, Trey was always picking on you."

Gia chuckled. "You have a good memory."

"I don't know if I agree with you on that. My recollection of events differs," Trey interjected. "I seem to remember Gia always in my face."

"Whatever..." she planted a kiss on his cheek.

Rayne laughed. "There was always some female in your face, but it wasn't Gia. Wait... I remember now. You had a huge crush on her."

"Did y'all see the wedding ring on her finger?" Trey said loudly.

She knew he was deflecting the conversation. "Really, Trey..."

"Rayne, did you get married?" Eleanor asked.

"And we didn't get an invite to the wedding," Trey interjected.

She gave him a narrowed, glinting glance.

He cracked up with laughter.

"Yes, ma'am, I'm married. We didn't have a wedding—that's why there wasn't an invitation."

"Is he here with you?" Leon asked.

"No, he's not. Auntie…the truth is that Taylor and I are separated. It's one of the reasons I came home. I want my children to grow up around family."

"Wait, are you moving back to the island?" Trey asked.

"I am," she responded. "Until this moment I didn't know what I was going to do, but yes… I want to raise the twins here."

"I'm so glad you finally decided to come home," Eleanor said. "This is where you belong, chile."

I hope you're right, Rayne thought silently.

Her eyes traveled around the room, studying the family that had gathered for the impromptu dinner. Leon was standing against the wall, looking at Misty as she cuddled Ivy. Rayne could literally feel the love for his wife radiating from him. Trey was seated nearby, playing with his son while Gia talked with Misty and Eleanor.

"Why are you standing over here by yourself?"

She looked over at Rusty. He'd dashed out

to the car to retrieve Eleanor's medication and had just walked back inside. "I've been gone a very long time. It feels a bit awkward."

"They're your family. Just dive right in," he responded. "They haven't changed a bit."

"You're right," Rayne said before excusing herself and walking over to Leon.

"You're a mother now...with twins...wow."

She laughed. "I can hardly believe it myself."

"Rayne, why didn't we hear from you?"

"To be honest, I had some growing up to do, Leon. I needed to get myself together—it took some time, but finally the lightbulb came on." She didn't tell him that her mother's experience shaped her opinion that they would never accept her unconditionally. She wasn't near perfect like them. Rayne had made mistake after mistake over the years.

"Well, whatever the reason, I'm glad to have you back."

"Rayne, how is my sister?" Eleanor asked. "I haven't talked to her in a while."

"Mama's fine." A thread of guilt snaked down her spine. Rayne stayed with Carol after finding out she was pregnant until she'd fully recovered from childbirth. She then up and left Texas, coming to Polk Island against her mother's wishes.

When her cousin Renee arrived, Rayne rushed over to hug her. "Oh, my goodness! What are you doing here? The last I heard, y'all had moved to New York."

"I live on the island," she responded. "I moved back here about four years ago. I own the boutique next to the bakery. My design company is based in Charleston."

"I can't believe it." Rayne could hardly contain her joy. She and Renee had always been close. In fact, she, Tray and Renee were inseparable.

Renee introduced the handsome man beside her. "This is my husband, Greg."

"Oh, my…all of you are married." Rayne held up her left hand. "So am I."

"Is he here…your husband?"

"No, unfortunately we're separated," she responded.

Renee smiled sympathetically."I'm sorry to hear that."

"It happens," Rayne responded. "At least I have my sweet babies."

"Where have you been?" Renee inquired.

"I was living in Los Angeles. I loved back to Texas when I found out I was pregnant." Rayne changed the subject by adding, "I read that you are one of the top up-and-coming designers. Congratulations. I'm so proud of you."

"How long will you be here?"

"I'm actually thinking about living here permanently," Rayne said. "After the holidays, I plan to look for a place to live and a job."

"That's wonderful. I've been trying to convince my brother to relocate down here, but he loves his life in New York."

They gathered in the dining room for dinner, where they made small talk while they ate.

Rayne hadn't laughed like this in such a long time. She'd really missed being around her family. She still resented her mother for taking her away from them.

After everyone left, Rayne walked into the family room, where Leon was watching television, and said, "I'd like to talk to you." She wanted to clear the air with him. She had always looked up to Leon and she really needed his support.

"Sure. Have a seat," he responded.

"Misty told me that it was fine to stay with y'all, but I wanted to check with you."

He seemed surprised by her words. "Rayne... you know you're more than welcome to stay here. You're my family. We have more than enough room."

"I really appreciate this, Leon. I intend to look for a job after the holidays and a place of my own."

"How long have you and your husband been separated?"

"To be honest with you, since I found out I was pregnant," Rayne admitted. "I realized really quickly that we weren't meant to be. Anyway, all I want to do now is raise my babies on Polk Island. I want them to grow up around family."

"You won't get opposition from me."

"Are you sure you're okay with two babies in the house?"

Leon nodded. "We love babies. I know Misty and Talei are going to enjoy having them here as well."

"Talei was a great help to me earlier. She's such a sweetheart."

"She helped when Leo and Fawn were babies. When they start walking and talking—she doesn't mess with them too much. I personally think it's because she can't get them to listen to her or do what she wants them to do." Leon reached for the television remote. "I'm sure you're tired, so I won't bombard you with questions, but at some point, I want us to have a conversation. A real conversation."

"We will," Rayne promised. "Thanks again for letting us stay."

"You don't have to thank me. Like I said… we're family."

As soon as she closed the door to the bedroom, Rayne released a sigh of relief. She should've known that her Polk Island relatives would welcome her with open arms. Despite what her mother had told her, the years apart hadn't changed that.

Rayne couldn't help but wonder how they would treat her if they knew the truth about her. She didn't want to find out.

SATURDAY AT ELEVEN in the morning, Taylor stood beside his friend Deacon as they awaited the start of the wedding, held in a beautiful cabin at Big Bear, complete with a burning fire and a tall spruce tree decorated in an array of red and gold Christmas ornaments. Lights throughout the cabin added to the holiday-themed ceremony. Fresh greenery was placed around the room and on the mantle of the brick fireplace.

He had been surprised to learn that Deacon and his fiancée, Nona, had decided to forego all the pomp and circumstance of an expensive wedding, choosing instead a simple and small service.

The harpist began to play.

The bride's sister, who was also her maid of honor, began her journey down the elegant staircase.

Nona then appeared in the doorway on her father's arm. She looked radiant in her simple gown, its velvety fabric perfect for a holiday wedding. Her locks had been styled in an elegant updo, accessorized with a pearl-and-rhinestone flower comb.

Taylor overheard Deacon's sharp intake of breath and smiled.

"She's so beautiful," his friend whispered. "And she chooses to marry me."

He thought about the wedding band that was hidden away in his drawer. No one knew about his marriage to Rayne, and Taylor wanted to keep it that way. He'd hoped to have the divorce finalized by now, but he couldn't file the petition without her signature.

He watched as Deacon took Nona's hand as they exchanged vows and rings.

Taylor was thrilled for his best friend. He smiled in appreciation of the commitment they'd just made. There was a small part of him that wished he could remember his own wedding ceremony.

The gathered friends and family clapped and cheered when the couple kissed. Love was in the air as if it were a special kind of electricity, intense and real. The melancholy that tried to overtake him during times like this was blocked out by his act of pretending it wasn't there. Still, it continued to call to Taylor softly, trying to pull him away from anything that brought him real joy, especially around the holidays.

After a myriad of photographs were taken, Taylor and the other guests ventured into another room where the air was filled with the fragrant scent of the orange pomander centerpieces on each table. The oranges, studded with clove, cinnamon and other warm spices, reminded him of his maternal grandmother's house. It was the only place he'd ever felt... safe. When she died, Taylor felt a part of him die along with her. It was a faded memory that had been revived by the aroma floating around the room.

After the bride and groom joined the guests for the wedding meal, they were served creamy tomato-basil soup with cheese on toast for starters. Guests had a choice of baked salmon, roast chicken or mushroom and cheese–stuffed ravioli for the main entrée, complemented with a rice pilaf and candied carrots. They dined on fruit tarts with clotted cream and toffee pudding served with hot espresso for dessert.

Deacon and Nona wanted their wedding elegant while keeping a warm and homey feel throughout, even in their choice of food.

The wedding cake was made by the bride's and groom's mothers, who owned a bakery together. It was all the couple's favorites together in different patterns and layers. Taylor presumed that every bite provided them a sense of home, security and nostalgic love—the bonds they both treasured.

For him, it was just cake. The melancholy Taylor felt was a cloak he couldn't just let take over his life. He tried not to hold on to the past so tight that he became cold and unfeeling, yet the pain of his childhood continued to cling. It was the anchor around his feet, the reason he couldn't seem to find the sunshine or that feeling of pure happiness that lived in other people's memories. Taylor wasn't a sad person; he'd lived much of his life in a space of contentment. He just wasn't giddy over family weddings and holidays.

When he'd had his fill of the romanticisms, well wishes and happiness radiating all around him, Taylor pushed away from the table and walked over to his friend. "Congratulations, again. I'm happy for you and Nona."

"You're not about to leave, are you?" Deacon asked.

He nodded. "Sorry, I'm going to head back to LA. I need to catch up on some paperwork. Enjoy your honeymoon."

Deacon grinned. "I really hope you can find the same happiness I've found with my love."

"Not everyone's that lucky," Taylor responded. "Go back to your reception."

He left because he didn't want to put a damper on Deacon and Nona's big day. Their happiness shined a bright light on the emptiness of his own life. Taylor couldn't help remembering the brief, startling moment when he'd first realized he and Rayne were married… The feeling of hope at the thought of a future with her.

CHAPTER TWO

Taylor sat in his Los Angeles office, staring at a months-old email from Rayne. Seven weeks into their marriage, he'd returned to Vegas so they could file the petition for divorce and found the apartment empty.

A week later, the email arrived.

Taylor,
I appreciate everything you've done for me, including the job as your executive assistant. However, I feel it's time to move in a different direction, therefore I'm resigning, effective immediately.

By now you have realized that I've left Las Vegas. Please understand that I have my reasons for doing so. Do not try to find me as I need time to process everything that's happened. I'll contact you when I'm ready to talk.
Rayne

After all this time, Taylor still struggled to make sense of her vague message. He wished he hadn't lost a great executive assistant, but mostly, he mourned the friend who had disappeared. He had no idea why she'd left.

He left the dealership shortly after seven o'clock and stopped at a restaurant to pick up dinner. He wasn't much of a cook, so Taylor usually ate out. In the past, Rayne would often take pity on him. She would either bring him meals or invite him over.

He and Rayne looked out for one another.

When Taylor pulled into his driveway, he spotted his neighbor on her porch. Despite being in her sixties, Alda loved technology. Her eyes were glued to her tablet.

"What are you watching?"

"A Christmas Gift," she responded. "It's just the sweetest romance movie."

"I don't understand what the deal is with these holiday movies. It's all fantasy."

"I love them," Alda stated. "I could watch them all year round because they make me so happy."

"But it's not real, Miss Alda," Taylor said. "Life isn't like that."

She clucked her tongue. "It's the possibility for me. I can't get enough of people finding love or their forever home and families being reunited. Movies like this fill me with hope. I wish Christmas was less commercial and more about making special memories instead of expensive gifts. You know…like making it about our gratitude, to respect creation and the earth…"

"Here we go…" Taylor responded with a chuckle. "You're about to get on your soapbox."

She laughed. "All I was going to say is that I wish the sense of Christmas was year-round. That we thought more of giving and less of receiving."

"Christmas is just another day to me," he said.

Alda eyed him in surprise. "Why is that?"

Shrugging in nonchalance, Taylor responded, "Because it's all I know."

He had spent his early years with parents who ignored him in favor of drugs and alcohol. When he was ten years old, his father beat him badly, breaking his arm. Taylor was removed from the filthy apartment and placed in a group home. During his time there, he hadn't experienced much hoopla when it came to Christmas. If the kids received a gift at all, it was one that had been donated from a local church. He was grateful he'd landed somewhere less dangerous, but he'd always wondered what it was like to grow up in a real family.

At thirty-one, Taylor no longer cared about such things. He preferred to spend the holiday serving food to the homeless. Every year, he donated a tree and gifts to the group home where he'd grown up because he wanted to make sure the kids there had a real Christmas—something he'd never experienced.

A FEW DAYS LATER, Trey and Gia returned to the house to spend some time with Rayne. Leon prepared a Caesar salad with blackened shrimp for lunch. Rayne couldn't help but notice how quiet the house was with the kids in school and Misty at the café. The sounds of the children's laughter, teasing, arguing—none of it bothered her. She relished the clatter of children underfoot. *It gives me something to look forward to, when my babies are walking, running and talking.*

After savoring a bite of shrimp, Rayne asked, "Leon, how much cooking do you do, since you're married to a chef?"

"We share the cooking," he responded. "I don't want Misty coming home to prepare meals for us after working all day. Sometimes she makes something there and brings it home, but we plan our meals and I help with the prepping."

"I see he hasn't changed at all," she said to Trey. Then she teased, "Leon, if you weren't my cousin—I'd marry you."

"Hey, don't sleep on me," Trey interjected. "Tell her, babe… I cook three days a week for you."

"He does," Gia confirmed.

Rayne wiped her mouth on her napkin. "Now I find that hard to believe. You never liked making a sandwich so I really can't imagine you cooking."

"That changed when I went into the military. I still enjoy eating, so I had to cook. I was a single man."

She laughed. "What? You didn't have women clamoring to cook for you in Oceanside?"

"They wanted me to cook for them," Trey responded with a chuckle.

When they finished eating, Gia said, "I'll clean up."

Rayne checked on the twins, who were asleep in the crib in the guest bedroom. She then joined Leon and Trey into the family room. She sat close to the fireplace to ward off the chill in the air.

"I still can't believe our long-lost cousin is back on the island," Trey said with a grin as he sat on the sofa beside her.

"I'm here."

"Did Leon tell you what happened to me?" Trey asked.

"You're the one who enjoys telling everybody's

business," she responded with a chuckle. "But seriously, you know he wouldn't do that. It's your story."

"I'ma let you have that, cousin." Trey took her hand in his own, then said, "My life changed during my last tour in Afghanistan."

"I gathered as much. You were injured."

"We were ambushed while on a peacekeeping mission. I lost my whole team and my legs."

Her mouth dropped open in shock. Blood pounded in her temples as she struggled to take in what he'd said. Finding her voice, Rayne uttered, "Both of them?"

He gave a slight nod.

Rayne's eyes filled with tears. "Does my mom know about this?"

"I'm not sure," he replied. "Aunt Eleanor sometimes forgets what happened to me. It's hard on her when I have to tell her all over again."

She couldn't stop her tears. "I'm so sorry I wasn't here for you. I…"

He gave her hand a gentle squeeze. "Don't cry. Don't… I'm good. In fact, I couldn't be better. I'm healthy."

"You do look good," Rayne said. "I just never expected to hear something like this. I knew you'd gone into the Marines. I feel terrible for not keeping in touch. I admire your strength and courage, Trey."

"Oh, I went through a real bad patch after it happened. I was angry, and I'd started drinking to dull the pain. Gia wanted to help me, but I even gave her a hard time. She wasn't having it—she pushed right back."

"Trey, I'm so sorry."

"Hey, I get it. You were out there doing your own thing. I actually tried to look you up when I was stationed at Camp Pendleton."

"I shut everybody out," she responded. "I'll never do that again. Leon did mention that it was your idea to open the Rothchild Museum. I think it's a wonderful idea. Polk and Hoss Rothchild left an incredible legacy behind. And now we can add to it. It's a wonderful way for our children to learn about our Rothchild ancestors."

Trey nodded in agreement. "We also renovated the Praise House—the church Polk built. We plan on rebuilding the house our parents were born in."

"I've got to go check everything out."

"I'm really sorry to hear that you're not with your husband," he responded. "But I'm really glad you decided to come be with us. Seventeen years is a long time to stay away from the people who love you."

"I can't tell you how happy I am to be back," she replied. "I'm so excited to spend the holidays with y'all."

"And we're glad to have you, Rayne," Leon said, joining them in the family room. "But what I'd really like to know is why you cut off all communications with us over the years. I know you were young when you and your mom left, but you knew where to find us."

Rayne had guessed this question would come up, and she was prepared to answer it to a certain extent. She didn't dare tell them everything. "I was a very angry person after Mama took me away from the island. I was a complete mess. I'm telling you—you and Trey wouldn't have liked me at all."

"You think we don't know how to handle you?" he responded. "You forget that we know all about that hot temper of yours. It wouldn't have fazed us."

"You couldn't have done anything so terrible that we wouldn't want you in our lives," Trey stated. "We all have been a mess of some sort at one time or another."

"I hope y'all can forgive me."

Leon gave her a level look. "There's nothing to forgive. You're home now—that's all that matters."

Rayne smiled at him. "Thank you for saying that. You didn't have to open your home to me and the babies, but you did. I appreciate it more than you know."

"How is Aunt Carol?" Trey questioned.

"She's fine," she responded tightly.

"I know she talks to Aunt Eleanor, but Leon and I haven't heard from her. We were kids back then, and it hurt to lose you both. We didn't have anything to do with the fight she had with Uncle Daniel and Aunt Maggie."

"Mama doesn't blame y'all. But to be honest, I think she's still really embarrassed that y'all were witness to all that drama back then."

Silence hung for a moment, and Leon seemed to decide to change the subject. "What does your husband do?" he asked.

"Taylor owns a car dealership. One in LA, and he just opened a second car dealership in Las Vegas."

"So he's out there, and you want to move here, right? What's your plan?"

She wasn't surprised by Leon's line of questioning. He had always been the most sensible of the three of them. Rayne found it comforting that he hadn't really changed much—just matured more. "I have money saved. It should carry me for the next six or seven months while I look for work and get a place of my own. In the meantime, maybe I could help at the café, especially over the Christmas holidays."

"You should focus on the twins," Trey said. "These months go by so fast."

Rayne picked up her phone when it began vibrating. "My first priority is my children, but I need to resume some sort of life. I can't just sit here and do nothing. I need to keep busy and earn my own way."

"Do you have any event-planning experience?" Gia inquired.

"I do," Rayne responded after checking her phone. She laid it back down. It wasn't important. "I did all the event-planning for my previous employer."

"We could use your help with the Christmas festival. Of course, it's a volunteer position. Two committee members had to resign due to family issues."

"That's perfect." Rayne was overjoyed that Gia would trust her with such an important event. Their acceptance meant the world to her.

"I don't want you to feel as if you need to rush," Leon said. "You're welcome to stay with us as long as necessary."

"I'm good," she responded. "I can take care of myself and my babies."

"What about your husband?" Leon inquired. "He's helping you financially, right?"

"No…" she said, trying to formulate a better response.

The expression on Leon's face clearly showed his disapproval. "He should be helping you with the twins at least."

"I don't want his help," Rayne blurted. "I don't need Taylor's money. This is my decision and it's final." Rayne's tone brooked no argument. She wanted her cousins to respect her wishes.

They had no idea that Taylor didn't even know about his children. Leon and Trey would never understand, so she didn't bother discussing this with them.

TAYLOR LEFT THE conference room after a meeting with his employees. He passed by the desk of his new executive assistant, granting her a tiny smile. Brenda was decent at her job but wasn't nearly as personable or efficient as Rayne. He silently chided himself for comparing her to the person who'd held her job previously—it wasn't right. He'd known of Brenda's shortcomings in the position but hired her anyway. In truth, she performed her job fairly well, but she wasn't Rayne.

As much as he tried to shut off his feelings where Rayne was concerned, Taylor couldn't escape his longtime struggle with rejection and bitterness. In both his professional and personal life, Taylor had thought of her as a friend and confidante, although there were parts of his life he didn't share with Rayne.

But if their friendship had been genuine—Rayne wouldn't have just left the way she did, without a real explanation.

Taylor wanted answers.

He'd replayed the last time they spoke before she disappeared so many times.

What did I do?

Taylor couldn't think of a plausible reason for Rayne to cut off all communication with him. And then there was the matter of the marriage. Initially, she was just as adamant as he was about dissolving what they both knew was a mistake. So, what changed?

Taylor had hoped to hear from Rayne at some point, but after eleven months of nothing, he was convinced that she wanted nothing to do with him. But if that was the case, why hadn't she been eager to sign the divorce papers?

He couldn't proceed without her signature, so Taylor was intent on finding Rayne. He was ready to put an end to their marriage. Only then could he move on with his life.

Taylor had hired a private detective to help him locate her. He'd recently discovered that Rayne was in Dallas. He'd left several messages for her with her mother, but they went unanswered.

Brenda knocked on his open door. "You wanted me to remind you about your meeting with Meridian Bank. It's coming up at two."

"Thanks." Taylor said. "I'll leave in a few. Traffic might be busy on that side of town."

"I've scheduled this Friday morning for the tree-trimming, and I ordered breakfast for the staff from Danny's."

"That's fine. Thank you," Taylor said.

"Did you want me to purchase gifts for the staff on your behalf?" Brenda asked.

"No," he answered thickly. "Everyone knows that I don't participate in the holiday festivities and gift giving."

She couldn't hide her surprise at that. "Oh, I had no idea."

When Brenda left his office, Taylor turned on his computer. As he'd done so many times over the past year, he pulled up the photographs from the party in Vegas. There were several of Rayne.

She was a hard worker and really knew how to throw a great party. Not only was she beautiful, Rayne was also smart and creative. He had always praised and rewarded her for her job performance. And he'd tried to be a friend to her when she desperately needed one. Taylor stuck by her during a very dark moment in her life.

So why did she leave me?

He settled back in his leather chair. *I'm not giving up. I'm going to find you, and when I do, you're going to tell me what happened between us. You leaving the way you did just doesn't make sense to me.*

"I HAVE TO say that while I'm happy to have Rayne home with us… I can't shake this feeling that she's not telling us everything," Leon said after Rayne went to her room to care for the babies.

"Well, whatever it is, apparently Rayne isn't ready tell us any more than what she's shared," Trey responded. "It's her story to tell when and if she ever ready."

Gia joined them and sat down beside Trey. "I agree with my husband. It's up to Rayne whether she wants to tell us anything more about her marriage."

Leon lowered his voice to a whisper. "Do you really believe that she's married?"

"You don't?" Trey asked. "She's wearing a wedding band. Surely, she wouldn't lie about something like this."

"She could've bought that herself. I guess it's

not that I think she's lying... I just think she's leaving something out."

"I don't think Rayne's lying," Trey said. "She'll open up when she feels she can. I'm just glad that she's back in our lives."

Leon fiddled with his phone. "I guess we'll just have to wait for her to come to us."

"And she will."

He eyed his brother. "You really think so? After all this time?"

"I do," Trey replied. "Rayne wouldn't have come home otherwise. I believe she's here because she needs her family. We have to be careful in our approach. Remember what happened with Aunt Carol... We don't want to repeat those old mistakes with Rayne."

"What happened?" Gia asked.

"Carol got into a really bad fight with her siblings. She basically believed that they'd turned their backs on her. I don't know how much of that is true—I just don't think we should turn our backs on Rayne now."

Their conversation turned to the upcoming holiday.

"I'm very excited about this year's Christmas festival," Gia said. "And I'm really looking forward to working with Rayne. She was telling me about the events she worked on for the car dealership and some of the volunteering she's done. We have a lot of stuff planned and can use her help."

Leon was glad Rayne wanted to help, too. He hoped his cousin knew she could count on her family. They would always be here whenever she needed them.

CHAPTER THREE

CAROL ROTHCHILD'S DAY began at five in the morning.

The first thing she did was check her phone. It wasn't that she expected to hear from Rayne. Of course not. She was only looking to see if any staff members weren't coming to school.

She was greeted by texts from two teachers calling out sick. They were already a sub short, which meant that she had to reassign some staff. It wasn't really that big of a deal, but it wasn't a good way to start her day, either. It left her feeling like she was already behind before setting foot on the high-school campus. However, Carol loved her job as assistant principal, and it kept her busy.

The morning flowed by. She stole a peek at the clock on the wall in her office. It was almost eleven thirty: time for lunch duty.

Carol exhaled, drank the last few sips of her coffee, then left her office.

In the cafeteria, she stood apart from the other three staff members on duty. She didn't feel like listening to their whining and complaints.

Carol's sorrow was a huge, painful knot inside her. It was a heartbreaking thought that her own daughter would betray her in this way. How could she go running to the family that had turned their backs on them?

Well, Eleanor and the boys hadn't—they didn't have anything to do with it—their only crime was being witness to her humiliation. Leon and Trey once looked up to her. She had no idea what they possibly thought of her now. Besides, seventeen years had come and gone. It was too late.

Rayne had taken off with Carol's grandbabies. She couldn't understand why her daughter wanted to spend the holidays on Polk Island instead of home with her. She and Rayne always spent Christmas together.

Carol swallowed her disappointment.

"Howdy, Miss Rothchild."

She smiled at the young man with locs. He was a senior who excelled on the football field and in the classroom. "Lance, what are you up to?"

"Nothing, ma'am. Nothing at all. I hadn't seen you in a few days."

"Is that your way of saying that you missed me?"

He laughed. "I wanted to let you know that

I got accepted into my first choice. Even got a decent scholarship offer."

"That's wonderful, Lance. I'm so proud of you."

"My momma 'bout had a hissy fit, though. She not crazy about me going to school in California. My dad said he's gonna talk to her."

"It was hard for me when my daughter up and announced that she was moving to Los Angeles, so I understand. It will work out as long as you do what you're supposed to do, Lance. Minimize the distractions."

He gave her a sheepish grin. "I know, Miss Rothchild. I be tryin', but the ladies won't leave me alone."

"Boy, go on and get to class…"

Lance broke into laughter. "See ya later, Miss Rothchild."

She returned to her office after lunch duty ended.

It was a few minutes after two when Carol finally took a break to eat her salad.

She eyed the photograph on her desk of her daughter. It had been a great joy having Rayne home and getting the chance to support her through the pregnancy.

Now she was gone again, leaving Carol feeling alone and empty.

How are my babies doing?

She missed the twins as much as she missed Rayne.

The holidays were always hard on her. Rayne knew this but had refused to change her mind. Instead, she wanted Carol to come to the island with her.

Carol missed Eleanor terribly.

She still communicated with her eldest sister, but every time they talked, Eleanor would try to convince her to forgive her other siblings. That wasn't happening. She intended to keep her distance where they were concerned.

And those siblings had never once tried to initiate a conversation with her, either.

Needing to talk with someone, Carol decided to call her sister.

Eleanor answered the telephone on the second ring. "Hello…"

"Hey, Ella…"

"Who is this?"

"It's me… Carol. Your little sister."

"Oh, my goodness. Carol, where on earth have you been? I haven't spoken to you in months."

"Ella, I know it's been a while, and I'm sorry. I don't have an excuse, but I'm so happy to hear your voice."

"Are you still in Dallas?" Eleanor asked.

"Yes, I am," she responded. "I still work at the high school. I'm an assistant principal."

"That's wonderful. Schools need people like you. You've always cared about children."

"I do love what I do," Carol stated.

"I told Rayne that you both should move back to the island."

Carol's breath caught in her throat, and she felt a shock go through her body. She didn't know why this hurt so much. "So, you saw her, huh?"

"And her beautiful babies."

She gritted her teeth. She'd wanted to talk, but now thinking about the rest of the family seeing Rayne and the grandbabies while she was left alone was too much. "Okay, well I have to go, but I'll call you again."

"It's sho' good to hear from you, Carol. I just wish you'd come home. At least for a visit."

There was a critical tone to her voice. "Ella, I remember everything that happened just like it was yesterday. The people on that island won't let you forget the mistakes of your past."

"You have to choose not to let the words of other people define who you are or keep you away from the people who care about you."

"Oh, you mean the same family who stood by while that woman told all my business in the middle of the café," Carol snapped. "I don't blame you, Ella. You were the only one who stuck up for me, but it was a little too late. The damage was already done. You may not remember this, but they dropped Rayne from *The Nutcracker* because of what happened. Other kids started bullying my child."

"You know how sorry I am that you were humiliated like that," Ella told her.

"I don't want to focus on the past right now. I just need to talk to my daughter. If you happen to hear from Rayne—tell her to call me, please."

"I will," Eleanor responded.

They ended the call.

After their mother died, Eleanor stepped up to raise her. The two sisters had been close, until Carol turned sixteen. She wanted to make her own decisions, good or bad.

She met Rayne's father, Roger, on her sixteenth birthday while visiting Charleston. It wasn't until after Carol found out she was pregnant that the love of her life revealed he was married. As if breaking her heart had not been enough, he also made it clear that he had no interest in the child she was carrying.

Carol had her child, and with the support of Eleanor and her sister's husband, Walter, she enrolled in college. Things were fine…until Rayne was twelve years old, and a woman stormed into the café identifying herself as the wife of the man she'd been involved with.

Carol didn't bother to deny the affair. She might have ended things with Rayne's father, but that didn't change the fact that she'd been part of this woman's pain. She stood there, arguing with the enraged woman, and fully expecting her siblings to speak in her defense.

Instead, Maggie and Daniel began to berate her, too. They stood in judgment of her behavior, taking the wife's side. It never really mattered to Carol what others thought of her, but she was deeply wounded by her siblings' judgment of her. They were supposed to know her better than anyone else in the world.

Only Eleanor offered her the support Carol so desperately needed in that moment, ushering the other woman out of the café and taking Carol into the kitchen, away from prying eyes.

But the damage had been done. Local residents started to shun Rayne—it started when Carol was told that her daughter wouldn't be able to perform with the Polk Island Dance Company any longer. Then she was being teased and picked on at school. That was when Carol decided to move away. She wasn't going to allow Rayne to pay for her mistakes.

Her phone rang.

She looked at the caller ID, and her eyebrows raised in surprised. Taylor Carrington, Rayne's former boss. The man she'd made a one-night mistake with that had brought Carol her sweet grandbabies.

Carol had met him four years ago when she was in the market for a car and liked him immediately. She'd always hoped that he and Rayne would end up together, but according to her daughter, she and Taylor didn't want the same things when it came to a relationship. This wasn't the first time Taylor had called looking for Rayne. As far as Carol knew, Rayne had never called him back.

Sighing, she answered. "Hello, Taylor."

"I was hoping to speak with Rayne."

"She's not here," Carol said.

"Do you have any idea where she is?" His tone was more tense than she'd ever heard it. "Please, it's very important that I speak with her."

A thought occurred to her. Rayne might not want a relationship with Taylor, but he'd always seemed like a good friend. Maybe he could bring Rayne home again. "Well, I do know where she is. If you promise to talk some sense into her—I'll tell you where to find her."

"I'll do what I can," he responded.

"Rayne is staying with family on Polk Island. Call the Polk Island Café. Ask for Misty Rothchild and ask her to put Rayne in touch with you."

"I'll do it in person," he said decisively. "I'll make plans to travel tomorrow. I really need to talk to your daughter."

"Thanks, Taylor. Rayne doesn't realize it yet, but she needs us. She needs both of us."

He seemed to care a great deal about her, but her daughter always insisted that they were only friends.

Carol prayed things would change between them once he arrived on the island. He was in for a bit of a surprise, however. Rayne never told him about the twins.

A DAY LATER, Taylor settled back in the seat of his rental vehicle and drove toward the freeway, following the directions of the GPS to Polk Island. He couldn't wait to come face-to-face with Rayne. He wanted answers, the first of which was why she left without signing the divorce petition.

Taylor wouldn't allow himself to believe that Rayne left because she wanted to stay married. She'd made it clear that she enjoyed being a single woman the morning after their nuptials.

It somehow felt even worse that this was happening over the holidays. Everywhere he looked, there were reminders of the holiday season. Bells with red and green ribbons and snowflake-shaped lighting adorned every pole on Main Street.

Once he arrived at the café Carol had told him about, Taylor wasted no time. He didn't pause to consider what he'd say to Rayne. He just wanted to lay eyes on her. His initial concern was making sure she was okay.

Taylor strode through the doors of the Polk Island Bakery & Café and was met by the lively sounds of holiday music playing in the background. He quickly scanned the dining area. Several people at tables engaged in laughter and conversation while eating or waiting for their food to arrive.

He could hear the clamor of pans as meals were being prepared. A server walking past a table paused to pick up a red cloth napkin that had fallen to the floor. Taylor's nose was immediately enticed by the mouthwatering scents of fresh baked goods. His eyes strayed in the direction of an array of muffins, brownies, cookies and cakes on display behind the glass counter.

A slender young woman wiping down a table looked up. "Are you eating in or picking up?"

"I'm looking for the owner," Taylor stated.

"I'll get her."

He turned his gaze away from the Christmas tree, focusing instead on the tasty offerings summoning him. Taylor's stomach protested, and he considered ordering a couple of muffins. Before he could decide, he was approached by a striking woman, her eyes filled with open curiosity.

"Hello, I'm Misty. How can I help you?"

Before he could speak, he heard a voice behind him. "Hey, Misty, I—"

He spun around. After eleven months, Taylor was finally face-to-face with Rayne.

Her thick lashes flew up. She stood there, surprised and looking uncertain.

An unexpected warmth surged through Taylor. He stared wordlessly, trying not to be distracted by Rayne's beauty.

Rayne surprised him by planting a quick kiss on his cheek. "What are you doing here?"

"I was looking for you. We need to work out some things, don't you agree?"

Looping her arm through his, Rayne wore a tight smile. "Where are my manners… Misty, this is my husband, Taylor Carrington. I had no idea that he was coming to the island."

Giving him a sidelong glance, she asked, "Why didn't you tell me?"

He was too stunned to speak.

"I'm glad you were able to come," Misty said. "I know the rest of the family can't wait to meet you."

He felt Rayne shudder.

Misty adjusted her apron. "I need to get back to work. Taylor, it's wonderful meeting you."

When she disappeared through the double doors, he turned to her asking, "What kind of game are you playing?"

She took his hand, leading him to one of the booths in the back of the dining area.

Keeping her voice low, she asked, "How did you know I was here? Did you hire a detective?"

"I hired one after I got your email and found out you'd gone to your mother's house. I figured I'd give you some space before reaching out, but when I did…you never responded. I even left messages with your mother."

"So, why are you here now? Is everything okay?"

He stared at her in astonishment. *Did she really just ask me that?* After all these months without a word from her.

Taylor couldn't ignore how her smooth caramel complexion glowed. Her hair was glossy and healthy—it had grown longer, reaching the middle of her back. When Rayne removed her coat, his eyes strayed to the slight roundness of her stomach.

Cold dread washed over him as his gaze traveled back to her face as he asked, "Are you pregnant?"

RAYNE'S BREATH CAUGHT in her lungs at his question. She thought she detected a hint of censure in Taylor's tone. "Can you keep your voice down, please?"

"You didn't answer me." There was an edge to his voice.

"Taylor, I'm not pregnant," Rayne responded. "Not anymore. I gave birth six weeks early in September to twins. A boy and a girl. They will be three months old on Sunday."

He stiffened as though she had struck him. "Are they—"

With both hands on her hips, Rayne responded, "Yes, they're yours. You're the father." She was irked by his cool, aloof manner.

Taylor seemed to retain his affability, but there was a distinct hardening of his gorgeous gray eyes. "How could you let something like this happen?"

"I didn't *let* anything happen. We're in this together, Taylor. The twins were conceived on our wedding night. If you remember, we'd had a lot to drink. Neither one of us was thinking clearly when we decided to stop at that chapel."

"Fine, I accept my part in this, but why didn't you tell me that you were pregnant?" Taylor asked. "Didn't you think I had a right to know?"

"I already know how you feel about children," Rayne responded. "So, I didn't really see the point in telling you right away. I wanted a stress-free pregnancy and delivery. That was what was more important to me at the time. I didn't think I would have that with you. Judging from your reaction—I was right."

"Is this why you held up the divorce?" Taylor asked.

I might as well tell the truth.

Rayne nodded. "Yeah. I wanted to be married when they were born. Look, I never told you this, but my mom was seventeen when she had me. Not only was I considered illegitimate, but my father was married at the time. He didn't tell my mom. She found out afterward. When some people on this island found out—they never let her forget it. I'm not about to let that happen to my children."

"That's a different situation. You weren't involved with a married man."

"Right, but I didn't want my children's birth certificate to have a blank space under *father*. With me as your wife, they have a right to your last name."

Taylor's stare drilled into her as he clenched his mouth tighter. "And you didn't think you could tell me about any of this?"

They glared at each other across a sudden ringing silence.

"What exactly did you tell your family about us?" Taylor asked, cutting through the quiet.

Rayne sighed. "Obviously, I didn't want my family to learn that we said vows while drunk. I just told them that we're separated. That's the truth of it."

"All of this is about what you want, regardless of how it affects anyone else. Rayne, you're really something else." His accusing gaze was riveted on her for a moment before he eased out of the booth. He was leaving.

"Taylor…" Rayne hesitated, blinking with bafflement. "Don't go."

"I'm sorry. I need time to process all this."

He strode through the door.

"Is everything okay?" Misty asked when she walked up to the booth.

"Oh, yeah," Rayne responded, trying to maintain her composure. "We haven't seen each other in a bit. It's a bit tense. He's going to a hotel to rest."

Misty looked perplexed. "A hotel? He doesn't have to go there. He can stay with us."

"You already have me and the twins…"

"He's your husband, no matter what you're going through right now. If you're okay with him staying with us, go catch up with him and let him know he's welcome, okay?"

"Taylor and I are separated. Are you sure?"

Misty nodded. "Of course. We have another guestroom upstairs. He can stay in there."

Rayne slid out of the booth and rushed out of the café. "Taylor, wait…"

He'd just opened the door to his vehicle.

Taylor looked up. "I can't do this right now."

She stood on the passenger side of the car. "Look, I know I just hit you with a lot. This is not the way I wanted you to find out."

"Apparently, you didn't want me to know anything about the twins."

"That's not true," she responded. She really had been planning to tell him in the new year, once she'd settled into life here. "I need you to hear me out."

"I'm going to a hotel. Then I'm flying back to California tomorrow. Right after you sign the divorce petition."

"Come to the house with me," Rayne said. "Misty insists. We might be separated, but she still wants you to know that you're part of the family now, too."

Taylor responded, "I don't think that's a good idea."

"There's another guestroom."

"I don't know…"

"You've come all this way, Taylor."

"I'll think about it."

"My mother told you where I was, didn't she?" Rayne asked. "It had to be her."

"I wish she'd also mentioned that you'd given birth. I had no idea."

"And if I'd told you I was pregnant?"

"You knew that I never wanted children."

Rayne felt a scream of frustration at the back of her throat. "Exactly. So, you can see why I made the choice I made! I wanted them, and I didn't want to burden you."

His glare burned through her. "Still...you ran off without telling me that you were pregnant. I can't believe you!"

"Right now, I'm getting the feeling that you're mostly worried about how this is going to make you look. That's the same thing my father did—worry about his reputation. He blamed my mother for everything and took no accountability that he was a married man."

Taylor walked over to where she was standing. "Rayne, I understand why you'd feel this way. Women seem to shoulder a lot of the blame in situations like this. It's unfortunate, but I'm not like the man who fathered you. You and I...we could've talked about this. I thought there was trust between us."

"What I know is that you wanted the divorce months ago, but I just couldn't sign those papers. I chose to protect my babies. They're not responsible for what you and I did." She paused a moment, then said, "It's not that I don't trust you. You know I do. But your feelings just weren't my priority. When I found out I was pregnant—it became all about my children. I am more than capable of taking care of them. I've always intended to do this alone."

He seemed to be considering her words.

"So, what happens now?" Rayne asked. She kept her expression as neutral as she could manage. "Will you please come to the house with me?"

"I honestly don't know what I'm about to do. I need some space."

She pulled out her cell phone. "I'll text you my new number. Please call me when you decide."

Taylor got into the car and drove away.

Rayne released a sigh. Why did he have to show up now?

She couldn't recall ever seeing him so angry. She hoped he would eventually calm down enough to hear her out. Rayne didn't want him exposing the ugly truth to her family. It had taken a lot for her to reappear in their lives, and she wanted them to see her as a woman who was without blemish.

In the short time she'd been around Misty, she could tell she was practically perfect. Beautiful, intelligent, most likely a devoted mother. Leon and Trey had both chosen well when it came to their spouses. Rayne had failed. She knew her marriage was going to end in divorce, despite the delay. But she didn't need her family to see her making the same kinds of mistakes her mother had.

CHAPTER FOUR

TWINS.

The word echoed in Taylor's mind repeatedly as he drove around in circles. The fact that he'd unknowingly fathered two children with a woman he cared for but had no intentions of remaining married to—he was still reeling from the shock and not paying attention to where he was going.

Not only that, Rayne had also hidden the truth of their marriage from her family. Was he supposed to play along with that?

Deep down, the last thing Taylor wanted to do was cause Rayne any embarrassment.

Maybe I should stay with her family, he reasoned. While there, he could convince her to sign the divorce petition.

He turned into the driveway of a bank and parked in an empty space.

Taylor called her.

"Text me the address," he said when Rayne answered. "Before I get there, is there anything I should know?"

"Can you please pretend that you knew about the pregnancy and the births."

"Rayne…"

"You don't owe me anything after everything that's happened, but I'm asking anyway. I don't want my family to think badly of me or the babies. Please…just do this for me."

"How long do you intend to carry on this charade?"

"Just let me get through Christmas, and then I'll sign the divorce papers."

"I hadn't planned to be here more than a day or two at most, Rayne."

"That's fine."

He didn't reply.

"Taylor, I give you my word—you will get your divorce. After Christmas."

"I know because I'm going to make sure you sign it this time. After I get your signature, I'm going to file the petition."

"Is our marriage preventing you from something? You seem to be in a big hurry."

"We decided *together* that a divorce was for the best," Taylor stated. "This was never more than a mistake."

She said archly, "So, you don't remember telling me that you loved me?"

Panic rioting within him, he asked, *"When did I say that?"*

"That's what you told me when we decided to get married." Rayne said. He could practically hear her roll her eyes. "It's fine. I'm just giving you a hard time. I didn't take you seriously. Well, I did at first. I married you, but then I realized you meant that you loved me as a friend."

Taylor felt like he should apologize to her. "I don't remember a whole lot about that night except marrying you."

He couldn't believe he'd acted so out of character and placed them both in such an awkward position. If only he could convince her to sign the papers so that they could move forward. Taylor's mind slid once more to the twins who were innocents in this situation.

What am I supposed to do about them?

"MISTY JUST TOLD me that your husband is in town," Leon said when Rayne arrived home ten minutes later.

"I had no idea Taylor was coming. He surprised me." She smiled, trying to settle some of the raw emotion she was feeling. "I wasn't expecting to see him until the new year."

Rayne glanced out the window. He would be arriving at any moment. "Misty invited him to stay here," Rayne went on. "I hope that's okay.

I know it might seem awkward, my husband who I'm separated from staying with us..."

"I'm looking forward to meeting him. I'm curious to see the type of man you married."

"You will find that the two of you have similar interests. He's into sports and is a voracious reader."

"I think he just pulled up," Leon said.

Rayne looked out the window. "Yeah, that's Taylor."

She walked briskly to the door and stepped onto the porch. "You made it."

"I'm here."

A wave of apprehension washed over her. "Thank you for doing this for me."

A chill black silence surrounded them.

Rayne swallowed hard. "C'mon in."

Leon was standing in the foyer when they entered the house.

She made the introductions. "This is my cousin Leon."

He shook Taylor's hand. "Good to meet you."

They made polite small talk in the living room.

Rayne remained on edge and nervous until she was able to usher Taylor into the guestroom.

"That wasn't too bad, was it?" she asked.

"No, I can see why you wanted me to stay here." He paused. "Can I see the babies?"

Her breath caught, but she nodded and changed direction to her own bedroom.

Taylor walked over to the crib, staring down at the tiny infants. "They look like balls of hair. You have them bundled up snugly."

"Mama says it reminds them of being in the womb," she responded.

"Twins."

Rayne nodded. "Yeah...can you believe it?"

Taylor shook his head no.

"Your son's name is Ian and your daughter is Ivy." She sank down into the warm softness of the upholstered bench at the foot of the bed. "Look, I realize how uncomfortable this is for you."

"I'm trying, Rayne. We've been friends for years. I just wish you'd known you could have come to me. We could've figured out everything together."

Arms folded across her chest, she said, "I already know how you feel about children and marriage. You wanted our marriage over the day after it happened."

"I recall that you felt the same way," he responded. "Or has that changed?"

"I already told you that I'll give you a divorce after Christmas."

He pointed toward the sleeping babies. "And the twins?"

"You can terminate your parental rights," she suggested. "I'm willing to raise them alone."

"That's out of the question," Taylor responded.

"But you don't want to be a father."

"That's true, but you took that decision away from me," he told her, and she could hear him trying to keep the anger out of his tone. "They're not just your children—they are also mine."

She couldn't deny the truth. "You're right."

The room grew pregnant with silence.

Rayne shook her head after a moment. "I don't know why my mom can't just mind her own business. I'm so tired of her interfering in my life."

"One thing I know about your mother. She loves you, and she's made you her whole world, Rayne. You don't realize just how lucky you are to have a mom."

"I don't mean to sound ungrateful. I know your parents weren't there for you. It's just that I'm no longer a little girl. I'm a grown woman. I left Dallas and moved to Los Angeles as soon as I graduated from high school, just so I could live my own life—of course, that's when I messed up big-time."

"Carol's love for you is unconditional."

"I know you're right. I think that what my mom really needs is a life of her own."

"Isn't she close to her family here?" Taylor asked.

"She and her oldest sister are close, but she had a terrible falling out with her other siblings. Mama calls Aunt Eleanor every few months, but she's vowed to never come back to the island."

He stared toward the crib for a moment, then said, "Rayne, help me understand why you don't want to sign the divorce petition now. Why can't we just get this over with?"

"Because I want to enjoy the holidays with my family. I don't want to think about anything sad or depressing. There's nothing happy about ending a marriage."

"Even though ours wasn't a real one?"

"I know you don't understand."

"I'm trying, Rayne. The twins were born within the marriage, and they have my name— you have everything you wanted. Don't you?"

She stood up saying, "It's almost time to feed them. I'd better get those bottles warmed before Ian and Ivy wake up."

Rayne stopped halfway to the door, then turned to face him. "I'm sorry you had to find out this way. You may not believe me, but I'd planned to tell you... I just needed some time."

The tense lines on his face relaxed. "I'd say that we're beyond that now. We have to figure out where to go from here." Taylor spoke calmly, with no lighting of his eyes, no smile of tenderness—all the things she missed about him. A heaviness centered in her chest. Rayne didn't like the tension surrounding them.

Once again, she'd messed up.

TAYLOR PUT HIS phone down on the tall walnut dresser. He studied his reflection in the mirror. Women loved his creamy, smooth, peanut-colored complexion, his greenish-gray eyes and his neatly trimmed wavy hair. Taylor's six-four height and muscular body had carried him through four years of basketball in college and forward. He looked like the same man on the outside, but inside, he felt different.

His world had changed.

Ian and Ivy.

He made a mental note to ask her inspiration behind their names. Taylor didn't know what to think or how to feel. He felt betrayed by Rayne; he was angry with her. How could she do something like this to him?

He hadn't known what to expect when he came to the island. Discovering that he and Rayne were the parents of a set of twins—it was not a scenario that had entered Taylor's mind. Even if she'd told him all those months ago, he had no idea how he would've reacted.

And he couldn't believe Carol had let him walk into this without telling him, either!

One of the babies started to cry, sending a shock wave through Taylor's body.

He walked over to the crib and stared down at the infant. This must be Ivy. She was dressed in a pink outfit with yellow butterflies all over it.

He didn't know what to do to comfort her. "Shh… You're going to wake up your brother. Your mom is warming your bottle. Try to be patient."

She looked up at him and stuck out her tongue.

Taylor's eyebrows rose a fraction.

"I'm back." Rayne brushed past him, bending to pick up the little girl effortlessly. "My sweet angel…" she cooed. "I have your bottle ready for you."

Minutes later, there was a knock on the door.

"That's probably Talei," she told him. "She likes to help me with the twins."

Taylor crossed the room and opened the door.

"Hi, Rayne… Oh…" A little girl stared up at him. One of the cousins' daughters? She looked as if she didn't know whether she should enter the room or leave. She began playing with her ponytail. "Sorry."

"C'mon in, sweetie," Rayne said from behind him. "That's Taylor. You're right on time because Ian's just waking up."

Talei glanced up at him. "Can I please feed your little boy?"

"Sure." He was impressed by her manners.

She walked straight to the crib, tossed a blue cloth over her shoulder, picked up Ian and sat down in the rocker. "Hey, little cousin...sweet boy. You ready for your bottle?"

Taylor was amazed at how well Talei handled the baby.

Rayne glanced over at him and said, "She's helped out with lots of siblings and cousins."

Taylor grinned. "I can tell that she's an expert."

Smiling, Talei nodded. "I love my little cousins."

"I'm sure they love you, too." He looked at Rayne to gauge if his response was appropriate.

She awarded Taylor a smile, before returning her gaze to her daughter.

"Rayne said you weren't going to come, but I'm glad you did," the girl said sweetly. "I hope you're going to stay for Christmas. We always have a lot of fun."

"Taylor's not going to be able to stay here that long," Rayne quickly interjected. "We're just going to have a good time without him."

"I'll just have to give you your present before you leave," Talei said, catching him completely off guard.

"Thank you," he responded. "But you don't have to go out of your way—"

"I want to do it. You're going to be away from your family. I don't want you not to have any presents to open on Christmas day."

Taylor broke into a sincere smile. "Talei, you're incredibly sweet and a very special girl. Thank you for thinking of me."

Talei had just put Ian back in the crib when her mother appeared in the doorway. "Okay, little lady…it's time for dinner."

"Aren't they coming, too?" she asked, pointing at Rayne and Taylor.

"We'll be right behind you," Rayne said. She watched as her little cousin skipped out of the room, then turned her attention back to Taylor. "You okay?"

He nodded. "That little girl met me not even an hour ago, and now she wants to give me a gift. I didn't have the heart to tell her that I don't celebrate the holidays."

"Don't ruin this for her, Taylor. Just accept the present."

"I won't hurt her feelings, Rayne. I guess I'll need to get one for her."

"I'll take care of it," she said while changing Ivy's diaper. "I'll put your name on whatever I buy for Talei and her siblings."

"Thanks. I don't really have any idea what to buy for her."

"I know," Rayne replied with a smile. "I always bought the toys for the group home you and Deacon sponsor. By the way, how is my replacement doing?"

"She's not you," Taylor responded. "I'll leave it at that."

"Not sure why, but that actually makes me happy," Rayne stated.

"I imagine it would."

She chuckled.

Rayne placed Ivy in the crib beside her brother. "We should join the family for dinner."

"I feel like I'm about to stand before a judge and jury."

"They're nothing like that, Taylor. They get that we're separated, and they'll appreciate that you're here for me and the twins today. Just relax and enjoy your food. Misty is a fantastic cook."

Leon and the children were seated at the table already.

A little girl with two curly puffs looked up and waved at them.

"Hey, Fawn, don't you look pretty," Rayne said.

"Yeah," she responded with a grin.

Taylor noticed Rayne seemed more comfortable around the children than she did with their parents, especially with Leon. Rayne was nervous, almost skittish.

"Hello," the little boy greeted. "Rayne, are the twins sleeping? I wanted to see them. Talei is always with them."

"Don't worry, Leo. I promise that when Ian and Ivy wake up, I'll make sure you get to spend some time with them."

"Okay."

"Me, too," Fawn said.

Talei handed her sister a napkin. "You can only look at the babies, Fawn. You're too little to hold them."

Leon walked in and sat down at the table.

Rayne's demeanor changed suddenly. She averted her gaze, staring down at her empty plate.

Misty walked out of the kitchen with a bowl of steaming vegetables and a plate of yeast rolls. She sat them on the table then went back to get the rest of the food.

"Everything smells delicious," Taylor said. He hadn't eaten anything since the morning.

"My mommy is the best cook in the world," Leo stated.

Leon chuckled. "I thought you said I was the best."

"You are, but Mommy is the bestest."

"Son, I agree with you."

Taylor enjoyed observing Leon with his children throughout dinner. He was also appreciative that he hadn't attempted to delve into his relationship with Rayne.

"Misty, how do you get this chicken to just fall apart like this?" he asked.

"Golden mushroom soup," she responded with a smile.

"It's really good."

"Taylor doesn't really eat a lot of chicken," Rayne interjected. "So for him to say it's good… that's saying a lot."

"I used to have to eat chicken all the time when I was growing up," he explained. "By the time I was grown, I'd had enough poultry to last me a lifetime. I have to say that I've never had it like this—it's really delicious."

"Whenever his company hosted a dinner, I'd always make sure the menu only had beef, seafood and vegetarian entrées," she laughed.

Rayne insisted on washing dishes after they finished eating, and she sent Taylor to the family room.

He joined Leon on the couch. They bonded over their love for the Lakers while a game played in the background.

At the end of the evening, he followed Rayne to her bedroom and leaned against the door frame. His eyes strayed to the crib, where the babies napped. "So..." he said.

Rayne peered up at him. "There is the guest-room upstairs if you'd prefer your own room, but...you can stay here with us, if you want."

He couldn't say why, but he did want that. He wanted to be close to her...and to the babies. "Can I? I can sleep in the rocker."

"If that's what you want to do," Rayne responded. "No one will mind that you're here. We're married. And I'm perfectly willing to share the bed with you. It'll be two friends sleeping—nothing more."

It would be too easy for him to get caught up in this story she was spinning, where they'd once been happily married. One of them had to keep a clear head about this situation. Taylor decided it would be him.

Rayne wanted her family to think the best of her; he understood her motives. But he didn't like feeling as if they were being dishonest. There had been a point when Taylor considered exploring a relationship with Rayne, but she'd always seemed intent on a platonic friendship. So he'd abandoned the idea. He'd had enough rejection in his life.

He settled down in the rocker for the night. *This chair isn't comfortable at all.*

Taylor shifted his position beneath the blanket. He sat forward and tried rearranging the pillow behind his head. Finally, he gave up on it altogether.

"Are you sure you don't want to sleep in the bed?" Rayne asked from across the room.

She seemed to be peering at him intently with the aid of light filtering through the open blinds. She looked almost ethereal in the moonlight, even with the silk bonnet on her head.

Something intense flared through Taylor. He swallowed the lump that lingered in his throat. "No, I'm good."

"G'night, Taylor."

"Good night."

He closed his eyes, praying for sleep to come. Rayne radiated a vitality that drew him like a magnet. Taylor spent the next hour fighting his overwhelming need to be close to her.

CHAPTER FIVE

RAYNE WAS MORE than a little irritated with Taylor. It had nothing to do with his refusal to sleep in the bed with her. It was his fierce determination to have little to no interaction with the twins. She could tell that he was uncomfortable when it came to holding or feeding them, so Rayne didn't pressure him to help. During the late-night feeding, Taylor had remained wide-awake until the twins went back to sleep, but Rayne believed it had more to do with his inability to get comfortable in the rocker. Although she was in a comfortable bed, she had some trouble sleeping as well, probably because of Taylor's commanding presence.

She tossed the heavy quilt off her body. Rayne didn't know what it was, but the air around them seemed electrified, wrapping around her like a warm blanket. Although she and Taylor were in an awkward space, Rayne drank in the comfort of his nearness on one hand, and on the other, she deliberately tried to shut out any awareness of him.

Shortly before six o'clock, Rayne gave up on sleeping and eased out of bed, careful not to disturb Taylor or the twins.

She showered, threw on a sweatshirt and matching pants then navigated to the kitchen and enjoyed a cup of ginger tea before Misty came downstairs.

Stifling a yawn, her cousin-in-law said, "You're up early."

Rayne took a sip of tea. "I couldn't sleep. Besides, Ian and Ivy will be waking up shortly."

"Is Taylor still sleeping?"

"Yeah. I think he's still on West Coast time."

Misty retrieved a carton of eggs, a tomato and a container of fresh spinach from the refrigerator. "I'm about to make omelets. Want one?"

Smiling, Rayne responded, "Yes, please."

She went back to the refrigerator and pulled out a container. "Leon and I like mushrooms in ours. How about you?"

"Same." Rayne finished off her tea. "Can I help with anything?"

"Just keep me company while I cook," Misty responded.

"I can do that."

"You must be thrilled to have your husband here."

"He's only going to be here a short while,"

Rayne stated. "We're not… This isn't a reconciliation, you know?"

Misty placed an omelet pan on top of the stove. "Well, make the most of your time together anyway. I can tell there's still something between you. I don't mind watching the babies if you two would like some time alone."

"You have enough on your plate, Misty. You have the restaurant, the children and a husband."

"You just have to find the right balance," she responded, pouring the egg mixture into the pan.

"So true," Rayne responded. "I'm already learning that with the twins. I've figured out that I need to nap when they do, or I tire really easy. I used to have so much energy."

"You're still recovering from childbirth," Misty stated.

"I feel like my hormones are still all over the place. Is that normal?"

"Yes. It's different with every woman and even every pregnancy. With Talei, I was super sensitive, and I cried all the time. I could be watching a movie or just talking to someone. With Leo and Fawn, I seemed to bounce back quicker."

"Thank you for telling me this, Misty. I wasn't sure what was going on." Placing a hand to her stomach, she said, "I'm ready to get back to exercising."

"Gia and I work out three days a week. You should join us. They even have a childcare center in-house. Whenever she has a free moment, Renee meets us at the gym."

Rayne was grateful to have women close in age to talk to about such things. She'd always wanted a sister. Now she had Misty, Gia and Renee.

"Do you remember any of your DuGrandpre relatives?" Misty asked.

Rayne nodded. That was the other branch of her family on the island.

"The gym we go to is owned by Jordin DuGrandpre's husband, Ethan. Oh, Aubrie just opened a restaurant here on the island. She and her husband own Paradis. She has two others—one in New Orleans and the other in Charleston."

Rayne was happy for all of them, but their achievements made her feel a little inferior. She hadn't accomplished anything. She quickly reminded herself that she wasn't in a race. That she shouldn't measure herself by the success of others. That was what Taylor would tell her.

"Good morning, ladies," Leon greeted when he entered the kitchen ten minutes later.

He planted a kiss on Misty's cheek.

"G'morning," Rayne said.

"Where's Taylor?"

"He's still sleeping. I'm sure the three-hour time difference probably caught up with him."

Leon nodded in understanding.

"He seems like a nice guy. Why are you two separating, if you don't mind my asking?"

She wasn't surprised the question had finally come up. She'd thought about how to answer without really lying. "We don't want the same things. For one, I don't want to raise my babies in Los Angeles. I intend to live here on the island. Taylor's dealerships are in Cali and Vegas. He's not leaving there."

Leon sat across from her at the table. "You didn't ask for my advice, but I'm going to give it anyway. Rayne, you said vows with this man. He's your husband. If he doesn't want to move to the island, then maybe now isn't the time to think about relocating. You have to think about the twins."

"I am thinking about them," she responded. "I'm tired of being away from family. I want Ian and Ivy to grow up with their cousins."

"I can't tell you how happy I am to have you home, but you must consider Taylor's feelings in this. You can't be selfish."

She folded her arms across her chest. "So, it's okay for him to be selfish?"

"I'm not saying that. Marriage is about compromise."

"I know you're right, Leon. But I need to be here. Start a new life here with my babies. That's all I want."

Leon nodded. "I'm crossing my fingers it'll work out between you anyway."

"If it's meant to be—it'll work out," she responded.

"What's on your agenda for today?"

"I have a meeting with the festival committee," Rayne said. "I'm so excited about helping to plan this event. I used to love going to the parade when I was younger and then spending the day at the Christmas festival. It was so much fun."

"Do you remember the time Trey left you near the reindeer?"

She laughed. "Of course, I remember. I was so scared."

"Oh, my goodness! What happened?" Misty asked.

"He saw a friend of his and just took off after him. There were so many people there—I couldn't find him, so I walked to the information booth where Aunt Eleanor was working. She was so mad at him."

"Trey got into some real trouble for that," Leon said before chuckling at the memory.

"Both Aunt Eleanor and Aunt Carol lit into him."

He took a long sip of his orange juice. "What time is your meeting?"

"One o'clock," Rayne responded. "Misty, are you still good with watching the twins?"

"Will Taylor be offended?" she asked. "I'm sure he probably wants to spend time with them."

"Not at all. I think he has a couple of meetings this afternoon." It was probably true; he always had meetings.

"Okay, great. I'm looking forward to cuddling with them."

"Misty's not going to have all the fun," Leon said. "I'll be back home around noon."

"We're meeting at the café."

"I think Gia mentioned that when I spoke with her last night," Misty stated. "I'll call Josh to make sure there's lots of herbal tea and banana nut muffins. I was told they're a committee favorite."

"It's definitely mine," Rayne said with a grin. She finished off her omelet. "This was so delicious, Misty. My omelets end up being a scramble."

"You need the right pan."

"You're probably right," she responded. "I tried making a frittata once, and it didn't go well at all."

Misty laughed. "How did you mess that up?"

"I don't know, but after that—I left it alone. I stick to frying eggs or scrambling them. I'll leave the omelets and frittatas to you."

"By Christmas, I'll have you making both," Misty said.

"I'd love that."

"When did you learn to cook?" Leon asked.

"Boy, I was cooking before we left the island," Rayne responded. "I used to stay in the kitchen with Aunt Eleanor. You and Trey always had me making grilled cheese sandwiches."

Leon smiled at the memory. "That's right. My cousin used to make the best grilled cheese sandwiches. Trey and I always burned them whenever we tried to do it. Rayne knew how to time it just right so that the bread wasn't burnt. She was only, what, seven or eight at the time. I had to supervise her when Aunt Eleanor or Aunt Carol wasn't around."

Being back on the island with her family meant the world to Rayne. But she still kept a part of her heart behind a wall—she had to learn to trust them again. Her mother had drilled caution into her for years. Carol had constantly reminded Rayne that family could sometimes become your worst enemy.

This was why she harbored some anger toward her mother. Carol had expected her to choose between her and the rest of the family. She didn't want Rayne to come back to the island because she feared losing her—at least this was the impression Rayne had gotten from their last conversation. She knew she should call her mother, but she didn't want to get into an argument. She didn't want Carol to make her feel as if she'd betrayed her.

TAYLOR WOKE UP with a start and a sore neck. He grimaced in pain as he looked around for Rayne. He shot to his feet when he heard a sound coming from the crib.

He looked inside.

Ivy was wide-awake and met his gaze straight on. She wiggled her body, then stuck her tongue out.

"Good morning to you, too," he said, trying not to panic. He had no idea what to do if she started to cry.

You get a bottle and feed her, the tiny voice in his head whispered.

That's just it, he told the voice. *I don't want to feed her. I don't want Ivy getting the wrong idea about me.*

When Rayne walked into the room, he almost sagged with relief. "Ivy's up."

She looked surprised. "I didn't hear her cry."

"She was just lying here. When I was watching her, Ivy stuck her tongue out at me. That's the second time she's done that. Does she ever do that to you?"

"Nope. Never," Rayne responded with a tiny laugh. "I'd better go make the bottles. Ian will be waking up soon."

By the time she returned, Ian was awake and starting to fuss.

"What's wrong, sweetie? Mommy's here."

The baby immediately calmed.

"He knows your voice," Taylor said in awe.

She glanced over at Taylor and said, "You really haven't been around babies at all."

"I haven't."

"All you have to do is make them feel safe," Rayne said while placing Ian in his carrier. She did the same with Ivy. "They love to cuddle, and when you talk—they listen." Then she handed him a baby and a bottle. "Just stick it in his mouth."

Taylor's nerves eased, and he laughed when Ian attacked the nipple. "He acts like he's starving."

"They both have good appetites." Rayne stroked Ivy's legs as she fed her.

"I don't think there were ever twins in my family," Taylor said. "I have no way of really knowing, though."

"They run in mine. I have twin cousins in Charleston. Jadin and Jordin."

"Hey, little man," Taylor whispered. "You keep drinking like this, you're going to end up with a milk belly."

Rayne laughed.

"Are you listening to our private conversation?" he asked.

"Sorry."

Taylor winked at Ian. "She's not really sorry."

The infant released a loud burp in response.

"He agrees with me."

His words sparked more laughter.

"Let's switch," Rayne said. "You can finish feeding Ivy while I change Ian and burp him."

Taylor was grateful for the suggestion. He certainly wasn't ready for diaper duty.

He was so awestruck with the babies that he kept her company while she bathed and dressed them.

"Ivy acts like she's at a spa," he stated. "Look how she just relaxes her body."

Rayne chuckled. "Her brother is the complete opposite. Ian doesn't like a dirty diaper, but he puts up a fuss whenever he's being changed. Ivy always tries to help—at least that's the way it looks. She's always grabbing for the diaper."

"They have more personality than I ever

imagined a baby would have this young. I always thought they were tiny, little dull people."

"I'm always fascinated by them," Rayne said.

"I'm curious. How did you choose their names?"

Rayne gave him a tender look. "You told me once about a friend of yours who was the closest thing to a brother."

Taylor's heart fluttered wildly in his chest, and his pulse skittered alarmingly. "You named him after my friend Ian?"

She nodded. "You always said that you, Ian and Deacon were the Three Musketeers. I hope you don't mind."

"Not at all," Taylor responded. "I can't believe you remember that. He died a few months after you started working for me."

"I remember how heartbroken you were. I thought naming your son after him would be a great way to honor his memory."

"I agree."

"My maternal grandmother's name was Ivory, but everyone in the family called her Ivy."

After the twins fell asleep, Rayne asked, "I know you're not a big breakfast person, but would you like something to eat?"

"Are there any muffins here?"

"Yes, and fruit," Rayne responded.

"Sounds good. I'll take a shower and get dressed first, though."

"Okay." She paused. "I'm not sure what your plans are today, but I have a meeting with the festival committee this afternoon."

He tried to hide his panic. "Are you leaving the babies here?"

"Relax… I've already asked Misty to watch them. She was concerned that she was intruding on your time with the twins."

"What did you tell her?"

"That you had a couple of meetings scheduled. However, it wouldn't hurt you to take some time to get to know your children."

That surprised him. Two days ago, he didn't even know where she was, let alone that he was a father of twins. Now she sounded almost accusing.

She walked over to the closet. "I need to figure out what I'm going to wear. Leon said it's cold. I don't have a lot of winter clothes."

"I almost didn't bring my coat. One of the managers suggested that I bring one because the weather is unpredictable."

"He was right," Rayne responded.

"I just scheduled a conference call with my general managers," Taylor announced as he put his phone down.

"They should keep you busy until I get back."

Rayne changed clothes then went to check on the twins. They were still asleep.

She found Taylor on the screened-in back porch.

"What are you doing out here?"

"Trying to get in some exercise," he replied.

"I need to do the same thing," Rayne said. "I'd like to get back to my pre-pregnancy size."

"You look good to me. I like the extra pounds on you."

She was surprised. "Really?"

"Yes. Do you have any pictures of you pregnant?"

"Yeah, I do," Rayne responded. "I embraced the weight gain, but I could do without the morning sickness."

"I feel sure that you looked stunning during your pregnancy," Taylor stated.

"What's up with the compliments?" she asked.

"Just trying to get back to the way we used to be. I don't like this tension between us."

"Neither do I."

"I guess you need to get ready for your meeting. You're helping with a Christmas festival?"

"Yeah, a couple of the committee members had to withdraw, and they needed some last-minute help. They're still trying to finalize the activities and attractions."

"I know you'll do well. Planning events is a strength of yours," Taylor said. "Have you considered starting your own business?"

"You mentioned that before," she responded. "Do you really believe I can do something like this?"

"I believe in you, Rayne. You can do anything you put your mind to doing. I've seen you in action."

His words and that million-dollar smile meant everything to her.

"YOU'RE BACK EARLY," Rayne said when Leon arrived home shortly after eleven o'clock.

"I'm off today, but I had to attend a training," he said.

"I'll be leaving in a few minutes. I've been craving chili from the café—I need that in my life right now."

"Now you got me wanting some."

"I'll bring it home for you."

He smiled. "Thanks, cousin."

"No problem. I really appreciate everything you and Misty have done for me."

"We're family."

She wished she could make herself believe in the acceptance he seemed to be offering. "I'm still eternally grateful to y'all." She gestured toward the back of the house. "Taylor's on the patio. He's in a meeting with his staff."

"That's fine," Leon said. "Misty and I will take care of the twins while you two are doing your thing."

"I should be back here by three at the latest."

"Take your time, Rayne. Everything is going to be fine," he assured her. "We'll be here if Taylor or the twins need anything."

She walked outside, got into her car and drove the short distance to the café.

Rayne slipped into a comfy booth and ordered a bowl of chili. She loved the café's tranquil, laidback atmosphere.

A few other people wandered in, but none were members of the festival committee. It was still early.

Rayne thought about Taylor, and a wave of guilt washed over her. She decided not to scold herself. She'd done what she thought was best for her children.

Her food arrived steaming and smelling delicious, with a slice of jalapeño corn bread and a generous portion of honey butter made locally. After saying a quick blessing over her food, Rayne enjoyed her meal.

She had almost finished eating when she became aware of someone sliding into the booth across from her. She looked up and saw it was Gia.

Wiping her mouth on a napkin, Rayne said, "I needed to put something in my stomach."

"I had the same thought. I left home with the intent to grab something for breakfast, but remembered I had an early morning meeting. And it just got busy from that moment forward."

Gia signaled for a server.

"I'd like the chili and corn bread as well," she ordered.

When the server walked away, Gia asked, "I'm loving the sweater. You've brought the holiday spirit with you, I see."

"I love Christmas. I'm super excited about this event. I remember when I was little how we'd go to the parade in the morning, then spend the rest of the day at the festival. It was so much fun."

Gia nodded in agreement. "Christmas is my favorite holiday. Do you remember when they used to have the Ferris wheel at the festival?"

"They don't anymore?" Rayne asked.

"Not for almost a decade now. My mom plans to suggest that we bring it back. It'll depend on the budget. However, we need some new attractions to build up our attendance. We can't keep doing the same things over and over."

"I have some ideas I'd like to pitch."

The server returned with another bowl of chili and corn bread. She placed it in front of Gia.

"That's great," she said. Then she leaned forward conspiratorially. "Misty told me that your hubby's in town."

Rayne smiled. "Yeah. I had no idea Taylor was coming, but I'm happy he's here."

"I'm sure. I know y'all are going through some things, but still. I don't like being away from Trey too long."

"You make him really happy," Rayne said. "I felt it when we were all together. After everything he's been through, I'm glad he has you and Trevon."

"He's a wonderful husband and father. After the meeting, let's pick a day for you and Taylor to come to the house for dinner. And you know you have to bring Ian and Ivy. We want some cuddle time with them."

"For sure. We'd absolutely love to spend time with you and Trey." Or at least, she would.

Rayne took a sip of her iced water, then said, "I am in awe of the way you take care of your clients, take care of Trey and your baby. And you're on different committees. Yet you seem to manage everything so effortlessly."

Gia wiped her mouth on the edge of her napkin. "I always feel like I don't have enough hours in the day. It can be challenging at times, but it's always rewarding."

Nodding in understanding, Rayne said, "Lately, I've been feeling overwhelmed. I love my babies…but working on the festival gives me an outlet I really need."

"You're trying to relocate from one coast to the other. You're a mother, and you're working through a tough time in your marriage. You have a lot going on. It's great that Taylor is here. That's a good sign, right?"

"Right," she responded.

"Maybe he can help you find a place. You want a place of your own, right?"

"He doesn't know the island like I do," Rayne murmured. "And I already have some ideas of what I want. I want new construction. I want to be the first person to live in my home. I don't like older homes."

"Trey said you always thought they were haunted."

"I believed it because that's what your husband told me when I was little. Trey was terrible."

They laughed.

Gia leaned back. "So, tell me a bit more about you and Taylor. How long have you known each other?"

"For about eight years," she responded. "Taylor believed in me when I didn't believe in myself. He's such a good man."

"Easy on the eyes, too. Sounds like you have a great husband, too, Rayne. I'm hoping the two of you will decide to stay and fight for your marriage. You're a great couple."

"Marriage isn't for everyone," she said before asking, "How did you and Trey reconnect?"

"It was after he came home from Afghanistan," Gia responded. "Trey was angry during that time. He tried to shut everybody out. He just wanted to be left alone."

"But you didn't give up on him."

She chuckled. "Girl, I thought about it a few times, but he's so worth the trouble."

Their conversation came to a halt when they were joined by more committee members.

Rayne hugged Gia's mother. "I remember you, Miss Patricia. You don't look like you've aged one bit." She looked like a slightly older version of her daughter. She had the same honey-blonde hair and hazel eyes. She possessed a curvier figure in contrast to her daughter's slender frame. Her festive sweater matched her personality.

They moved to the reserved seating area.

"Thank you, sweetie. I'm so glad to have you on our team. Gia mentioned that you have some great ideas for the festival. We can't wait to hear them."

Rayne smiled. She had always enjoyed event planning and felt it was one of her strengths. After the holidays, she intended to approach Trey, who worked at the museum, with a proposal to assist him with fundraising for the museum.

"Gia was telling me she'd like to have some new activities for the children, and after reviewing what previous festivals offered for the past five years, I agree with her. We should debut something fresh and new each year. It doesn't have to be anything huge."

"Do you have something in mind?" Patricia asked.

"Actually, I do," Rayne responded. "What do you think about a candy cane hunt?"

"Is it similar to the Easter egg hunt?"

She smiled at Patricia. "Yeah… We make it really simple for the younger children to find the candy and more challenging for the older group."

"I love this idea," Gia said.

"I do, too." Patricia took a sip of her water.

Rayne relaxed. She was thrilled about the chance to help with the final plans for the festival. Most of the planning had taken place earlier in the year. They were only a couple weeks away from the event.

Her thoughts centered on Taylor and how things were going at the house. Rayne prayed he would stay away from Misty and Leon. She didn't know how well he'd hold up if they started questioning him.

Taylor was even-tempered for the most part, and she didn't believe he would do anything to deliberately hurt her, but although he tried to hide it, she knew he was angry with her.

CHAPTER SIX

TAYLOR PERFORMED A series of kicks, punches and other karate movements called *kata*. He'd earned a third-degree black belt and even taught classes from time to time. After he completed his workout on the screened-in patio, Taylor stayed out there for another thirty minutes. It was almost time for his next virtual meeting. He'd scheduled one for the staff in Los Angeles and a second one for the Vegas crew.

Taylor's mind was plagued with thoughts of Rayne and her children. Once more, the prick of betrayal stabbed at him. He was deeply disappointed in her. Taylor had always regarded Rayne as honest and forthcoming. He never thought she would keep a secret this huge from him. He had a right to be told that about the pregnancy. The twins complicated an already difficult situation, but they were a tangible bond between them now.

He reminded himself of what Rayne had been through—this was the reason she was navigating in this manner with her family. The time he spent around her family only served to make Taylor feel guiltier. *How will they feel about me when the truth comes out? How will they feel about Rayne?*

Taylor knew that Rayne was keeping another secret from them. It was something she never wanted any of them to find out. He promised to take what he knew to the grave, and Taylor intended to keep his word.

He was about to enter the house but heard one of the babies crying. He froze. Was he supposed to instinctively run to his babies? Before he could move, he heard Misty's cooing tones, and a moment later, he received a call from his assistant. "Brenda, what can I do for you?"

"I'm having a problem with my laptop. I've been trying to save a spreadsheet for an hour."

"Have you spoken to Andy?" He was the tech person.

"No, I haven't."

"Give him a call," Taylor said. "He'll walk you through."

He made a mental note to enroll Brenda in one of the Excel classes at the community college. He'd done the same for Rayne when she began working for him. Someone had given him a chance in life, and he continued to pay it forward.

"HERE'S LUNCH," Rayne told Leon when she entered the house. "I bought enough for you, Misty and Taylor. That chili was so good…best I've had in a long time."

"Josh makes the greatest as far as I'm concerned," Leon responded.

"I heard my name," Taylor said when he walked into the kitchen.

"I brought you something to eat," she told him. "It's the absolute best chili and corn bread on the East Coast."

"I can't wait to dive into that. Tell me more about the corn bread."

Rayne grinned. "It's jalapeño corn bread. One of your favorites."

Taylor planted himself in one of the chairs at the table. "It smells good."

She sat down across from him.

"Where's yours?" he asked.

"I ate mine at the café."

"How did your meeting go?" Taylor inquired.

"Great," she responded. "And yours?"

He wiped his mouth on a napkin. "They were both good. We're set for the end-of-the-year sale at both locations."

Rayne glanced over at Misty and asked, "How were the twins?"

"They woke up once while you were gone. I fed and changed them, then they went back to sleep much to my disappointment. I wanted more cuddle time with them."

She gave a short laugh. "I know the feeling well. They try to sleep all day then be up at night when I want to sleep. But I'm glad they weren't a bother."

"Babies are never bothersome," Leon said.

She stole a peek at Taylor, who was beginning to look extremely uncomfortable.

"The twins and I are going to visit with Aunt Eleanor," Rayne announced. "I told Rusty we'd be there within the hour."

"Do you want me to drop you off?" Taylor asked.

"I'm good," she responded, though she was touched by his offer. "I can drive myself."

"I don't mind. I'd like to meet your aunt. You talk about her all the time."

She hadn't expected Taylor to want to meet more of her family because he wasn't comfortable with discussing their marital situation.

"I really hate that she's dealing with Alzheimer's. Her short-term memory is affected, so I'm not sure she will remember the twins or you."

"Maybe she will," Taylor said. "But even if she doesn't, I'd still like to meet her. She's very important to you."

"Yeah. Me and my mom both."

"Speaking of... When I talked to Carol, she sounded upset. She misses you."

She sighed. "I don't want to argue with her about my decision to come to the island. Maybe I'll call her later tonight."

He pointed to her sweater, apparently deciding to change the subject. "You're not seriously wearing that to your aunt's house?"

"What's wrong with it?"

"I thought you put it on for your meeting," Taylor stated.

"What don't you like about my sweater?"

"You have ornaments dangling down the front."

"All right, Grinch. I'll change it this time, but I'm warning you. I'm not about to let you kill my Christmas buzz."

Taylor laughed. "Just don't try to convert me."

She gave him a sidelong glance. "I make no promises."

They bundled up the twins and placed them in their carriers. Twenty minutes later, they were comfortably ensconced at Aunt Eleanor's.

"How are you feeling, Auntie?" Rayne inquired after they settled on a sofa with a floral pattern. Eleanor was one of a handful of people she knew who still had a formal living room.

"I can't complain. I feel pretty good. I'm a bit forgetful these days, but I suppose that comes with age."

"As I get older, I find that I'm always forgetting something, too," she responded with a chuckle. Rayne was devastated by the news of her aunt's condition. She felt guilty for not staying in better touch with Eleanor.

"Are these your babies, Rayne?"

"Yes, ma'am," she responded. Her eyes filled with tears. "I have a boy and a girl, Auntie." Pointing to her son, she said, "His name is Ian. My daughter is Ivy."

She seemed to be searching her memory before saying, "Yeah, I think I remember you mentioning that you'd had twins. You've been doubly blessed. A boy and a girl…that's just wonderful." Eleanor looked down at Rayne's hand. "I see you wearing a wedding ring. Chile, when did you get married, and why am I just hearing about it?"

"We got married last January. It was spur of the moment, I guess you can say," Rayne replied. "Auntie, this is my husband, Taylor."

Eleanor studied him a moment from head to toe before saying, "You a mighty handsome man."

Taylor broke into a grin. "Why thank you, Miss Eleanor. I appreciate the compliment."

"Rayne, I sho' hope you treating him right."

She broke into a short laugh. "I'm doing my best, Auntie."

"Glad to hear it," Eleanor stated. "You've got a nice-looking family, Rayne. Cherish them."

Rayne stole a quick peek at Taylor before replying, "That's exactly what I'm doing. They're my primary focus, Auntie. I know what life was like for me, and I won't have my children going through that."

"Times are different now, chile."

Rayne bent over to pick up her daughter. "She's waking up. I'd better feed her before she wakes up her brother."

Eleanor held the baby while Rayne warmed a bottle in the kitchen. She could hear their conversation continuing in the living room.

"Taylor, how are you enjoying Polk Island?"

"It's beautiful here," he replied. "I noticed that the island seems very family-oriented."

"Family is important."

"I agree," Taylor said.

"Where is your family?"

"I never knew many of my parents' relatives," he responded. "I ended up in a group home for the most part." Rayne knew he took ownership of his past, never trying to hide it. She appreciated that about him. He'd never shared too many of the details with her, though.

Rayne returned with two bottles. She sat one on the table. "That one is for Ian when he wakes up."

She took Ivy from Eleanor and sat down to feed her.

"You've very good with them."

"Thank you for saying that, Aunt Eleanor. I really want to be a good mother."

"You gwine do just fine. Give em' lots of love and your attention…that's what any child wants most."

"I couldn't agree more," Taylor stated.

Rayne eyed him until he looked away, trying not to judge him. He said he knew children needed love, yet he seemed to be too scared even to hold the babies. Sure, he felt they were his responsibility, but that was it. Just a responsibility.

"I made a big pot of collards, baked chicken and candied yams," Eleanor announced. "I hope you brought your appetites."

"Auntie, I hope you didn't go through all this for us."

"I love cooking for my family. Everybody knows when they come to my house—they better come hungry."

"I don't know about Taylor, but I definitely brought my appetite," Rayne responded. "Auntie, I didn't want you going out of your way just for us."

"Sugar, my husband and I eat like this every day."

Ian let out a squeal.

"Look who's up…" Rayne said. "I knew it wouldn't be long. He pretty much sticks to his schedule."

"Taylor, you feed your son," Eleanor stated as she rose to her feet. "I need to check on dinner."

Fear, stark and vivid, glittered in his eyes when he looked at Rayne.

"Just do what I'm doing," she whispered.

Taylor got up and cautiously picked up the baby boy. He held the infant away from him as he returned to his seat.

He took the bottle in one hand and cradled Ian with the other.

After a moment, Taylor said, "Either I'm not doing it right, or Ian's trying to hold it himself."

Rayne chuckled. "He's very independent. I can tell that already. The doctor had to catch him when he was born. He was moving like he had somewhere to go."

"You mean he was trying to bust out?"

"Something like that. I had to have a Caesarian birth. When they cut me, he started crawling out."

His eyes widened. "That must have been a scary time for you."

"It was," she confirmed. "But my mom was with me through the entire pregnancy. She was even my Lamaze coach."

"I'm glad you weren't alone," he responded.

She glimpsed a flash of raw emotion in his eyes and felt a sliver of guilt. "Taylor…"

"Dinner's ready," Eleanor announced, her voice adding warmth to the chilled temperature in the air.

"I can't change what happened," Rayne whispered. "But now that you're here… I do wish I'd handled it differently."

All he could do was nod. There wasn't anything to say.

Determined not to put a damper on the evening, Taylor swallowed his emotions and was intent on enjoying their time with Eleanor and Rusty.

They settled down in the family room to watch a movie after dinner.

She could feel Taylor's body heat as they sat together. The baby carriers were on the floor beside them. Every now and then, she would engage him in conversation.

As they readied to leave when the movie ended, Eleanor said, "I'm so glad y'all came by. I really enjoyed this visit. When y'all plan on leaving out?"

"Auntie, I'll be here," Rayne said. "I'm moving back to the island."

Taylor's eyebrows rose a fraction. They hadn't yet discussed her plans for the future.

"Oh, that's wonderful. I sho' wish I could get your mother to come home."

"I'm working on her."

"Now that she got those grandbabies, she just might do it," Eleanor stated as she walked them to the door.

"I'll call you tomorrow, Auntie."

"Okay, sugar. Y'all drive safe."

It was almost nine o'clock when they returned to Leon's house.

"I really like your aunt and Rusty. It's sad that she has to fight such a dreadful disease."

"I wish you could've met Aunt Eleanor before Alzheimer's," Rayne said while getting the twins settled in the crib.

She grabbed a pair of pajamas, saying, "I'm going to get ready for bed. I'm tired."

Taylor grabbed the folded blankets from a trunk inside the closet. He placed them on the floor. "I can't take another night in that chair."

"Taylor, come on. You can sleep in the bed."

"I'll be fine on the floor."

Rayne sighed in resignation.

The tension between them was gnawing away at her confidence. Taylor had always been easy to talk to, but they couldn't seem to find any common ground now. She wondered if she'd broken the bond they'd once had.

When she returned to the room, Taylor took

one look at her and broke into a grin. "I'm loving that bonnet on you."

She knew it was an attempt at a truce. "Laugh all you want. I'll do whatever it takes to keep my hair healthy."

"I've always loved your hair," Taylor confessed.

Rayne climbed into bed, pulling the covers over herself. "You never told me that before."

Taylor sat down on the upholstered bench. "I wasn't sure it was appropriate because you were my employee."

She smiled, then said, "That's why I never told you how much I liked your beard."

"Anything else you like about me?"

"Are you really fishing for compliments?"

Grinning, Taylor responded, "It's been a while since I've had one."

"I find that hard to believe," she teased.

But he said seriously, "You know I haven't seen anyone for a while now. Romantically, I mean. It seemed like I just kept meeting women with children or women who wanted to have them."

"You know how my last one ended," Rayne said. "The one before you, that is. After all that mess, I decided to focus on being a better version of myself."

"I know. And in case no one's told you, you've

done a fantastic job of turning your life around. I'm very proud of you."

"I couldn't have done it without you, Taylor. Most people wouldn't have given me my job back after being arrested. They wouldn't have paid my attorney fees or supported me the way you did." She blinked several times, fighting back tears.

He gave her a tender look. "Rayne, I knew you were innocent."

Wiping away her tears, she said, "You really care about people. I see how you are with your employees, with the kids at the group home... I love that about you."

"I simply treat people the way I'd like to be treated," he responded.

Silence fell for a few moments. She moved to a lighter topic, asking, "How was Deacon's wedding?"

"It was nice," Taylor said. "They got married in a cabin at Big Bear Lake. A small, intimate ceremony."

"Sounds like it was very romantic."

He yawned.

"I guess we really should try to get some sleep before the twins wake up," Rayne stated. She tried to stifle her own yawn by putting a hand over her mouth.

"I understand why you wanted to bring the

twins here…with your family. They're surrounded by love."

"I didn't just do it for them, Taylor. I need my family, too."

Taylor made a pallet on the floor and lay down on it.

Rayne stretched and yawned. "I hope it's more comfortable for you on the floor."

"Me, too."

Wallowing in the softness of her pillow, she squeezed her eyes tightly closed and sought the sweetness of sleep. It didn't take long.

TAYLOR AWOKE SUDDENLY. A glance at the clock indicated that he'd been sleeping for only a couple hours. He raised up just enough to see that Rayne was sound asleep. No sound came from the crib.

He lay back down, hoping to grab another two or three hours of sleep before Ian and Ivy demanded their attention.

When he woke up a second time, it was almost seven o'clock.

Taylor was grateful to wake up without a stiff neck. He got up and stretched. He was surprised to find Rayne still in bed sound asleep. She lay on her side with her back to him.

He crept out to the bathroom.

She was up and moving around when he returned fully dressed. Taylor noticed that she'd already removed the bonnet; her hair hung freely down her back.

"You're up early," Rayne said.

"I guess I'm over the jet lag."

"I'm going to get dressed before the twins wake up. I've already fixed their bottles." She pointed to them. "They're on the nightstand."

"When did you do that?"

"About ten minutes ago," she responded.

He must have looked worried because Rayne said, "Relax, I'll get dressed and feed them." She shook her head. "You've always been the one to reassure me of my capabilities. I'm not used to seeing you like this."

"There's a good reason for that. I've never been around babies."

"I'm sure you can learn, Taylor. If they cry, just give them a bottle. I'll be right across the hall. Knock on the door if you need me."

"You're right," he responded. He was being ridiculous. "I can handle Ian and Ivy. No problem."

"That's right. They're only babies."

Taylor watched her leave the room before turning to the crib. He felt the infant's gaze on him.

"Hey, little man...do you know who I am?" he asked, stroking his cheek.

Ian grabbed his thumb.

Keeping his voice low, he whispered, "You and your sister deserve all the best that life has to offer. That's what I want for you both. But I have to be honest with you—it's not me, so don't go getting any ideas. You deserve to have someone like Leon or Trey in your lives. But this doesn't mean that I'm going to abandon you. *I'm not.* I'd never do that. Just letting you know that I might mess up sometimes, but I hope you won't give up on me."

"That won't happen, Taylor."

He glanced over his shoulder at Rayne. He hadn't heard her enter the room.

"I forgot something," she said.

When she headed back out, she teased, "Carry on…"

Ian started kicking and making noises.

"You heard your mom's sweet voice. I'll tell you a secret…that's how I feel when I hear her voice. You won the lottery when you got Rayne for a mother. She's smart and funny. She's loyal… Ian, she's incredible."

Taylor picked up his son, cradling him in his arms. He sat down in the rocker. "You and your sister have her eyes. I'm not sure who you really look like more, but it doesn't matter. I'm glad you're both healthy and happy."

When Rayne returned to the bedroom, she found them still seated in the rocker.

"Ian didn't want his bottle?" she asked.

"He hasn't made a fuss. I think he just wanted some guy time. In fact, Ian was just telling me that he's really not into Christmas, either."

She broke into a grin. "Oh, really? Ian said that?"

Taylor nodded. "I asked if he'd written a letter to Santa Claus, and he was like 'Who's that?'"

Rayne laughed. "Give him a couple of years."

Ivy woke up protesting, so she quickly attended to her daughter.

Taylor picked up the other bottle and poised the nipple to Ian's lips. He latched on quickly.

He continued his conversation with the infant, whose gaze was glued to Rayne.

"Hey, young man... I'd like some of your attention, too."

Ian looked up at him.

"That's better. I understand... Your mother distracts me, too."

Taylor glanced up to see if Rayne was listening to them, but she had her head down and seemed to be having a conversation of her own with Ivy as she changed her diaper.

He turned his attention back to Ian. "Now, your mom...she's going to give you all the love she has. She's a great person. She will always be there for you and Ivy. You can count on that."

Ian tried to put Taylor's thumb into his mouth.

"You don't want to put that in your mouth," Taylor said. "Where's his pacifier?"

"Here you go." Rayne handed one to him.

"How do you know this one belongs to him?"

"His are all blue, and Ivy's are pink."

"Oh. That makes sense."

"It's not scientific—it's just my way."

Shrugging, Taylor said, "As long as it works."

He kept Ian in his arms until the baby was asleep. "Is it me or are they staying awake longer?"

"Last night, they only woke up for one feeding," Rayne said.

"I didn't even notice."

"That's because you were knocked out on the floor. You were actually snoring."

Taylor shook his head in denial. "No, I don't think so."

She laughed. "It was you."

"I guess I was making up for the other night in that chair." He was ready to check into a hotel, but he didn't want to be away from the twins.

Rayne's voice cut into his thoughts. "You haven't said what you think of your son and daughter."

"They're, you know, good," he replied.

"Good?" she laughed.

He sighed. "Look, you know I'm bad at this. You were right, I'm not really father material. I never wanted kids. But I intend to be there for the twins."

Rayne turned away from him. "If you don't want them, why do you want to be in their lives? This doesn't make sense to me."

A sudden feeling of guilt overwhelmed Taylor. "None of this really makes sense, if you think about it. All I know is that I'm not going to walk away from my children."

He thought the emotion he saw in her gaze was one of disappointment. Taylor bit back his hurt. Even Rayne thought he wasn't father material. Why else would she want him to terminate his parental rights?

It was perfectly clear that she only wanted his name for the babies, not him for himself.

RAYNE STRUGGLED TO keep her expression blank during breakfast. Rayne was confused by Taylor's insistence on being in the twins' lives. But then she never understood how he could be so loving and caring to children but not want to have his own. She knew it stemmed from whatever happened to him growing up. Rayne didn't know the depths of his pain—he would always stop short of discussing his childhood with her.

She'd tried to get him to open up more about his parents, but Taylor would just change the subject. Rayne wouldn't press him; instead, she respected his boundaries. It was one of the reasons they got along so well.

She thought of his dedication to the kids at the group home; Taylor always made sure they had whatever was needed and more. He and his best friend, Deacon, volunteered on a regular basis as tutors and mentors. Rayne knew that Taylor had the older boys shadow the staff in various areas. He employed a couple of them at the dealership.

Rayne had always believed he'd make a great father, even though she knew he was adamant about not wanting kids of his own.

How did I ever think I could change his mind?

This question had come up again and again. She still had no answer.

Her eyes watered. She blinked rapidly to keep tears from slipping down her cheeks. Rayne wasn't about to let him see her cry. At least not over him.

Somewhere deep down, Rayne must have believed Taylor would suddenly embrace fatherhood and plead to become a part of their lives.

She was wrong. He wasn't coming along willingly. Taylor was a reluctant husband and father.

After breakfast, Rayne went back to the bedroom.

Taylor cut into her turbulent thoughts by asking, "Why are you so quiet?"

"I was playing around with some ideas for the festival," she fibbed. Her contemplations were consumed by him, but she refused to tell Taylor that.

"You're good at things like that. Remember the fundraiser you worked on a couple of years ago?"

"You mean the one where we collected prom dresses?"

"Yeah. You spearheaded the event, and it was a huge success."

"I was thinking about asking Renee to donate a couple of dresses. She owns the boutique next to the café."

"She's the fashion designer?"

Rayne nodded. "Yeah."

"That's a good idea," he said.

Taylor sat down beside her. "Rayne, I didn't mean to disappoint you earlier."

"What are you talking about?"

"I think it's time we had an honest conversation," he said.

"I've told you the truth about everything, Taylor," Rayne answered thickly.

"You kept the twins' existence from me, like you didn't want me to be part of your lives. But since I got here, it almost feels like you're going back and forth between being angry I'm not here for them and...*hoping* I don't want to raise them. That I'd just walk away from them."

"I never saw myself as a mother," Rayne responded after a few moments. "I wasn't even sure I wanted children, but the first time I heard their heartbeats and saw them during a sonogram... Taylor, I felt such an abundance of love for them. It was like all my love had been stored up for them. I think maybe I was afraid that if I shared that with you and you didn't feel the same way, it would break something in me. But now that you're here, I think you feel that connection, after all."

"I don't," he responded, then winced. "I'm not saying this to be mean or to upset you. I'm being honest, Rayne. It's still very new for me. Don't misunderstand me. I care for Ian and Ivy. I really do. I just... We both know I'm not the dad they need."

She glared. "So, why are you still even here? I've already told you that I'd sign the paperwork after Christmas. Why haven't you left yet?"

"I haven't seen you in eleven months. Did it ever occur to you that I missed my friend?"

She started to cry.

"Rayne…"

"It's nothing. My emotions are all over the place," she said. "I'll be fine."

Taylor wrapped an arm around her. "I wish I could tell you what you want to hear, but I'd be lying. Why don't we table this discussion for now?"

"I don't really care what you do," she responded. Rayne sighed, clasped her slender hands together and stared at them. Her clamped lips imprisoned a sob.

"I'll give you some space," he said quietly.

She ached with an inner pain. She'd been lying to herself all these months. She *had* wanted him to be a part of their lives. But no amount of Christmas magic could make him want to stay married and help her raise their twins. He wanted out, and she refused to beg him to stay.

CHAPTER SEVEN

EARLIER, WHEN RAYNE looked at him, there was no lighting of her eyes, no tender smile—just pain flickering there. So Taylor left the guest-room to give Rayne some privacy.

He walked into the kitchen and found Leon at the table eating a breakfast sandwich.

"Do you mind if I make a cup of tea for Rayne?" he asked.

"Not at all. Make yourself at home. Rayne mentioned you opened a second dealership in Las Vegas earlier this year. Congratulations."

"Thanks. It's always been a dream to have several across the country."

"Looks like you're off to a good start."

"That was my first job," Taylor said. "I worked at this tiny car lot. It was just the owner and his wife running the place. They didn't have any children, so Jim taught me everything, and I was able to take over after he was diagnosed with cancer. The business grew stronger just as he was becoming weaker. After Jim died, his wife and I continued running the company. At that point, we needed to hire a couple employees. Before Myrna passed away, she placed everything in my name."

He leaned against the counter. "I wish she and Jim could've lived long enough to see how far we've come from that little lot."

"I believe they know," Leon said.

They talked for a few minutes more before Taylor went back to the guestroom.

Rayne was staring out the window, her back to him.

"I brought you a cup of tea," he said.

"You can leave it on the nightstand."

He crossed the room to stand beside her. "I hate being the cause of your sadness."

She didn't respond.

Taylor swung her into the circle of his arms. He held her snugly. "Rayne, you know that I care about you. A year ago, you were one of my best friends. I know you're disappointed in me, but you also know I'm not father material." He wanted to add, *But I'm willing to learn.*

Looking up at him, Rayne asked, "Why won't you tell me what happened to make you believe that?"

"Just trust me on this." All Taylor felt in this moment was the weight of being forced into fatherhood. He wished he felt differently for Rayne's sake, but he didn't. He didn't believe he had anything to offer those two innocent babies. Of course, he wasn't going to just disappear into the night. He was going to find a way to support them. Maybe even to earn their trust and respect. They were beautiful. He could hardly believe that he'd had such a major role in their conception.

When Rayne walked away from him, he said, "I think it's best that I leave. My presence here is only upsetting you."

"I'm still not signing those papers until after Christmas," Rayne stated.

"I'll come back then."

"You do realize that neither one of us lives in Las Vegas."

"I'll stay there for the required six weeks," he responded. "I can check to see if they'd consider the time you lived there."

She shrugged in nonchalance. "Do whatever you want."

"Rayne, you're confusing me. Now you're acting as if you don't want this divorce to happen."

"Why would I want to stay married to a man who doesn't love his own children?"

Taylor stiffened. "Wow…" He felt an instant's squeezing hurt.

"That was unfair," Rayne said after a moment. "I'm sorry." She folded her arms across her chest. "Maybe you're right. It's best you go back to Los Angeles."

"Do you need help with securing a place for you and the twins?"

"I'll be fine."

"Rayne, let me at least do that for you."

"No," she responded, then she seemed to come to a decision. "Look, maybe you're right that I shouldn't have kept the twins a secret from you. Maybe we could have worked something out months ago. I didn't think you'd want them, and I thought I was okay with that. But things have changed. If you walk out on us now—don't look back, Taylor. If being here with our children hasn't opened your heart just a little—then leaving is the right thing to do. You might as well terminate your parental rights. You can't be half in and half out. I won't allow it."

Rayne turned toward the door. "I'll leave you to your packing. Try not to wake the twins."

When she was gone, Taylor sank down on the edge of the bed, his face in his hands.

RAYNE TOOK SOLACE in the warmth of the family room. She sat down on the sofa with Leon and Misty's wedding album on her lap. Her eyes filled with tears as she looked at photo after photo of their wedding ceremony on the beach at sunset.

Since when did I start thinking about marriage? It was never a part of my plans. Rayne gave herself a mental shake.

She and Taylor had both agreed that terminating the marriage was the right thing to do. He wasn't blindsiding her with the decision. In fact, she was the one who'd initiated the idea. And she'd been sure all these months that he wouldn't want to be a father. He was only proving her right.

I can't be angry with him.

The right thing to do would be to let him leave. Leave the marriage and the twins behind.

She'd assumed giving them Taylor's name would be enough. But just the thought of her children with no real father broke her heart.

Rayne wiped away her tears when she heard Misty in the kitchen. She got up to join her.

"I just finished looking at your wedding album. You were a beautiful bride, and you looked so happy. Leon, too."

"I think every bride and groom look happy on their wedding day," Misty said while making sandwiches. "It's what happens after that day that tells the true story. Earlier this year, I made this beautiful cake for a couple. It was very extravagant and expensive. I saw the wife last week, and she told me that they aren't together anymore. They're getting divorced."

"That's really sad," Rayne responded.

"I don't have anything against lavish weddings or cakes—they keep us in business. Too often it's more about the wedding than the marriage. I thought about that when Leon proposed. Had a really nice wedding the first time. The marriage...not so much."

"I never thought about weddings or getting married, period," she confided. "I was focused on making my place in this world now that I was finally on track."

"But then you met Taylor."

Rayne nodded. "I married my best friend."

"Those are often the best marriages," Misty responded.

Rayne helped carry plates to the table.

"Talei, there's lunch for y'all," Misty called out to the children.

They heard Leo and Fawn running toward the kitchen.

Soon after, they heard Talei yell, "No running in the house."

Rayne and Misty chuckled.

Trey and Gia came into the house with their son.

"Trevon, are you hungry?" Misty asked the little boy.

He nodded.

"Son, speak with your mouth," Trey said.

"Yeh."

A little later, Taylor emerged and joined them in the living room. He seemed composed, like nothing had happened between him and Rayne.

"How long will you be in town?" Trey asked him.

"Until later tonight."

"You should consider spending Christmas with us. The family would love to get to know its newest member. At least think about it."

"I will," Taylor responded.

Rayne knew he'd already made his decision. He was leaving. They would all have to accept it.

"I tell him all the time that his employees think they can't function without him," she said.

"It was better when Rayne worked there," he responded. "She kept the place running smoothly. I think I took my first real vacation six months after she came to the company."

Smiling, she said, "They used to call me head of security."

"I can believe it," Trey responded. "You've always been bossy."

She dismissed his comment with a slight wave of her hand.

Everyone seemed to be enjoying the conversation going on except Taylor. He looked tense and was quiet unless someone asked him a question. Rayne was sure Leon and Trey noticed it as well.

She was relieved when he had to excuse himself to take a phone call. Rayne waited twenty minutes before going out after him.

He was pacing the floor when she joined him outside.

"I've never felt so uncomfortable in my life," he stated. "They keep looking at us like they hope we're going to work it out, and I feel like I'm lying to them."

"We haven't lied," she protested.

"But you know that our marriage has never been a real one."

She winced. "Yeah, I know. You certainly won't let me forget it."

"Those are good people in there. I believe they'd understand what really happened."

"Taylor, I'm really not trying to make you out to be a villain. I ask that you don't make me one, either. Just let me handle my family, please."

Talei rushed out of the house. "Rayne, Ian is waking up. I think he's hungry. Can I give him his bottle when it's ready?"

"You sure can," she said.

They could hear him crying when they walked inside.

Rayne retrieved two bottles from the fridge, placing them in the warmer. "He's going to wake Ivy, fussing like that."

Taylor glanced at Talei. "You have such a unique name."

She smiled. "My mom says that it means *precious one*."

Rayne sat the bottles on the table in the breakfast area. "I'll be right back."

Talei walked with her toward the first-floor guestroom.

They returned minutes later with the babies.

After Talei was settled in a chair with Ian, Rayne handed her a bottle. She then grabbed the other bottle and sat down across from her.

"Talei really seems to know what to do. She has a natural instinct," Taylor observed as he watched her make eye contact with Ian and talk softly while feeding him.

"Yes, she does," Rayne responded. "She's been great. I've never met a little girl who loves babies as much as she does."

"She certainly knows more about them than I do." Taylor eyed the infants. "I'm glad you've got help here. I don't know how you manage it...taking care of two babies."

"I love them, so I don't mind that they command so much of my attention," Rayne responded. She looked at him seriously. "Would you like to hold your daughter one last time before you leave?"

He took the baby from Rayne.

The little girl snuggled up against him, placing her head on his chest.

"That's your daddy, Ivy," Talei said.

His breath caught when the infant opened her eyes to stare at him. It was as if she'd understood the introduction. Ivy seemed to be studying Taylor. The heat from her tiny body radiated a warmness throughout his body.

"She didn't stick her tongue out at me this time." He had hardly gotten the words out when Ivy did just that. "Uh…change that. She just did it."

"Ivy doesn't do that with me," Rayne said.

"I don't think she likes you," Talei blurted. "She doesn't do that to anyone else."

They laughed, but when she glimpsed a glimmer of hurt in Taylor's expression, Rayne felt a thread of guilt. "It's not personal," she explained. "It's a tongue-thrust reflex. I read that it helps facilitate breast or bottle feeding."

"If it's a reflex, why does Ivy only do it whenever she's with me?"

"I don't have the answer to that."

"I think Talei's right. She doesn't like me. I've heard that young children have an innate sense about people." Taylor gave Ivy back to Rayne. "I need to finish packing."

HE CHIDED HIMSELF for feeling rejected by Ivy. She was a baby. But he couldn't help but wonder why she didn't care for him. She didn't cry whenever he held her—just stared and stuck her tongue out.

His thoughts were interrupted by a phone call from Deacon.

"I hate calling you about this, but your assistant just messed up big-time."

"What happened?" Taylor asked.

"She never booked a caterer for the Christmas party, and she didn't buy toys. We have the ones that were donated. That's it."

After listening to what Deacon had to say and promising to get back to him with a solution, Taylor ended his phone call in frustration.

"Whoa...little people entering the area," Rayne said.

"I'm sorry," he responded tightly.

"What's wrong?"

"Deacon just called to let me know that my executive assistant forgot to order food for Kline's annual Christmas party. Oh, and she forgot about the toys. I can't believe it!"

"Taylor, breathe..." she said. "The party is next weekend, right?"

He nodded.

"I'll call Petra at Three Sisters Catering to see if she can pull together a menu of turkey, ham and veggie sliders, maybe some sweet-potato fries or chips… Something quick and simple." Rayne handed Ivy to him.

Taylor put the baby on his chest and sat down on the edge of the bed. "If there's a rush fee—that's fine," he said. "I can't let those boys down."

Talei sat in the rocker with Ian, who was still wide-awake. She was so quiet; he'd almost forgotten she was in the room with them.

Rayne called her friend and went over what she needed. When she ended the conversation, she announced, "Food's taken care of, and Petra said she's waiving the rush fee. She had a last-minute cancellation. She's going to throw in some peppermint bark for the boys."

"Thank you. Now what can we do about gifts?"

She smiled. "We go shopping. There's a Barnaby Toy Store in Charleston. We can buy everything on this end and have Kline pick the order up at the store's location in Los Angeles."

"I'm good with that."

"The only thing is that I usually have a list I work off of with ages and wishes. We're going to have to wing it, so I'm going to need you and Talei to help."

"I love shopping for gifts," the little girl interjected. "I know all the toys that boys like. I hear them talking about stuff all the time at school."

"Great," Rayne responded. "I'll ask your mom if you can go with us. I'll also see if she is okay with watching the twins while we're gone. If not, I'll check with Aunt Eleanor and Rusty."

Thirty minutes later, they were driving to Charleston.

"Thank you," Taylor said. "I don't know how Brenda missed this. I sent an email reminding her last week."

"It can be daunting if you're not used to doing stuff like this," Rayne responded. "Don't be too hard on her."

"I'm not entrusting any of this to her again. This could've ended up a disaster."

"It won't be. Everything is going to be fine. Those boys are going to have a great time like they do every year."

"Thanks to you and Talei."

She glanced at him and smiled. "Relax..."

Taylor leaned back in his seat with his eyes closed.

When they pulled into the parking lot of Barnaby's, Talei gushed, "I love this place."

He shared a look with Rayne and laughed.

Inside the store, they grabbed a shopping cart. Rayne wanted to pick up gifts for the children in her family.

Taylor was impressed with Talei's suggestions for both family members and the boys in the group home.

"Only the younger boys want superheroes. The boys in my class are all about video and computer games. But some of them really like science stuff like microscopes or those lab kits. My friend Randy has a rock collection."

"I hadn't really thought of that before," he said. "There's a couple of boys there who collect rocks."

"You should get them this kit," Talei responded. "It's for beginners."

He looked over at Rayne. They were both infected by the little girl's enthusiasm.

Taylor took Rayne's hand. "I owe you bigtime for all this."

"No, I owed you," she responded. "I know we can't exactly call it even, but I'm hoping it's a start."

They spent an hour looking and selecting items that would be picked up from the California store.

For her help, Talei was allowed to pick out something for herself.

"This is not your Christmas present," Taylor

said. "This is for helping us with this and for helping Rayne with the twins."

"Can I choose something for Fawn and Leo instead?"

He smiled. "Yes, you can…as long as you also pick out a toy for yourself."

Talei wrapped her arms around him. *"Wado."*

"It means *thank you*," Rayne explained.

"You're quite welcome, Precious One."

That evening, Rayne brought him a cup of hot chocolate while he reviewed company reports.

"Those spreadsheets don't look right."

"They're not Brenda's strength."

"Why did you hire her?" she asked.

"She lost her previous job and was about to be homeless."

Rayne gave him a knowing smile. "You've always been so compassionate. It's one of the qualities I lo—" She stopped short. "That I like about you."

His gaze traveled over her face and searched her eyes.

"Tonight's your last night on the island. Your last night with me and your children."

"You make it sound so permanent."

"It truly feels that way," she replied.

He took a sip of the warm liquid. "I know

you don't believe this, but you and the twins will be in my life forever."

Looking over at him, she asked, "Do you really have to leave?"

Taylor nodded. "I don't feel good being around your family in this situation."

"And I'm not ready to tell them what really happened between us." She sighed. "I'll miss you."

"We'll keep talking, okay? I'm not walking out on you."

"I can't help but feel like you're abandoning me and the twins."

Something flickered in Taylor's eyes. "I've never *abandoned* anyone, Rayne. I won't start now. Trust me, I know what that feels like."

HIS SUITCASE NEAR the door, Taylor sat down on the edge of the bed. "I thought it didn't snow in this region."

"It has on rare occasions," Rayne responded. "They mentioned there was just a slight chance of it on the weather channel."

"It's enough to cancel flights."

"I'm not going to say I'm sad about this because I'm not."

He met her gaze. "There's something I have to ask you."

"What is it?"

"Will you please reconsider signing the papers now? We can get this taken care of and not have it hanging over us."

Rayne shook her head no. "I'm not going to change my mind."

"Why are you delaying the inevitable?" Taylor asked.

"Why do we have to rush into this divorce?" she countered. "Have you met someone?"

"No, there's not someone else," he responded. "I just figured it would be better for us to rectify what we both know was a mistake."

She sighed. "I'd promised myself that I'd reach out to you in the new year. I wanted my life settled and stable on the island before becoming a divorced woman."

"And is that still what you want?"

She frowned. "Yes. But also... I don't know. Some part of me feels like rushing into this divorce is a mistake."

"We've been married for eleven months—almost a year," Taylor said. "We've never lived together or even been a real couple."

"I know that," Rayne said.

"Is this your way of telling me that you don't want a divorce at all?" Here it was. This was her chance.

"I don't know what I'm saying right now." She put her hands to her face.

"Look, maybe we're both on edge."

Rayne nodded. "You're probably right."

"What would you like me to do?" he asked after a moment.

"I'd like for you to stay here for the holidays. Continue to get to know your children. We can sign the papers in the new year and…if you want to help support the children financially, I can accept that. No regrets if you want to be out of their lives otherwise."

He considered her words. "I guess I can do that. My GMs can handle the business, and if something comes up—I'm only a video meeting away."

"So, do we have a deal?" Rayne asked.

He nodded. "Just until after the holidays."

"I'll keep my word." Holding her hand out to him, she said, "Let's shake on it."

Taylor pulled her into his arms, kissing her instead.

THAT UNEXPECTED KISS had her senses spiraling.

There were moments when Rayne wondered what it would feel like to be kissed by him. She only had a few fractured memories of what happened the night they got married. She'd decided a while back that it would be the pinnacle of foolishness to romanticize their relationship.

It was probably pure stupidity to have allowed this kiss to take place.

Taylor slowly stepped back from her. "I won't apologize for kissing you," he said.

"I would be insulted if you did," Rayne responded.

"I guess we need to let your family know that I'll be here for Christmas."

"They're going to be very happy to hear this. Especially Talei." She was the happiest of all, but she didn't say it aloud.

With a nod of his head, he followed her to the family room, where Leon and Misty sat watching television.

"The movie just started," Misty announced. "Come join us."

Taylor sank down beside Rayne, who said, "Taylor's not leaving. He's going to stay through Christmas."

"That's wonderful," Misty exclaimed.

Rayne felt him shift his position in the space beside her once more. He'd done that at least three times now; he seemed restless.

The kiss she'd shared with Taylor floated to the forefront of her mind. It would have been very easy for Rayne to allow the kiss to take on greater importance, but she didn't trust it. She knew that he wasn't trying to start something with her—why would he want someone like her?

She knew the truth.

Taylor Carrington was a good friend. She knew that. Maybe there had been more attraction between them than she'd ever admitted before. But sharing a kiss like that after all this time was foolish. She knew why he was here: his precious divorce.

CHAPTER EIGHT

THE NEXT DAY, Taylor opened his suitcase to unpack. He was surprised to find a small box inside. It was a gift from Talei with instructions not to open it until Christmas.

"She gave it to me to sneak in your suitcase when we thought you were leaving," Rayne said. "Here, give it back, and I'll make sure it's under the tree on Christmas morning."

His phone rang. It was Deacon.

"I need to take this call," he said. "I'll be on the back porch so I don't disturb anyone."

"So, Rayne saved the day for us," he said when Taylor answered the phone.

"Yes, she did," he said. "She really came through for us."

"Were you able to convince her to come back to work?" Deacon asked. "If not, you need to— Brenda needs to be a receptionist or something. I know you're not going to fire her. Maybe Rayne can train her to eventually be an executive assistant. But right now, she's not ready."

"She's not that bad. I just can't expect her to do everything that Rayne used to do."

"What's going on with Rayne? Why did she quit in the first place?"

Taylor glanced over his shoulder. "Right now, she wants to focus on her family." He still hadn't told his best friend about the marriage or the babies. He wasn't being completely honest with his friend, just like Rayne hadn't told her family the complete truth.

"I can respect that," Deacon responded.

No response.

"Taylor, you still here? You seem a bit distracted."

"Huh… I'm sorry… My mind is all over the place."

"When are you coming back home?" Deacon asked.

"I'm not sure right now?"

"You know I always thought the two of you would end up together."

"We were friends," Taylor responded. "Nothing more. I wasn't going to risk everything I'd built on a relationship with an employee."

"I'm not saying anything inappropriate was going on between you and Rayne. Besides, she's no longer your employee."

"We're feeling everything out right now, Deacon."

"She's the one for you, Taylor. Don't let her get away a second time."

They talked a few minutes more before hanging up.

Taylor returned to the bedroom and found Rayne gone. He heard laughter coming from upstairs in the loft.

He left the bedroom and called out to her from the bottom of the stairs.

"Taylor, come up here," Talei said. "We're about to watch a Christmas movie."

He groaned, then said, "You go ahead. I think I'll catch up on some reading."

"You'll like this one," Rayne said. "It's *How the Grinch Stole Christmas*." She chuckled then sang a song about how the Grinch was a mean one.

Shaking his head, Taylor slowly made his way to the second level. *I just need to get through this month.* It wouldn't be so bad if he didn't have to fight through the many painful holiday memories of his youth.

SATURDAY MORNING, a sleep-deprived Rayne followed the mouthwatering sound of bacon sizzling on the stovetop grill and the smell of fresh coffee to the kitchen, where her gaze landed on a stack of pancakes and fresh fruit.

Misty handed her a plate. "You look exhausted."

"I didn't get much sleep between the feedings, changing diapers and the cuddle time. The twins were off their schedule. Ian wanted to play, and he kept Ivy up with his crying whenever I tried to put him down." She yawned. "I have a meeting regarding the festival in a couple of hours. I'll get the twins ready after I put some food in my stomach." Rayne placed two strips of bacon, two pancakes and fruit on her plate.

"Why don't you leave them here with me?" Misty suggested. "You and Taylor take some time for yourselves."

"You're not working today?" Rayne asked.

"No, Leon's working an extra shift, so I'm home with the kids. I'm sure Talei will be eager to help me with the twins."

"Misty, are you sure about this?"

She nodded. "I love having them here. Leon thinks I'm getting baby fever."

"Are you?"

Misty shrugged. "Maybe...we've been talking about having another baby. It's just talk for now, though. We haven't really decided yet."

"You're great parents." She sighed and then confessed, "I wasn't sure I'd be a good mom. I didn't want to be like my mom. I know now that she was a good mother, but back then I saw her as weak. I lost respect for her the day she decided to take me off the island. I was twelve at the time, and it stuck with me. I was so rebellious during my teen years. And angry. Angry because I hungered for a father's love, frustrated with my mother for being so controlling."

"My dad wasn't in my life, either, Rayne. And it affected me. I blamed my mom for a while and had moments of rebellion," Misty said. "But my mom—Oma didn't play. She sent me to spend the summer with her sister who lived on tribal lands. That was a real education for me."

"It took a really dark moment in my life to change my perspective."

Misty sat down at the table across from Rayne. "Those defining moments make or break us."

She nodded in agreement. "That's for sure."

"I'm glad Taylor decided to stay. It'll give you two a chance to work on your marriage."

"Me, too," Rayne responded.

She stuck a piece of bacon in her mouth.

"How is it that you always beat me to the kitchen for breakfast?" Taylor asked.

"Hmm…just happens that way."

He fixed his plate, then joined them at the breakfast table.

"After my meeting, I'd like to take you somewhere," Rayne said after wiping her mouth on a napkin.

She poured Taylor a glass of juice.

"Where are we going?" he inquired.

"You'll see."

Taylor glanced over at Misty, who merely shrugged.

Rayne was going to take him on a tour of the island. She hoped it would help him appreciate why her family was so important to her, why she wanted to raise Ian and Ivy on the island, surrounded by a village of love.

TAYLOR STARED OUT the passenger-side window as Rayne drove to the historic section of the island. They got out of the vehicle.

Pointing to the skeletal structure, she said, "This is Polk Rothchild's original house. As you can see, it was built from a mixture of lime, shells and water. A cyclone hit the island in the late 1800s, leaving behind a lot of damage on this street."

"Why didn't they rebuild?" Taylor asked.

"I'm not sure," Rayne responded. "That's a question for Trey. All I know is that instead of rebuilding here, the family moved to the south side of the island. I do know that all this land over here still belongs to the family."

He pointed to a sign. "The Praise House. Is that supposed to be a church?"

"Yeah, it is. Polk was the pastor."

He peered through one of the windows. "Looks like it's been renovated."

Rayne took a look as well. "Trey did tell me that he had some work done on it but wanted to keep it close to the original building. I can show you the old photographs. What I have always found amazing about this church is that it wasn't touched during the cyclone. Only the other four houses across the street."

"That's interesting," Taylor said. "I think the chapel where we got married is larger than this church. I don't think I've ever seen one so tiny."

"It's tiny, but I'm sure it does whatever it's supposed to do. This is where Gia and Trey got married."

His eyebrows rose in surprise. "Really? You can't get all of your family in that building— not to mention her family members."

Rayne shrugged. "It worked for them."

Taylor walked ahead a few yards. "Is that a cemetery in the back of the church?"

She nodded. "It's where Polk and Hoss are buried along with other family members."

"I think it's nice that you're able to trace your family back so many generations," he said.

Rayne saw the expression on his face and

gave his arm a squeeze. She knew he didn't have any extended family of his own. Taylor did not enjoy talking about that part of his life. She wondered if his parents were still alive, and if so, where they were.

He caught her by surprise when he said, "I really liked my grandmother, but I only saw her maybe two or three times. My mom had a brother, but I think he died of a drug overdose."

She touched his arm again. "Well, you have Deacon. And before he died, you had Ian. They're your brothers."

Taylor agreed. "The three of us met when we were ten years old. They are definitely my brothers."

They walked back toward the car and got inside.

"This area is North Beach," Rayne said at their next stop. "This is where you'll find the more upscale houses."

"This is where the wealthy live," he responded.

"Yeah. My DuGrandpre cousins have a house on this side of the island. Renee and Greg are building their new home over here, too."

Taylor's eyes bounced around. "This is a nice neighborhood."

They drove to the downtown area next.

They made a left turn down another street. "That's the museum," she said.

"It's obvious just how much you love this island. Why did you wait so long to come back here? Your family...they love you, Rayne."

"Taylor, when I left here, I was so young, and I bought into my mama's hurt and anger. When I was growing up, I'd brag about everything I was going to accomplish... I was going to do big things. Instead, I got involved with a drug dealer and ended up in jail—almost went to prison. I'm pretty much a complete failure. Leon's a dedicated firefighter, a great husband and a father. Look at Trey... He lost both his legs, but he didn't let that stop him. He's built a museum to honor our family's legacy. Renee is a fashion designer..."

"I'm going to stop you right here," Taylor replied. "Rayne, you turned your life around. I'm a witness to that. That's success. You went back to school and got a business degree."

"And if my family knew the half of it— they'd either judge me or look at me with pity. I don't want any of that. I'm more than capable of taking care of myself."

"They will only look at you with pity if you're pitiful," Taylor stated.

Rayne offered him a small smile. "I've heard you say that many times. I know you think that I'm just feeling sorry for myself."

"Aren't you?"

She stole a peek at him. "I don't think so. They accept me now, the version I'm letting them see. I don't know what they'd think about the rest of me. Taylor, I know I messed up with you. With our marriage. There's no forgetting that, as much as I would love to dismiss it."

"Trust in your family's love, Rayne."

"I do," she responded.

But did she really?

RAYNE SAT ACROSS from Taylor in a booth at the café, the man who made her heart thump rapidly in her chest.

"Here you are…" The waitress, whose name tag read Joyce, set their plates in front of them.

Her stomach growled loudly as she gazed down at the crab cakes with steamed vegetables and herbed potatoes. Taylor had ordered the same. "This really smells good," Rayne said. "Obviously, my belly agrees."

He chuckled. "I can't wait to try these crab cakes Leon's been bragging about."

Rayne sliced into the lump crab patty and stuck a forkful in her mouth. "Okay, this is delicious."

"I have to agree with you."

They ate the rest of their meal and made small talk. "That was great," Rayne said as they walked out to the car after leaving the café. "I enjoyed hanging out with you, but I'm ready to get back to the babies."

"I can't believe I'm saying this, but me, too."

Rayne bit back her smile. She didn't want to get her hopes up that the walls around Taylor's heart were beginning to dissolve. She could admit it now. She wanted him to fall in love with their babies—it was her one Christmas wish.

"How WERE THEY?" Rayne asked when they walked into the house after their two-and-a-half-hour excursion.

"Wonderful," Misty responded. "Ian and Ivy are just the sweetest babies. I've just put them down for a nap."

"Thank you for watching them. Taylor and I appreciate it. We had a nice time out. I took him to the historic section and to North Beach."

"I remember the first time Leon took me to see Polk Rothchild's house," Misty said. "I found it interesting that the brothers built their houses with identical floor plans. Aunt Eleanor told me that Polk's was larger because he had ten children while Hoss only had six."

"The bedrooms where the children slept were bigger in Polk's house," Rayne responded. "Their rooms were larger than Polk's bedroom. It was about function for him."

"Why won't your family rebuild those houses?" Taylor inquired.

"Trey and Greg have been talking about it. They want to use the original materials. The houses will be a part of the museum and available for tours."

As soon as they arrived home an hour later, Talei and Fawn rushed Taylor, nearly knocking him down.

Laughing, he embraced them. "I missed you, too."

Leo walked by him and gave him a fist bump.

"They adore Taylor," Misty whispered to Rayne.

"He has that effect on children. You should see him whenever he visits this group home the company supports. Those kids love him. Taylor doesn't just help them financially—he volunteers his time. He and his best friend. They even coach the football team every year."

"That's really sweet. He truly has a heart for children."

Except when it comes to his own, she thought sadly.

Taylor cares for the twins, her heart argued. *He's just afraid.*

But of what, she wasn't sure.

CHAPTER NINE

THE SOUND OF Ivy crying was like music, beckoning him. "I'll get her," Taylor said.

He grew more comfortable handling the twins every day. He actually looked forward to his time with them.

Taylor sat with Ivy in his arms. "When I was a little boy, I used to wonder what angels looked like. I wondered if they were real. When I look at you and Ian...you both have the faces of angels. I heard somewhere that they play with you." His gaze followed hers. "Is there one here in the room with us now?"

Ivy turned her attention to him.

"I don't remember ever feeling this safe and secure when I was younger. I was afraid all the time. My parents...they don't even deserve that title because they weren't parents at all. I liked when they were getting high because they'd ignore me. But when they'd been drinking...they only had to look at me and they'd beat me." His eyes watered at the memory.

Taylor swallowed his emotions. "I was glad

when they took me out of that house. I knew my parents wouldn't try to get me back. They could care less about raising children. It was always about the high."

He looked down at Ivy. "You will never have to worry about something like that happening to you or Ian. Your mother and I will always make sure that you feel loved and safe."

She released a string of unintelligible sounds.

"I'm glad you approve," Taylor said with a grin.

Ivy suddenly frowned, and he heard a low rumbling followed by an unpleasant scent.

"Little girl, why didn't you hold off on pooping until you were with your mother? You know she's better at diaper duty."

When Ivy looked as if she was about to cry, he said, "Okay…okay. I got you."

Taylor stood up and carried her over to the bed. He laid her down on a protective pad, then grabbed a diaper, box of wipes and ointment.

"Your mom doesn't mind doing this without gloves, but not me—I have to wear protective gear. You'll understand when you become a mother."

"What are you doing to my daughter?" Rayne asked from the doorway.

"She pooped. I'm changing her."

"Have you ever changed a diaper before?"

"I've avoided it until now." Frowning, he said, "You can step in at any time."

"And ruin it for you? Naw, I'll just stand way over here and watch."

"See...your mom is offended by your stinky bottom," Taylor said, unfastening the soiled diaper. "Me, I'm fighting through the smell."

At that, Ivy raised her legs high.

"How can such a beautiful little girl do all that?"

Rayne laughed and snapped a photo of him changing Ivy. "I'm so proud of you, Taylor."

He finished cleaning her bottom, placed a fresh diaper on Ivy then fastened her clothing.

"You should feel much better now. I know I do."

Taylor carried her over to Rayne. "Spend some time with Mommy while I dispose of your stinky diaper."

"You did great. Now you're on full diaper duty."

"I have my gloves... Just need a face mask, and I'm good to go."

She chuckled. "What are we gonna do with your daddy?"

Taylor had enjoyed his time with Rayne earlier. So much that he'd almost crossed the line with her. She was no longer his employee, but he was still reluctant to venture into the romantic relationship arena. He didn't want to screw things up with her for fear it would affect their friendship and also his future in the twins' lives.

WHEN LEON CAME home that evening, Rayne left the house with Misty. They were meeting Gia in Charleston for a strength training class at the Boot Camp Gym. She wasn't worried about the twins. She felt secure that they were in good hands with Taylor.

"It's been months since I worked out with weights," Rayne said.

"It's a beginner's class," Misty responded. "I'm used to taking aerobic classes. This is all new to me. Ethan says it's better for you."

Twenty minutes later, they walked through the doors of the gym.

Rayne admired the Christmas tree in the foyer. It was decorated with brightly colored ornaments and bows.

"Are you going to have a tree-decorating party?" she asked Misty.

"Of course," she responded. "It's a Rothchild tradition. We don't do it early because of the kids. When Fawn is a bit older, we might, but she's too touchy right now. She wants to touch everything."

"She likes textures."

Misty agreed. "She does. Fawn loves going to fabric stores with my mom. She can spend hours in there just running her fingers over the different textures."

Rayne picked up a brochure at the counter. "This Tabata training looks pretty interesting. Taylor used to take something like this in Los Angeles."

"It's a little too intense for me," Misty responded. "I was thinking about it until Ethan told me that they use twenty-second bursts of maximum-intensity work with a ten-second rest period, repeated eight times."

Rayne continued reading through the brochure. "I wouldn't mind the cardio kickboxing class. Water aerobics for sure as long as it's an indoor pool."

"They have a saltwater hydrotherapy pool here."

"Nice."

They found Gia sitting at the juice bar.

"How long have you been here?" Misty asked.

"About ten minutes," she responded. "I got finished earlier than expected with my client."

Rayne was enjoying this time out with the women. She'd had friends in LA, but she only allowed them to get just so close to her. Somehow, Taylor was the only one who'd ever gotten under her defense.

They performed a series of warm-ups at the start of the kickboxing class.

While the first half of the routines seemed manageable, the second half was more intense.

Rayne patted her face dry with her towel while trying to recover from her workout. She was grateful when it was over. She sat down on a nearby bench and groaned softly. Before the pregnancy, Rayne exercised on a regular basis. Taking those months off while carrying the twins…she was going to have to build up her endurance again.

Her body screamed in protest the entire ride back to the island.

"I'm telling myself no pain…no gain…" Misty said.

"That isn't working for me," Rayne responded with a grunt. "I can't remember the last time I was so sore."

When she walked into the house, Taylor opened his mouth to say something, but Rayne held her hand up to stop him.

She headed straight to the room to grab a change of clothes.

Rayne showered and dressed in a pair of sweats.

Her hair was damp from her shower, so she allowed it to hang freely in soft ringlets.

Walking into the family room, she said, "Okay, now I feel like myself."

"That must have been some class," Taylor said.

"It would be nothing for you."

"I remember you working out three or four days a week faithfully."

"I stopped when I found out I was pregnant. I took a yoga class for expectant moms but stopped when I went into preterm labor."

He frowned. "I never asked you this, but was it a difficult pregnancy?"

She met Taylor's gaze. "Not more than usual for twins. I had morning sickness until I was in my fourth month and went into preterm labor in my sixth month."

"I would've been there for you."

"I'd like to believe that, Taylor."

"Wow…" he uttered softly.

She rubbed her aching muscles. "I didn't mean it the way it sounded. I'm just trying to say that it would have been a difficult time for you."

"You're right, but I wouldn't have abandoned you."

"You know what we need right now?" Rayne asked. "Wine and charcuterie."

She and Taylor used to have a glass of red

wine after work to relax. They would often dine in and watch a movie together.

He remained in the family room while Rayne went to the kitchen.

She returned a few minutes later with a plate of cheese, pepperoni, sliced salami and crackers, which she put down on the coffee table. "I'll be right back with plates and red wine."

When she returned, Rayne sat down beside Taylor. "Did you find a movie?"

He sat up and reached for his wineglass. "Nothing on but Christmas movies."

"What's wrong with that?" she asked.

Taylor met her gaze. "I'm the Grinch, remember?"

She chuckled. "You're right about that. I'm expecting you to turn green at any moment."

They settled on one titled *Almost Christmas.*

Rayne took a long sip of wine. "I had my doubts about coming here, but I have to say now that I'm really glad I did."

"You seem happier than I've ever seen you."

She looked over at Taylor. "Really?"

He nodded.

When the movie was over, he said, "You look tired."

"Honestly, I'm exhausted," Rayne stated. "I think today wore me out. I took a shower earlier, but to be honest, all I really want right now is a soak in a hot bubble bath and some sleep."

"Then do it," he said. "I'll bring the twins out here and take care of them. If I need you, I'll wake you up."

Rayne's heart leapt in her chest. She felt hope surge through her, but she cautioned herself to take it day by day. Taylor didn't mind spending time with the twins now, but how would he feel as they got closer to the new year?

"I'll most likely be up anyway. If they whimper, I wake up. It's like my body knows."

"Go..." he said.

"Thank you, Taylor."

He kissed her on the cheek.

After her bath, Rayne found him in the bedroom, putting the twins in their carriers. She sat down on the left side of the bed. "That felt so good."

He smiled. "Good. Now try to get some sleep."

She eased under the covers.

"We'll be in the family room," Taylor said.

Rayne closed her eyes as sleep carried her away.

TAYLOR EASED HIMSELF down on the bed, careful not to disturb Rayne, who appeared to be sleeping peacefully.

He knew she was willing to take care of the

twins on her own, but he couldn't allow her to do that—he couldn't abandon his children. He knew Rayne felt her childhood was miserable because of the absence of a father. She spoke of missing out on father-daughter dances, not having her father's surname—it bothered her.

Taylor still considered her luckier than many because she had a mother who loved her dearly along with a host of relatives in her life, at least in the early years. Rayne only saw their absence.

He would have preferred to be included when it came to her pregnancy—but there was nothing they could do about that now. She was aware that his last relationship ended because his ex-girlfriend wanted to have a child. But he was surprised she'd believed he would abandon his own children. Taylor couldn't punish two innocent babies for the choices he and Rayne made. He just wasn't sure what this meant exactly.

What am I offering? Child support? Co-parenting? What do I do now?

The only thing Taylor knew for sure: he wasn't going to terminate his parental rights. He didn't want the twins to ever feel he didn't want to be in their lives. Taylor just didn't want to hurt or disappoint them. He never wanted Ian or Ivy to regret being born.

He glanced over at Rayne.

Taylor couldn't have asked for a better person to be the mother of his children.

"What time is it?"

"Hey, you…it's a little after midnight."

Rayne sat up in bed. "I didn't realize how much I needed this. I must have been running on fumes."

"I can believe that," Taylor said. "You have been known to be overzealous at times."

She laughed. "The pot calling the kettle black…"

Rayne got out of bed. "How long have they been asleep?"

"A couple of hours."

"Now that I'm up, you feel like late-night/early-morning breakfast?"

"Sure."

They quietly navigated to the kitchen, keeping it down so they didn't disturb the rest of the household.

Rayne set the pans on the cooktop while Taylor raided the refrigerator for eggs, bacon, onions and milk.

"I know y'all are not about to have the Rothchild Midnight Feast without us," Leon said from the doorway.

Rayne jumped at the sound of her cousin's voice. "Did we wake you?"

"My wife has a sixth sense when it comes to her kitchen."

"Yes, I do," Misty said, joining them. "Is this what I think it is?"

"It's about to be," Leon replied.

"So, this is a thing?" Taylor asked. "Eating breakfast late at night?"

"Yes," Rayne responded. "C'mon, let's get busy."

Misty had bacon duty while Taylor sliced up tomatoes, onions and mushrooms. Leon mixed fresh blueberries into pancake batter. Rayne whipped heavy cream into a bowl with eggs.

They soon sat down to eat.

"I like this tradition," Taylor stated while helping Rayne clean the kitchen.

"I've missed all of this."

After they finished, she and Taylor walked down the hall to their room.

Rayne peeked into the crib. "They slept through everything."

"I wasn't sure they would," he said. "I just knew as soon as I took a long-awaited bite of my blueberry pancakes, a cry was going to tear through the air."

"A bit dramatic but okay," she replied with a short laugh.

A hushed quiet soon settled over the room.

Without warning, Taylor pulled her closer to him.

He took her mouth, making it his own in a way that had Rayne's hands rising of their own volition, her fingers curling into his shirt. Her moan slid free of her mouth and into Taylor's.

The kiss was explosive, consuming and intense.

Taylor released her slowly, leaving Rayne breathless and hungry for more of his kisses.

He drew a slow breath.

She gazed into his beautiful gray eyes.

"You are irresistible," Taylor murmured, as though having reached some internal understanding with himself.

He lowered his head down to hers and pressed a single kiss on her lips.

Their gazes locked. Rayne and Taylor glimpsed the attraction mirrored in the other's eyes.

He kissed her again, lingering, savoring every moment.

"I have always been drawn to you," Taylor whispered. "From the first moment I laid eyes on you, but I couldn't act on it. I didn't want to cross that boundary."

"I understand. We're friends, and until recently, I was your assistant," Rayne responded.

"And now?"

"Do you see me differently?"

"I think we're getting there."

Taylor touched his lips to hers.

Rayne's entire body trembled as his arms drew her closer to him.

They *were* friends, and while she really didn't want to tamper with that friendship, she couldn't tear herself away from his kisses.

She allowed her head to rule her heart and broke the kiss. Rayne didn't want to confuse the situation since she and Taylor were still trying to find what their new normal would be.

CHAPTER TEN

WHEN RAYNE OPENED her eyes, it was six forty-five. She hadn't heard the twins cry, which worried her. She glanced over at Taylor, who was sleeping soundly beside her. She eased out of bed and crept over to the crib.

Ian and Ivy were sleeping. Had they slept the entire night? she wondered.

"Good morning."

Rayne turned around. "Hey, Taylor. Did they wake up during the night? I didn't hear anything."

"No. I got up a couple times to check on them."

"They took pity on us. Good thing, too. After that late-night breakfast… I was dead tired."

Ivy began squirming.

"It's time to get bottles ready," she said. "Ivy's waking up."

Taylor swung his legs out of bed. "I'll get the bottles."

Smiling, she said, "I see you decided to get some sleep in a real bed."

"I couldn't take the floor or that chair anymore." He walked to the door. "I'll be right back."

"Ian's up now," Rayne announced when Taylor returned.

While they fed the twins, he said, "I've been really thinking about our situation."

"Okay…"

"What do you think about us staying married?"

She blinked in surprise. "Excuse me? Did I hear you correctly?"

"We're friends, and we get along great, which is good for the twins. I trust you, Rayne. It just makes sense."

"You want us to be married in name only. Is that what you're saying?"

He nodded. "I think it's the perfect solution. Neither one of us ever planned on marrying. Our marriage will be based on friendship. It will probably be better than some of the ones based on love. Last night proved that we're attracted to one another. Dating would be a great start, don't you think?"

"I'm not so sure," Rayne responded. "How long do you want this marriage of convenience?"

"We can take it day by day."

"Taylor, you know that I don't intend to raise the twins in Los Angeles. I'm staying here, on Polk Island." He nodded but didn't say anything. So she said, "I suppose we could try it. But...Taylor, I don't want you doing this out of pity."

"I'm not. Rayne, you know that I care deeply for you, and I don't want the twins growing up feeling as if they're mistakes."

"I know what that feels like." She hoped this meant he felt something for the twins, too. It certainly seemed like he did, and she wanted him to welcome Ian and Ivy into his life for real, not out of a sense of duty.

Her phone began vibrating.

Rayne read the text, then said, "Trey just invited us to dinner tomorrow night."

"Do you have plans?" he asked.

"No," she responded. "I know that Leon and Misty will be in Savannah. I'll text Trey to let him know that we're accepting their invitation."

"Rayne, you don't seem happy about what I suggested."

"I'm just a little taken aback by all this," she responded. "The truth is that I would rather tell my children that we tried to make it work but ended up going our separate ways than having them wonder why we're married but not really together."

"Why would we have to say anything?" asked Taylor.

"Do you think Ian and Ivy won't one day realize that we don't act like some of the other couples around them? Take Leon and Misty or Trey and Gia…even Aunt Eleanor and Rusty. They love each other, and it's obvious."

"How do you know that what we have won't turn to love?"

"I don't have an answer for you."

He sighed. "I don't know what else to do. This…marriage…babies. None of this was supposed to happen. But I don't want to walk away from any of you."

"I don't have any answers, either," she responded.

"You have a lot of family on this island," Taylor said as he pulled behind another SUV and parked. There were several cars parked on the street and in the driveway. "I assumed we were the only guests."

"They don't all live here," she responded. "I think you're about to meet my cousins who live in Charleston."

"The ones who own the house on the north side?"

"Yeah. They're really cool people, Taylor."

"I'm good," he responded. "So far everyone in your family has been friendly and down-to-earth."

While they were liberating the twins from

their car seats, a young woman with long dark hair walked up to the SUV.

"Rayne Rothchild," she began, "it's about time you returned home. What did we do that prompted you to stop talking to us? I know they have phones in Texas."

She turned around. "Jordin! I'm so happy to see you. No one did anything. I just needed space to get myself together. That's all."

"I hear you're a married woman now."

Rayne introduced Taylor, then said, "This is my cousin Jordin DuGrandpre."

"It's Holbrooke now. My husband's in the house with the kids. We have three." Jordin peered at the infant in Rayne's arms. "She's beautiful."

"This is Ivy. Her brother is Ian."

"I have a set of twins, too."

"Jordin is also a twin," she told Taylor. "Is Jadin here?"

"Not yet, but she's on the way," Jordin responded. "They should be arriving any minute."

"I didn't know y'all were going to be here," Rayne said to Misty. "I thought you and Leon would spend the night in Savannah. Enjoy some quality time alone."

"It was a last-minute decision for us," she responded. "Leon was able to finish up his training early, so we decided to head back home to relieve Gia. My three can be a handful at times."

When Jadin arrived, one glance was enough for Taylor to recognize they were identical twin sisters.

Rayne accompanied the sisters and Misty into the kitchen.

"That's where the magic happens," Talei leaned into him and whispered with a giggle. "Aunt Gia is going to make her candied yams. Jordin is making pasta salad, and Jadin will make my favorite...macaroni and cheese."

"I love mac and cheese, too."

"Can Rayne cook?" the little girl asked.

"Oh, yes. She makes the best chocolate chip muffins I've ever tasted," Taylor responded. "She used to bring them to work every Monday morning. Rayne used to say that it was the best way to start the week."

"Ooooh, I love muffins, especially chocolate chip, strawberry and lemon."

Taylor was enjoying Talei's company while the twins slept in their carriers. He stole a peek into the kitchen.

Bowls, measuring cups and ingredients lined up, Misty worked at the kitchen island chopping bell pepper and onion. Across from her, Rayne measured flour. They were engaged in conversation while they worked.

Jordin set a large white mixing bowl filled with steaming pasta on the island. Her eyes met his, and she gave him a friendly smile before returning her attention back to her task.

Talei left to join her cousins in another room. Fawn stood a few yards away, watching him.

He smiled at her and waved.

As if his smile was the sign she'd been waiting for, Fawn made her approach.

"Tayla," she murmured the attempt at his name. "Babies sleep…" she said, then put a hand to her lips. "Shh…"

He nodded.

Rayne walked out of the kitchen, asking, "Everything okay?"

"We're fine," Taylor responded. "Fawn's helping me with the twins."

The little girl grinned. "I helping…"

Rayne embraced her. "Thanks, sweetie."

Fawn ran off five minutes later.

Taylor chuckled. "I guess she's done."

"Looks like it," Rayne responded with a short laugh. "There are two bottles ready in the diaper bag if they wake up."

"Okay. You go do your thing. I have Ian and Ivy covered."

He was attracted to Rayne like he'd never been attracted to any woman. Taylor had searched inside his heart to ensure his fascination with her wasn't because he felt a kinship because they were both fatherless. Nor did he pity her.

The truth was that Rayne had no idea just how great she had it.

TAYLOR WAS SEATED beside Eleanor. She kept him laughing all through dinner. It was good to see that despite the symptoms of Alzheimer's, she maintained her sense of humor.

"Leon and Trey kept me so busy... I enjoyed raising them, though. I didn't have any children of my own. Two stillbirths."

"I've heard that you were a fantastic mother."

"I tried to do what I could for my boys," she responded.

"You were kind of a mother to Rayne as well."

Eleanor nodded. "I loved that girl like she was my own. It nearly broke my heart when Carol left the island. I tried to get her to stay. Rayne pleaded with me. She didn't want to leave, but there wasn't anything I could do." She took a sip of water. "But my girl is home now, where she belongs."

Taylor smiled. "Yes, she is."

A few minutes later, Eleanor said, "I raised Leon and Trey..."

Rusty leaned over and planted a kiss on her cheek. "I love this woman right here."

"I couldn't tell at all," Taylor responded with a chuckle.

His gaze traveled to Rayne.

She was in a conversation with Jordin. Her features were animated as she talked. She looked so happy.

After dinner, they sat around talking.

"Where did you grow up?" Jordin asked him.

"In Los Angeles," Taylor responded while hoping they wouldn't pry any deeper.

When they didn't, he relaxed and was able to continue enjoying his evening.

At the end of the evening, as they got ready for bed, Rayne said, "I realize that you don't like talking about your family. Will you tell me why?"

"I just don't," he replied.

"Taylor, it's me. You know my secrets."

"I don't have anything to say about that part of my life. It's best forgotten."

A few moments passed in silence, and then he said, "But speaking of mothers."

Rayne groaned.

"No, listen. You put a lot of emphasis on family, but you've excluded Carol."

"You're deflecting. Are you going to keep running away?"

He gave a bark of laughter. "Instead of telling me about the pregnancy—that's exactly what you did. You ran away."

She huffed. "Let's just leave it."

He agreed. Rayne was absolutely right. He was deflecting because he didn't want to talk about his childhood. He didn't want or need pity.

CHAPTER ELEVEN

Rayne closed her laptop and placed it on the sofa. She'd spent the last two and a half hours in a virtual meeting with the committee.

While the babies were sleeping, she took a quick shower.

Beneath the hot spray of water, she thought about Taylor and everything they'd been through. Everything that had happened because of the choices she'd made. Rayne knew he'd been ambushed by the news of the twins. She might have been upset with how he'd kept the babies at arm's length at first, but Rayne was grateful to him for the way he'd handled all this.

But she was becoming frustrated with him because he was always bringing up her mother.

Rayne was grateful for the distraction of helping the Christmas festival committee. It helped to take her mind off Carol. It wasn't that she didn't want her mother in her life. She loved her, and she appreciated that Carol had been there all during the pregnancy. But she didn't want to fight with her, and she knew her decision to come to the island—and her sub-sequent one to stay here—would eventually bring about a fight.

When she checked on Eleanor, Rayne promised her aunt that she'd bring the babies for another visit, so she bundled them up and placed them in the car.

Taylor was on an outing with Leon, Trey and Greg. Rayne had a feeling they were Christmas shopping, which meant that he was probably miserable with her cousins. Taylor wasn't one for giving gifts, not even on birthdays, but he always acknowledged hers by bringing her a cupcake.

At her aunt's house, a sleeping Ian seemed content with Eleanor's cuddling, while Ivy lay in Rusty's arms, wide-eyed and looking around. The babies cared for, Rayne scooped up a bowl of red beans and rice and a piece of hot, buttered corn bread.

"Auntie, I can't tell you how much I've missed your cooking."

"I'm so glad you decided to finally come home, Rayne. There were many nights that I prayed you'd reach out to us."

"I used to beg my mom to send me back here, but she wouldn't."

"I can understand that," Eleanor said. "Carol didn't want to be separated from you. I would've felt the same way about the boys. But you coulda come back once you were grown."

"I wasn't ready until now," Rayne responded. "But I never stopped thinking about y'all. I missed you so much, but I was a mess. A hot mess. It wasn't until I started working with Taylor that I began getting my life together."

As she satisfied her hunger, Rayne studied her aunt from under her eyelashes and tried to quell her fear. She feared that Eleanor would always view her as a disappointment. That was why she'd chosen to remain estranged from the family.

"I regret the way my sister left town and took you with her...away from the family. I pleaded with her to stay."

"She had a broken heart, and then to be humiliated by the wife she never knew about—I don't know how I would've responded if it had been me," Rayne stated. "I probably wouldn't have taken it as quietly as Mama. I don't know why she let that hateful woman talk to her the way she did."

"Oh, she wanted to light into that woman," Eleanor said. "So did I, but it was best to just stay silent. I always told Carol to just let folk act a fool all by themselves."

"But people still judged my mother. Even Aunt Maggie and Uncle Daniel. She told me how the pastor wanted her to go before the whole congregation to ask for forgiveness," Rayne said. "I remember being dropped from the ballet company and hearing my teacher Miss Reynolds gossiping about Mama with some of the other teachers and parents."

"I made sure Patty Reynolds was fired," Eleanor stated.

She was surprised by the news. "Really?"

"I sure did," Eleanor said. "Her actions were cruel and unprofessional. I wasn't about to stay quiet after that."

"Did Mama know?"

"I'm not sure. I don't think I ever told her. She was really upset with Maggie and Daniel when she left."

"Have you ever talked to them about what happened?" she asked.

"I did," Eleanor said. "I didn't like the way things went down. Regardless of personal feelings, I thought we should have stood together as a family. When Polk decided to stay here on this island—after his first wife died—Hoss could've kept going. He was the one who really wanted to head north. But he put aside his dreams to be there for his brother. He eventually moved to New York, but he believed in family first. They both did."

Then Eleanor pointed to her hand. "You wearing a wedding band. When do we get to meet this man?"

"You've already met him, Auntie. His name is Taylor Carrington."

Eleanor glanced over at Rusty before saying, "My memory sho' ain't what it used to be."

"Mine ain't, either," he responded. "Just don't you go forgetting that I love you."

They sat in companionable silence for a while.

"This little lady needs her diaper changed." Rising to her feet, Eleanor said, "I'll take her in the bedroom."

When she left the dining room, Rusty stated, "These babies have sure put a light back in her eyes. Eleanor really enjoys feeling needed."

"It's hard knowing she has Alzheimer's, but there are times when she seems like her old self."

He nodded in agreement. "My wife craves her independence, which makes it challenging for her. Eleanor doesn't understand why she has to be driven everywhere or why someone has to be with her most times."

"I can't imagine what it's like to be a caregiver."

"I love your aunt through sickness and in health," Rusty stated. "There's nowhere else I'd rather be than by Eleanor's side. Caregiving isn't for the faint at heart. I'm fortunate that I can be home with her most of the time. Leon, Trey and their wives help whenever I need them."

"That's great. Now that I'm back, what can I do to help?" Rayne inquired.

"Just keep bringing the twins over to spend time with Eleanor. It'll do her a world of good."

Smiling, she responded, "You can count on it, but I'm going to really need to exercise if she keeps feeding me."

He chuckled. "Eleanor loves to cook. It brings her joy."

"It's good she can still do it."

"I'm usually in the kitchen with her when she's cooking because sometimes," Rusty said, "she gets confused."

When she returned, Eleanor said, "Did I tell you that I talked to Maggie the other day? I told her that you were back. Suga, she wants to see you."

Rayne glanced over at Rusty, who looked confused. "First I'm hearing about this," he whispered.

"How is she doing?"

"Maggie's fine. She misses Carol. She always tells me that. She feels bad about what happened." Eleanor planted a kiss on Ivy's forehead. "I want our family to come together."

Rayne knew that her mother wasn't interested in ever seeing Maggie or her brother,

Daniel. However, over the years, she often caught Carol looking at family photographs and becoming emotional. Although she would never admit it—her mother was lonely, and she missed her siblings.

Rayne desired the opportunity to sit down with her aunt and uncle; she wanted to hear what they had to say in their own words. She'd reached out to both Maggie and Daniel, asking that they come to the island for the holidays. Rayne hoped that she'd be able to bring her family back together. Not just for her, but for her mother.

Of course, she'd never tell Carol this—her mother would view it as a betrayal.

TAYLOR STARED AT the phone in his hand and braced himself before answering.

"Taylor, it's Carol. Did you have any luck on the island?"

"Yes, I'm here with her now," he responded.

"You're still there?"

He heard the surprise in her voice. "Yes. I'm planning to be here until after the holidays."

"Why? Wait, have you two decided to give your marriage a chance?"

"Rayne asked that we postpone the divorce until after Christmas. She just wants to focus on the holidays and family."

"It's her way of avoiding the things she doesn't want to do," Carol responded. "You should've figured out by now that Rayne is a runner. In all fairness, I guess she gets it from me. I don't know what happened between you and my daughter, but I hope you two work it out. Those babies deserve a mother and a father."

"Finding out about the twins was a shock to me, but they're here. Now, we're just trying to sort everything out," Taylor responded.

"I told Rayne that I wouldn't interfere, so I'm not going to—I just want what's best for my grandchildren."

"I understand. Carol, I really appreciate you giving us the space we need."

"I'm sure Rayne's angry with me for telling you that she was on the island. I don't regret it because you needed to know about your children."

"She knows your actions were from a place of love."

"I hope so," Carol said. "How is Rayne?"

"She's great. She looks good. Happy."

"Is she staying with my sister?"

"No, she's with Leon and Misty."

"I'm not surprised. They have always been close. More like siblings than cousins. I know that she missed them a lot."

"I got the impression that he missed her just

as much. Leon and his wife have been very welcoming and supportive to both me and Rayne."

"That's good to hear."

"I know that Rayne would love to have you spend Christmas with her and the twins. You should consider coming to the island."

"I don't know about that. It's been seventeen years."

"Your sister would really enjoy seeing you as well," Taylor said. "Miss Eleanor talked a lot about how much she misses you."

"I miss her, too."

They talked a few minutes more before hanging up.

Taylor had second thoughts about what he'd just done. Rayne was going to be furious with him for inviting her mother to the island without talking to her first. She had worked hard to establish firm boundaries when it came to Carol.

He found it touching to witness how much she loved her daughter, especially since Taylor hadn't ever experienced what parental love looked or felt like.

He hoped it wasn't too late for them. Taylor wanted Carol and Rayne to repair whatever was wrong in their relationship. What they had was something special...if only they had the sense to see it.

CAROL GULPED HARD, hot tears slipping down her cheeks. She released a low, tortured sob as the depths of her heartbreak rose to the forefront. She had done everything possible to be a good mother to Rayne. She left the island all those years ago to protect her only child. Carol didn't want any black marks against her daughter's name.

She'd sacrificed everything to give Rayne a decent life. She gave up on the idea of love and loving because she didn't want to risk bringing a man into their lives who would one day disappoint them.

"I did everything for you," Carol told the photo of her daughter on the sideboard. "I can't believe you would do this to me…shut me out of your life like this." She hadn't heard from Rayne since she left Dallas, except for the text letting her know that she made it safely to the island.

Pacing, Carol gathered her composure as she debated whether to just give Rayne the space she wanted or to go see her daughter and grandchildren.

Even if Rayne didn't need her, the grandbabies did, she decided.

She went to the bathroom and washed her face.

When she returned to the living room, Carol

opened an airline app on her tablet and booked a ticket.

She wasn't going to let Rayne keep her from her grandchildren. Even if it meant having to face her past.

AFTER PUTTING THE twins to bed, Rayne went looking for Taylor.

"What are you doing out here?" she asked.

"Nothing," he responded. "I just thought I'd sit out here until I couldn't take the cold anymore."

"From the way you're shaking, I don't think it's going to be much longer." Rayne rubbed her arms. The jacket she was wearing wasn't heavy enough to ward off the bite of the weather. "I could use a cup of hot chocolate. What about you?"

"Sure. How did your meeting go?" he asked.

"Great. We don't have as many sponsors as last year, but things are going well."

Taylor got up and followed her inside the house to the kitchen.

"You should come back to the island when the weather's warm," Rayne said as she retrieved two mugs from a cabinet near the refrigerator. "It's really beautiful then. The trees are green and flowers are blooming everywhere."

"I think I will. I'd like to see it during the summer time. I'm sure there's lots of tourists."

She nodded as she poured milk into the cups, then added chocolate. "What's going on with you, Taylor? You've been really quiet today."

"Trying to wrap my mind around the fact that I'm celebrating Christmas this year. You have to know this is a first for me."

"Don't worry," she said. "You're going to have the best time."

He accepted the hot chocolate. "I hope so."

"I'm looking forward to it," Rayne stated with a huge grin on her face. "A real Rothchild family Christmas. This is exactly what I need in my life right now."

"Rayne, your mom—"

"No, I don't want to hear any negativity."

"But you should—"

She cut him off by saying, "Taylor, I don't want to hear anything that will upset me. I'm in a great space. Just let me enjoy this moment."

He gave a slight nod. "I'm almost afraid to ask what's got you in such a good mood."

"The parade and Christmas festival are next weekend. We're decorating the Christmas tree in a couple nights. It just makes me happy."

A frown forming on his face, he asked, "We're not going to be singing Christmas carols and stuff, are we?"

"Stop being a Grinch," Rayne said.

"I don't know any other way to be," Taylor responded.

"Jingle Bells...jingle bells...jingle all the way..." she sang.

Rayne ran into Leon in the hallway.

"Why are you tormenting your husband?" he asked.

She laughed. "I'm going to convert Taylor. Just wait and see."

"I don't think so," Leon laughed.

"Give it time," she responded, then sobered. "I'm sure you're tired of hearing me say this, but I'm super grateful that you didn't just close the door in my face when I showed up. I regret allowing Mama's issues to color our relationship."

He eyed her. "I'd never do that to you or anyone in my family," he stated, his voice firm. "Rayne, we're bonded by blood. The only way I'd cut you out of my life is if you tried to harm my wife and kids. Even then, I'd try to forgive, but I'd have to love you from a distance."

"I guess I assumed Mama was telling Aunt Eleanor everything that I was doing because she was always telling me how good you and Trey were doing. I was too ashamed to face y'all because the only person messing up was me. I felt like a bad seed."

"I love you, cousin," Leon said. "Flaws and all. We all got 'em. If Aunt Carol told Auntie anything, she never told us. Trey and I made mistakes—stupid ones. We weren't exempt." He gave her a smile. "Rayne, you have to remember that nobody is perfect. I don't know what all you've done, but from where I'm standing, it looks like you turned your life around."

"I did," she responded. "I went through a real wild phase a few years back, but I'm not that person anymore. I stopped running around with the wrong types of people a while ago, went back to college and graduated with a degree in business."

"We don't have to keep talking about this, Rayne," Leon said. "Your past is just that. The past. Continue to look forward, cousin."

She hugged him.

Rayne hummed softly as she headed to the family room. She was so looking forward to Christmas.

CHAPTER TWELVE

TAYLOR WOULD ATTEMPT once more to tell Rayne that he'd asked her mother to consider coming to the island for Christmas. She'd be upset initially, but he didn't believe she'd stay angry. Besides, it was highly unlikely that Carol was actually going to come.

When Deacon called, Taylor was happy to hear from him. They normally met for dinner every other week, but with Taylor being away, he hadn't seen him since the wedding.

"How are things going?" Deacon inquired.

"Great," Taylor responded. "I'm glad you called. I have something to tell you."

"What's up?"

"Remember the party to celebrate the opening of the Vegas dealership?"

"Of course."

"A lot happened that night, Deacon."

"I didn't notice anything unusual. Nona and I had a great time. I hated that we had to fly out early the next morning."

"I think things would've turned out differently if you hadn't left," Taylor said.

"Okay, what happened?"

"Rayne and I got married in a chapel on the strip."

"Say what?"

Taylor imagined his best friend's mouth was wide-open in his astonishment. "Rayne is my wife."

"Man, I never saw that coming," Deacon said. *"Wow."*

"It's not what you think," he responded. "We finished off a bottle of champagne after everyone left. We weren't exactly thinking clearly, so the next morning, we decided to terminate the marriage. That's why I never said anything to you about it."

"So, then you're no longer married."

"The divorce didn't happen. As you know, Rayne quit the company unexpectedly. She moved back to Dallas. I now know the reason why she left the way she did."

"I can't wait to hear this," Deacon uttered. "But I'm sure it's because she wants the marriage to be real."

"Actually, it's because she was pregnant. Rayne gave birth to twins three months ago. A boy and a girl."

"Twins! I have to say that Nona called it.

She said that something happened between you two. She even guessed that Rayne was probably pregnant."

"I wished she'd mentioned her theory to me. She could've saved me from being shocked to the core."

"I don't mean to be indelicate, but are you sure…"

"That they're mine? Yes. I know Rayne," Taylor responded. "She wouldn't lie about anything like this."

"I know you never wanted to be a father. How do you feel about everything now?"

"I wasn't happy about it at first," he said. "But when I saw them… Deacon, before I even realized what was happening, Ian and Ivy had taken root in my heart."

"Ian?"

"Rayne named our son after Ian."

"I like it," Deacon said. "Ian and Ivy. Wow… I have a niece and nephew. You'll have to send me some pictures."

"I will." Taylor paused a moment, then said, "I can't just walk away from them. They look at you with such trust. Well… Ian does. I don't think Ivy likes me much. Whenever she sees me or I'm holding her, she sticks out her tongue at me. She doesn't do that with anyone else."

"I don't know much about babies, but I'm

sure it's not what you're thinking. All they know is love when they're that small."

"Maybe Ivy senses something about me. I feel like she knows I'm broken."

"I think you're putting too much thought into this."

"You're probably right."

"I'm assuming you and Rayne have discussed what this means for your relationship."

"We're still trying to figure everything out. That's another reason why we want to keep quiet about the marriage."

"What's to figure out?" he asked. "You're married, and you have a family. You're either in or you're out. Taylor, you do know that this isn't a half in or half out type of situation?"

He sighed. "Rayne said the same thing. But.... she doesn't want to come back to LA. She wants to live here on the island. I can't say I blame her—this place is beautiful, Deacon. It's the perfect place to raise children, and she's surrounded by family."

"Do you intend to stay married and live apart?"

"We haven't figured anything out," Taylor repeated.

"I have to ask… Do you love Rayne?"

"Deacon, I…I walled up my feelings for her a long time ago because she was my employee." He paused. "I do care for her. Always have. The truth is that love has never been in the cards for me, and I've accepted that. But more than that, Rayne only sees me as a friend. But we are committed to doing what we feel is right for the twins."

"Tell me about them," Deacon said. "I can't wait to meet my little niece and nephew. Y'all better make me godfather to them."

He laughed. "I'd love for you to be their god-father. Of course, I have to run this by Rayne."

Taylor happily lapsed into a conversation about the babies, something he'd never imag-ined himself doing before.

After the call ended, he found Rayne in the kitchen making bottles.

"I see that my gym has a location in Charles-ton, so I'm going to work out. Do you need any-thing while I'm out?"

"No, I'm good," she responded. "I plan on going tomorrow morning with Misty and Gia. Have fun."

Forty minutes later, Taylor strode into a mar-tial arts circuit-training class. He chose a spot near the back to warm up.

The class took his mind off his conflicting emotions about Rayne and the twins.

Time passed quickly. Before he knew it, Tay-lor was performing cool-down exercises. He performed chin-to-chest stretches, standing side reaches and lunges.

During the drive back to the island, he tried to think of the best way to bring up Carol. Taylor wanted to tell Rayne what he'd done. It was better to hear it straight from him than her mother.

Rayne was in the family room helping Talei prepare for her school's Christmas party when he returned to the house. They were putting miniature candy canes and chocolate kisses into little red bags.

He waved before heading to the bedroom.

Taylor checked on the twins before jumping into the shower.

Rayne was in the room with the infants when he came out.

"How was your workout?" she asked.

"Invigorating," he responded. "I'm glad you're here because there's something I need to tell you. It's important."

His words seemed to capture her full attention. "What is it?"

"Your mother called me."

She let out a soft sigh of frustration. "I don't know why she just can't stay out of this. She's done enough already."

"Carol was worried about you, Rayne. And

I'm sure she misses Ian and Ivy. Why haven't you called her?"

"Because I'm not exactly thrilled with her right now."

"You shouldn't blame her for telling me where you were," Taylor said. "She wasn't trying to start any trouble. I think she just wanted to help."

"It's not about her sending you my way. It's that being here, reconnecting with these amazing people, I can't help the old anger at her from coming up. She denied me these connections for so long."

"If she hadn't, I wouldn't be here with you and the twins."

"You're right," Rayne responded. "And I am glad that you're here. I really am. I just would've preferred that it had been me who reached out."

"Who knows when that would've been," Taylor stated.

She folded her arms. "That's a fair statement."

"I'm not picking a fight. I just wanted you to know that I spoke with your mother. I also asked her to consider coming to the island for the holidays."

Rayne gave a short laugh. "That's not gonna happen, Taylor. I asked her to come with me, and she flat-out refused. Carol Rachel Rothchild meant it when she said that her life on

Polk Island was over." She paused a moment before adding, "I hate it, though. I heard back from Aunt Maggie earlier. She and Uncle Daniel are coming for Christmas. It would be great if Mama would come, too. They could finally sit down and talk through what happened. That's really all I want for Christmas—my family together again."

Her eyes traveled to his face. "All of us."

Taylor hoped deep down that this included him. He was relieved that Rayne wasn't upset that he'd invited her mother to the island without consulting her.

PAINFUL MEMORIES FLOODED Carol's mind as she eyed the sign welcoming her to Polk Island at the end of the bridge connecting the island to Charleston.

Why did you have to come here, Rayne? You know I never wanted to come back to this place.

Carol released a sigh of resignation as she drove down Main Street.

She pulled into an empty parking space across from the café and sat there, looking up and down the street.

There were a couple of familiar stores; they had been around since her childhood, like Stanley Hardware, owned by her brother-in-law, Rusty. The florist beside it didn't look as if it had changed at all. She knew the clothing boutique beside the café was owned by her niece Renee. The other stores were all new.

Coming home felt strange, but Carol had to follow through. She'd come too far to turn back now.

She turned the ignition and pulled out of the parking space.

It was time to face her past.

Carol parked in front of the Stanley house. She smiled at the sight of two large pots of poinsettias on the porch. Her sister had always been able to grow the most beautiful plants and flowers. Eleanor was gifted in the kitchen and when it came to flowers.

She took a deep, calming breath, got out of the rental, walked up the steps and knocked on the door.

Rusty's eyes widened in surprise. *"Carol?"*

"It's me," she responded. "May I come in?"

"Sure. Eleanor's gonna be over the darn moon to see you."

Carol smiled. "I hope so."

He led her to the family room.

Her heart warmed at the sight of Eleanor sitting near the window, reading. Her big sister didn't look as if she'd aged much. She now wore her hair short, but she looked younger than her sixty-seven years.

"Hey, Ella," she murmured tearfully.

Frowning, Eleanor glanced up. "Carol…is that you?"

"It's me. I've come home."

Eleanor leapt to her feet. "Praise the Lawd… Oh, it's so good to see you." She stood there for a moment, surveying her younger sister. "It's about time you came back to the island. Are you here to stay?"

"No, I'm not," Carol stated. "I just came for the holidays. I have to go back to Dallas. I go back to work the day after New Year's." Eleanor looked confused, so Carol reminded her, "I'm an assistant principal at a high school."

The two women embraced. "I've missed you so much. I really wish you'd move back. We have a pretty good school system here, Carol. They need educators like you."

"I haven't forgotten how I was humiliated in front of my daughter. And how they started to treat Rayne back then. Polk Island just wasn't some blissful escape for me, Ella. It was my home—only it no longer felt that way."

"Times have changed."

"Maybe, but not for me," she uttered. "I'll never forget how I was treated back then. The good people of this island came short of branding me the town tramp."

"It was that woman who came here and caused

all the trouble, Carol. No one knew the whole story. She was the wife of an unfaithful man—she blamed you and wanted to get even. You know, they never did have any children. As far as I know, Rayne is his only child."

Carol could care less if he ever sired another child. "He denied my daughter before she was born. As far as I'm concerned, he can keep denying her."

"Suga, it's long past time to let go of that bitterness."

"Ella, that's so easy for you to say. Rayne was the innocent in what happened. My child was devastated by that woman's drama."

"Carol, do you accept any blame in all this?"

"Excuse me?"

Eleanor sat down on the plush, floral-patterned sofa. "I don't remember a lot of stuff, but I do remember that day. You gave as much as you got. That's why it ended up so ugly. Carol, I tried to convince you to just keep your mouth shut and leave the café, but you wouldn't do it. The only time you stopped talking was when Rayne walked in."

Carol sat down beside her. "I wasn't gonna let that woman stand there and talk badly about me. Her husband is the one who lied and seduced me. He told me he'd never been married, Ella. He said people were lying to me because they didn't want us together. I believed him. I was so in love with that man—I believed his every word."

"When you first told me about him, what did I tell you? I told you to leave him alone. I felt deep down that he wasn't being truthful with you."

"I know," Carol responded. "I was so stupid."

"He also claimed that he wasn't the father of your child. Remember that?"

"Of course, I remember," she snapped. "That's something I'll never forget as long as I have breath in my body. Or forgive."

"Carol, you can't really move past the pain until you forgive—it's for you. Not him."

She didn't want to continue this conversation. "Let's change the subject because we're never going to agree on this. Have you seen Rayne lately?"

"I think I spoke with her sometime last week," Eleanor responded.

Carol ran her fingers across the raised texture of the sofa. "When was the last time you saw her?"

Eleanor frowned. "She's still in Los Angeles, isn't she?"

"Ella, Rayne is here on the island."

Eleanor looked completely confused. "She is? How long she been here?"

"A couple of weeks."

"Oooh," she uttered. "She must be staying with Leon or Trey."

"I'm a grandmother now. Rayne has a set of twins."

"I think I remember her telling me that."

Taking her sister's hand, Carol asked, "Ella, do you mind if I stay here at the house?"

"I don't mind at all. I'd be offended if you didn't. I'm so glad to have my baby sister home."

"How often do you talk to our siblings?" Carol asked.

"Maggie checks on me regularly," Eleanor responded. "Daniel and I talk maybe once a month. He's never been a huge communicator. Reminds me of you."

"I feel a little shade in that statement."

"Naw, it's just the unfiltered truth."

"I see time hasn't changed you much," Carol stated with a chuckle.

The two women embraced a second time.

"My…my…my… It's so good to have you home, baby sister."

Carol wished she could say the same about returning to the island, but she couldn't. It was a painful reminder of her shame.

"I need to check on my daughter and the twins," she said after getting settled in the guest bedroom. "Rusty, can you give me Leon's address?"

"Sure. It's 244 Tiger Lily Street."

"I think I'll head over there now." *I might as well get this over with*, she decided.

"THEY'RE BOTH FINALLY ASLEEP," Rayne said when she entered the living room, where Leon and Talei were watching television. "Where's Leo and Fawn?"

"They're sleeping, too. They still take naps."

She sat down beside Talei. "I thought about taking one myself, but if I do, I'll be up most of the night."

They heard a car outside.

Leon rose. "We're not expecting company."

"It's probably my friend Sherry," Talei said. "I told her she could come over and watch a movie with me."

Leon went to answer the door.

"Hello, Leon."

The sound of her mother's voice sent shock waves coursing through Rayne's veins.

She stood up and walked to the entrance of the family room. "I can't believe my eyes. Mama, I can't believe that you're really here."

"Me, either," Carol responded.

"I had no idea you were in town," Leon responded.

"I arrived not too long ago. I went to Ella's house first."

"Taylor told me he'd invited you, but I didn't believe you'd come," Rayne said.

"I wanted to see for myself how you and the twins were doing. Especially since you didn't seem to be taking my calls."

"I didn't know what to say to you, Mama. I knew you didn't want me to come here."

Leon gestured for Talei. "C'mon, sweetie... we'll finish the movie upstairs."

Carol eyed her daughter. "Why are you so angry with me?"

They walked over to the sofa and sat down.

"Mom, you made me believe that everyone on the island would never let me live down the circumstances of my birth. I got tired of arguing with you. I don't want my babies to grow up in the same isolation I did. And then I got here, and all I found was people who wanted to love me. Love my babies. And I got angrier."

"Rayne, I don't understand you at all," Carol stated. "Sure, your cousins might be happy to see you, but you need me. Handling one baby is challenging enough—you had two. I only wanted to help you because you didn't have a clue about being a mother. You've always been so independent."

"That should make you happy," Rayne said.

"I don't understand you," Carol said again. "You want independence, but you also want all these people who turned their backs on us."

"They never turned their backs on me! You took me away from them."

"I was trying to be a good mother."

"You didn't have to try so hard," she said, trying to keep the irritation out of her tone. "Mama, you're a great mother, but you hurt me when you cut off contact with our family."

Carol sat down in a nearby chair. "You look good," she stated after a moment of tense silence.

"Thank you," Rayne replied.

"When do I get to see my grandchildren?" Carol asked. "I've come a long way."

"They're sleeping right now."

Another tense silence passed. Finally, Rayne said, "You might not believe me, but I am glad you came. I hope you plan on staying for Christmas. I've been helping with the festival. It's gonna be great."

"I've missed you, too, my darling daughter," Carol responded. "I just wish I could get you to understand that I only want to support you. You're my only child…"

"And you need to respect that my wanting to know our family doesn't mean I love you any less."

"I hear you."

Rayne sent Taylor a sharp glare when he walked into the house.

"Hello, Carol," he greeted.

Before he could escape, Rayne grabbed his arm. "Taylor, I'd like to speak with you outside."

"Sure."

She led him to the end of the driveway.

"What did you say to her? I couldn't get Mama to budge ever when it came to Polk Island."

"I just asked her to consider coming to spend the holidays with her family. This is a good thing, right? Her being here?"

"Yeah, but how do I prepare her for Uncle Daniel and Aunt Maggie's visit?" Rayne asked. "I don't want to keep this from her, but if I tell her—Taylor, she'll leave. Now that she's here, the thought of her turning tail and running scares me."

"Maybe she wants to see them," he suggested. "It's been seventeen years."

Rayne had serious doubts. "Naw… I know my mama. She will be on the first flight leaving Charleston."

"You never thought Carol would come back in the first place. I believe she's ready to face whatever they went through head-on, Rayne. I think I'll give you two some time alone. I'm going to go to the museum."

"Oh, no, you're not about to leave me alone with her," Rayne stated as she blocked his exit. "You brought her to the island, so now we're going to deal with the fallout together."

TAYLOR ACCOMPANIED RAYNE back into the house. He really hoped that Carol would be receptive to the news that her siblings would be there for the holidays. He could tell this reunion meant a lot to Rayne.

Carol broke down into tears when she saw her grandchildren. Watching the play of emotions on her face removed any doubt that he'd been right in asking her to join them.

When his eyes met Rayne's troubled gaze, Taylor offered her a reassuring smile. He felt positive that everything would work out. This wasn't just about Carol's relationship with her siblings—it was also a chance for her and Rayne to work out the kinks in theirs as well. He had no doubt that she loved her mother, but she seemed to take her for granted at times, which irked him. Taylor felt he could have benefitted from someone like Carol in his life.

When they were alone, Rayne said, "Aunt Maggie will be here tomorrow."

"When are you going to tell your mom?"

"I don't know. I thought I'd have this time to sit down with my aunt and uncle—hear their side of things. You know… I thought I'd have time to ease Mama into a conversation with them."

"Just rip the Band-Aid off and tell her."

Rayne looked up at him. "Really? That's your advice?"

"Would you rather she be blindsided when they show up?" Taylor asked.

"No, but then again, that just might be the way to go about this. Think about it… She can't just leave without facing them. It will force them to have that much-needed conversation."

"I think you should prepare your mother."

"I don't agree," Rayne responded. "I'm going to do my part to keep Christmas drama-free. I just hope my mother will do the same."

CHAPTER THIRTEEN

AFTER CAROL LEFT to go back to Eleanor's house, Rayne sat down with Leon and Misty.

"I had no idea that she was coming here. Mama said that she'd never come back to the island. But here's the thing. I called Aunt Maggie and Uncle Daniel. They're coming for Christmas."

"Is that bad?" Misty asked.

"Well, they're a big part of the reason we left in the first place."

"Oh."

Rayne eyed Leon. "Aunt Maggie will be here tomorrow, and I haven't told Mama. I don't want Mama to leave, but I'm also worried throwing them all together is a mistake."

"I don't think so," he responded. "The three of them need to sit down and talk like adults. If they don't want to do it, they can leave. I'm not letting them put a damper on the holidays for my family. I know Trey will feel the same way. You and Taylor shouldn't, either."

Rayne glanced over at Taylor.

"You have my support," he said.

"Tomorrow's going to be a busy day for you, Rayne," Misty said. "You have brunch with the committee and then the tree-trimming party later. We'll understand if you want to skip the tree-trimming."

"I'm not about to do that. I'm very excited about the brunch and the party."

She glanced over at Taylor when Misty and Leon left the room. "Mama's got to stop running away from her problems."

He gave a choked laugh, and she glared.

"Don't start with me again," she said.

Taylor shook his head. "I'm sorry. It's sort of funny. You did the same thing. Instead of talking to me, you made the choice to disappear and withhold your pregnancy from me."

Rayne's eyes grew as big as saucers as she looked past Taylor.

Leon and Misty stood there looking astonished.

"I guess I'd better explain," Rayne said.

They sat down at the dining-room table. She really hadn't wanted it to come out this way, or at all.

"Taylor and I had too much to drink after a party in Vegas," she began. "We were celebrating the opening of the new dealership. Anyway, we saw this chapel on the strip and decided to get married."

Rayne glanced over at Taylor, who said, "We woke up and decided that we'd made a huge mistake. The plan was to file for the divorce quietly."

"But one of us would have to stay in Vegas for six weeks," she interjected. "I was going to work from there remotely."

Leon and Misty sat quietly, listening.

"During that time, I found out I was pregnant. I knew that I didn't want to have my baby without being married, and I knew that Taylor didn't want the marriage, or kids. So I quit my job, left Vegas and went to my mom's. I was scared, and I wanted to delay the divorce until the babies were born." Rayne paused, then added, "Taylor had no idea why I'd disappeared. He had no idea that he was going to be a father."

"I didn't find out until the day I walked into the restaurant. Carol only told me where to find Rayne. She didn't tell me about the babies."

"Your reaction makes more sense to me now," Misty stated.

Rayne's eyes filled with tears. "I'm sorry. I didn't want y'all to think less of me and the babies when I showed up after all this time. I wanted you to believe that I'd had this normal marriage. I would rather have you believe that we were separated, than..." Her voice died. "All of y'all have beautiful marriages..."

"I've known Rayne for eight years," Taylor said. "She has always made you and Trey out to be larger than life, Leon. She really looks up to you. She didn't want you to see her as a failure, even in marriage. I want you to know that Rayne wasn't just one of my employees. We have a solid friendship, and I care about her. What we have is better than some marriages."

"I'm not disappointed in you for your personal life, Rayne," Leon said. "I'm disappointed that you felt you had to hide the truth from us. Honey, I meant what I said about loving you, mistakes and all."

A tear slipped down her cheek. "I'm really ashamed of my actions. Taylor tried to convince me to tell the truth. I was embarrassed."

"This will stay between us," Leon stated. "Unless you decide to tell Trey or anyone else."

"We have another guestroom upstairs," Misty said. "If it's needed."

Rayne peered at Taylor.

"I'd rather stay down here to help her with the twins."

Wiping her eyes, she nodded in agreement. "I'm sorry."

"We understand," Misty said. "I'm curious though... Are you still planning to get the divorce?"

Taylor shrugged. "We're still trying to navigate the best scenario for the twins. I know Rayne wants to stay here on the island. We both agree this is a great place to raise them, but my businesses are on the West Coast. There's a lot to figure out."

"You didn't ask my advice, but I'm going to give it anyway," Leon said. "Don't rush into anything. Take your time because you have two young children depending on you both."

Later, when they were in the bedroom, Rayne sat down on the bed. "That went way better than I thought it would." She looked up at him. "Thanks for not throwing me under the bus. I really couldn't blame you if you had."

"I'd never do that to you. I'll always have your back, Rayne. I thought you'd know that by now."

"I guess I forget sometimes. Taylor, you've always been a good friend to me, even when I wasn't such a nice person. I still remember the day you were going to fire me after my ex made a scene at the office. You'd called the police, and I got angry with you. You told me to pack my stuff and get out. I'd never seen you so upset, but worse, I saw disappointment written all over your face, and I felt awful."

"I was surprised when you came back, apologized and asked for your job back. But it confirmed for me that my instincts were right about you."

Rayne gave a wry smile. "You've always had more faith in me than I had in myself."

"It's because I really believe in you."

In that moment, Rayne knew she loved him. Taylor was good and pure. Despite all she'd put him through, he never failed her. He had never given up on her. The truth was that she didn't deserve a man like him.

"Your instincts were right," Misty told Leon as they prepared for bed. "You said that she was hiding something."

"I noticed something tonight," he responded.

"What's that?"

"Rayne's in love with Taylor. And I believe he feels the same way, but for whatever reason, something's holding them back from admitting it to themselves."

"Maybe they're both afraid."

Leon eyed his wife. "I think you're right."

"They're a beautiful family—I hope they stay together." Misty climbed into bed. "But with him in Los Angeles and Rayne here on the island, I'm not sure it can work."

Leon slid into bed beside her. "Maybe they'll split their time. Half here and half on the West

Coast. I wouldn't want to live that way, but it might work for them."

"Maybe," Misty murmured.

"I only hope Aunt Carol won't pack up and leave when she comes face-to-face with her siblings. Sounds like she's still very bitter over what happened."

"It's been seventeen years, right?" she asked.

"Yep, but she was really hurt back then."

Misty reached out to turn off the light. "We're going to need a lot of Christmas miracles this year."

"It's definitely going to take a miracle for Aunt Carol to forgive her brother and sister."

GIA'S MOTHER DUSTED a speck of flour on her sleeve and grinned at the guests gathered in her living room. "We're having roast chicken with a range of side dishes."

Rayne hadn't realized that the annual brunch for the festival committee was such an elaborate affair. She was glad she'd chosen to wear a dress. Wearing black was always a safe choice for any occasion.

She sent a quick text to Misty, checking on the twins. Rayne felt a thread of guilt over leaving them. Ian seemed not to be feeling well. Earlier, he refused to take his bottle, but the response from Misty made her feel better. Ian had taken a couple of ounces of the formula.

Rayne walked around, admiring the decor.

With Gia's assistance, Patricia had transformed her home into a Christmas wonderland with elegant, festive decorations in crystal and silver. A sideboard was covered with hors d'oeuvres and an array of mouthwatering Christmas cookies and candies. There was also champagne and wine.

"Everything looks beautiful," Rayne said, accepting a glass of red wine from Gia. "You and your mother did a fantastic job with the decorations."

"Thanks. I hope you're having a good time."

"I am. Ian's got a bit of a cold, so I was thinking of staying home with him, but I'm glad I came."

"Oh, I hope he feels better soon," Gia said. "Trevon had a cold around Thanksgiving, and he was so miserable."

Rayne nibbled on cheese-stuffed cherry tomatoes and prosciutto-wrapped asparagus with raspberry sauce while chatting with some of the other guests.

At the dining-room table, she was drawn into a conversation with one of the other committee members.

"Are you here just for the holidays?"

Rayne took a sip of water. "For now, but I'm actually considering making it permanent." She didn't want to reveal too much of her private life.

"I'm sure a lot of that will depend on your husband."

She gave a slight nod. "Yes."

"It took some convincing on my part to get my husband to leave Atlanta, but he finally agreed. We haven't regretted it one bit."

"That's great to hear," Rayne responded.

Misty met her at the front door when she arrived home two hours later.

Rayne could tell something was wrong by the expression on her face. "Are my babies okay?" she asked.

"They're great. Aunt Maggie just arrived."

"Where is she?"

"She's in the family room talking to Leon," Misty said.

"I didn't expect her so soon. Does my mom know that she's here?"

Misty shook her head. "Not yet."

Rayne walked through the house to where her aunt and Leon were seated.

Maggie and Eleanor favored one another greatly, except Maggie's salt-and-pepper hair fell down to her shoulders. They were both full-figured and tall in stature, but both were elegant women in their sixties.

"Hey, Auntie," she greeted. "I'm so glad you were able to come."

"When you told me that you were here—I had to see you. I've missed you so much. Carol may have given birth to you, but you were all of ours."

"I was very lucky to have three moms," Rayne said. "Have you met my babies?"

"Yes, I have. Oh, they're so beautiful," Maggie responded. "I met your husband, too. He was on his way out, so we didn't get to talk. He's quite handsome."

"Thank you," Rayne said.

"How is your mother?"

She looked away from her aunt. "She's fine."

"I'd really love to see her."

Rayne took a cleansing breath before saying, "That's great to hear because she's here."

Maggie looked surprised. "Carol's on the island?"

"Yes. I didn't know she would be here when I spoke with you. She and my husband had a conversation."

"I'm glad she's here, Rayne. She and I need to have a conversation. It's long overdue."

"I agree, Aunt Maggie. It's just that Mama's not ready."

"She's always been stubborn and strong-willed."

"The same can be said about all of you," she responded.

Maggie laughed.

"We're not going to think negatively," Leon declared. "I'm hoping that once they see each other, love will take over."

"I love Carol, and I want her back in my life."

"She's staying with Aunt Eleanor, so I think you should stay here with us," Leon said.

"Nonsense. I'm going to stay with Ella, too. It's childish to avoid one another—we're grown women. We know how to conduct ourselves."

"Leon, maybe you should call Rusty," Misty suggested. "Just to make him aware of the situation."

"You should also let him know that Daniel will be arriving sometime tonight," Maggie said.

When Rayne looked out the window, the shades of the sunset were beginning to merge with the darkening sky. She quivered, feeling cold, and pulled the folds of her sweater together. She had a bad feeling about this little reunion.

CHAPTER FOURTEEN

"WHAT SHOULD WE DO?" a nervous Rayne asked Leon. "I'm not sure how my mom is going to react when she sees her sister."

He shook his head. "Don't worry. Aunt Maggie's got it under control."

"Misty just invited me to stay for the tree-trimming," Maggie said, joining them.

"I'm so glad," Rayne responded. "You can get to know the twins better. Besides, I'd like to sit down and talk to you." She wanted to prepare her aunt that her mother's feelings toward her hadn't changed over the years.

"I'd love that. Will Carol be joining us?"

Shaking his head, Leon stated, "I don't think so, unless Rayne's mentioned it."

Rayne shook her head. "I didn't."

"Why don't we sit and have that chat?" Maggie suggested.

She nodded.

They settled in the family room.

"I want you to know that I have the purest of intentions, Aunt Maggie," Rayne began. "I was telling the truth when I said that Mama wasn't coming to the island."

"Honey, I know that. It's all right. I'm glad that she's here. We need to sort this out face-to-face."

"I love all of you. I want you to know that. I want my babies to get to know you and Uncle Daniel. I want us to be a real family again."

"We all want the same things," Maggie responded.

"I'm so glad to hear you say this. Mama doesn't know about you or Uncle Daniel coming here. I didn't have the nerve to tell her."

Maggie took her hand and gave it a gentle squeeze. "Stop worrying, sweetie. This is between your mother and me. We will sort this out."

"Thank you for understanding."

"Carol is my sister. We will always be family no matter what."

"I'm glad we're doing this. I'm…" Rayne sighed, then admitted, "I'm angry with Mom. My life would've turned out very differently if we'd stayed here, and I can't help feeling that leaving the island was a mistake."

"I understand, but, sweetie…maybe it was the best thing for your mother at the time. Carol and I will get this all sorted out. I'm staying at Eleanor's so we will all have a chance to talk."

"Mom's staying over there, too." Rayne prayed Taylor would show up soon. She didn't like this uneasy feeling swirling around her stomach.

She nearly sagged with relief when he walked into the house fifteen minutes later. "I'm so glad you're back."

"What happened?"

"Nothing yet," Rayne responded. "Aunt Maggie's planning on staying with her sister. So is Uncle Daniel."

"Wow."

"Right," she uttered. "I know my mom. She's not going to stay in that house with them. She will want to come here or go to Trey's. She may just go to a hotel. Worst, she might leave. Taylor, I don't want her to miss the twins' first Christmas."

"Maybe you should tell her that," he suggested, embracing her. "Stay out of it. Let them work it out."

An hour later, they prepared to finally put ornaments on the tree.

"Leon, I think you found the tallest tree out there," Maggie said. "It's huge."

He laughed. "My wife likes them tall and full."

"I sure do," Misty said as she entered the living room. "Good job, honey."

"I've never decorated a tree before," Taylor said.

Shocked, Rayne turned to face him. "Like never ever? I just thought you didn't care for them."

"Don't get me wrong. I can hang an ornament on a branch. But we never had Christmas trees when I was growing up, so it's just not something I've ever wanted to do. I didn't see much point in it."

"Well, don't say that too loudly over here. It turns into a party when we start tree decorating."

Taylor chuckled. "Well, I certainly don't want to be a party pooper."

Rayne had been right about it being a party. Misty brought out a tray of assorted slider sandwiches, raw veggies with dip and fresh-baked gingerbread cookies.

"This is my very first ornament," Talei said. "It was a gift from my grandma when I was a baby. Can you hang it someplace high please?"

Taylor recognized that the Christmas ornament was a simple handmade gift of the heart and was more special for it. "How about I pick you up so you can put it exactly where you'd like it to go?"

"Wado."

He noticed that all the ornaments were handmade. Taylor picked up one, rubbing his finger across the fabric. He'd never had a personal ornament—his parents never made much of Christmas, so this was all new to him. When Rayne worked for him, she suggested that he throw the employees an annual Christmas party, but he responded that he didn't celebrate the holiday. Outside of giving each of them a Christmas bonus—he didn't participate in any holiday festivities except the holiday party he sponsored at the group home.

Leon walked over to where he stood, saying, "Each year, we make a Christmas ornament to remind us of a blessing or a happy memory that we're thankful for. We want our children to understand that while the Christmas holidays can be a fun time, it should also be a time of reflection on how best to act in the ways of love."

"I think that's a great idea." As he glanced around, Taylor glimpsed what it looked like to be part of a family. Talei and her siblings' delightful chatter kept him engaged and laughing. Even Maggie was fun to be around.

Rayne walked over to the dining-room table, where Talei was helping Leon and Fawn with their ornaments.

"You and Taylor should make some for the twins and for y'all, too," the little girl said.

"Think you can handle it?" Rayne asked him.

"Of course," he responded. "But I'm going to need some pointers."

Smirking, she sat down across from him. "Taylor's going to need your help, Talei."

"I'm sure we both can use your expertise in ornament making," he responded. "You may have to help Rayne paint within the lines."

Talei laughed.

"Ooh, give Taylor that green feather," Rayne said.

Frowning in confusion, Taylor asked, "What do you want me to do with it?"

"Take one of the glass ornament balls and put the feathers inside."

He did as she instructed. "What now?"

Rayne took the ornament from him. "Talei, pass me the scissors, the black marker and that yellow one please."

She drew what looked like a face, then showed it to Taylor.

He burst into laughter.

Talei walked over to her and peered at the ornament. "It's the Grinch."

Taylor met her amused gaze, and they burst into another round of laughter.

He peered across the table where Rayne was working. "What are you making?"

"A snowman."

He watched as she created her snowman's

body out of a glass salt shaker filled with artificial snow and glitter. The head was made of a small foam ball. She fashioned a scarf out of a piece of tartan plaid fabric.

"Now all I need is a little black button," Rayne stated.

"That's super cool," Talei said. "You're good at making ornaments."

Taylor agreed. "She sure is."

Talei went back to helping Fawn make an ornament out of buttons. When they finished, she held it up for them to see.

"That looks like a Christmas tree," Rayne said. "Good job, Fawn."

The little girl grinned then hid her face.

"I made a button superhero," Leo announced while showing them his project.

"You did a great job on that," Taylor said.

He and Rayne led the children over to the tree, and they placed their ornaments on it.

"I think these are the prettiest ornaments so far," Misty told them. "My babies are talented."

"Talei, which ornament did you create for this year?" Rayne asked.

"I made a stocking," she responded and pointed to it. "It has the same pattern as the new ribbon skirt my grandmother made for me."

"Ribbon skirts symbolize resilience, survival

and identity for Indigenous people," Misty explained.

"That's super cool," Rayne said.

They were having such a good time that she didn't hear the doorbell.

Her mother's voice cut through the laughter.

Carol blew through the front door. "Hey, everybody, I came by to spend some quality time with my daughter and grandchildren."

Her smile disappeared when her gaze landed on Maggie. "What is she doing here?"

"I have every right to be here, the same as you," Maggie responded. "It's good to see you."

"I can't say the same," Carol replied stiffly. "Rayne, I'll talk to you later."

"Mama, stop. You don't have to leave."

She looked at her daughter.

"I'd like for you to stay," Rayne said. "We're trimming the tree. You and I haven't done that in a long time. Remember how much fun we used to have?"

"How can you expect me to stay here with her?"

"She's your sister. She's family, Mama."

"Maggie may be your family, but she's not mine," Carol responded.

"Let's not involve the kids in this," Maggie said. "We should talk and try to figure this out amongst ourselves."

"I don't have anything to say to you." Carol headed toward the door.

"You're not going to be able to escape me so easily. I'm staying with Rusty and Eleanor, too."

Carol turned. "Then I'll go to a hotel."

"Mama…"

"I don't want to hear it, Rayne."

"I'm sorry, but this time you're going to listen to me." She blocked her mother's exit. "This is stupid. You have young kids watching the two of you. If you're not ready to talk to Aunt Maggie, that's fine. I'm sure you can at least manage to be pleasant to one another."

"I can do that," her aunt responded.

Carol gave a curt nod. "Fine."

Rayne took her mother by the hand and led her to the opposite side of the room from Maggie. "Thank you, Mama."

"There were a few times when I really wanted to come home for the holidays, but I couldn't afford the airfare."

Rayne gasped in surprise. "You never told me this."

"I didn't want to disappoint you, Rayne. I knew how much you wanted to come home."

"Mama, why are you still so angry with your sister?" she asked.

"They believed what Roger's wife said about

me. You have no idea about the things they said to me. They judged me."

"I regret my words, Carol."

Rayne looked past her mother to her aunt. "I'd like to apologize for what I said to you back then. I'm truly sorry."

"You hurt me deeply."

"I realize that now."

Shaking her head, Carol replied, "I'm not interested."

Maggie shrugged, then said, "I want you to know that I love you. That has never changed."

She walked away.

"Mama, it's been years. We all make mistakes," Rayne said. "She realizes that she and Uncle Daniel didn't handle things right. At least listen to what she has to say. You can't keep running away."

"Really? This coming from you?"

"Mama, we can point fingers at one another all day long, but now isn't the time. You're right, though. We both need to stop running. Maybe you can start with Aunt Maggie."

"Some things you just never forget," Carol said. "I will accept her apology before the night is over, but I'm not sure I'll ever forgive her. She and Daniel broke my heart. People will hold your sins over your head. They expect you to be perfect."

"We can't do it now, but I do want to finish this conversation," Rayne whispered. "Mama, I'm going to ask you to do something for me."

"What is it?"

"This is the twins' first Christmas. I know they won't remember it, but Taylor and I will. We want this to be a nice memory for them."

"I want that as well," Carol responded. "I had no idea Maggie would be here. If I'd known, I never would've come."

"Not even for Ian and Ivy?" Rayne asked. "You would let your anger keep you away from your grandchildren?"

"I sound silly, don't I?"

"I don't think I have to answer that."

A smiled tugged at Carol's lips. "No, you don't."

"C'mon, let's make the best of this evening. It's supposed to be a party."

TAYLOR TOOK OFF his sweater. "I have to say that you handled the situation with your mother and aunt extremely well."

"It got pretty contentious for a minute there," Rayne responded as she removed her shoes.

"I don't suppose you told Carol that her brother was on his way to the island?"

"I sure didn't. I don't think she could've handled the news."

"I'm inclined to agree with you," he said.

"She'll probably catch the first flight out of Charleston."

"Maybe she won't, Rayne."

"I wanted this Christmas to be perfect."

"I can't believe I'm saying this, but it's not over yet," Taylor said.

Rayne looked over at him. "I can't believe it, either."

He wrapped an arm around her. "Everything will work out fine."

"The last time you told me that—we were in court because I'd been arrested!"

"And it did," Taylor responded. "I was right."

"You were."

"I have a feeling that you're going to get your Christmas miracle."

"I hope so," Rayne said. "I truly hope that she can get past the hurt and find a way to forgive them. It's not for Aunt Maggie or Uncle Daniel. She needs to forgive so that she can move on."

"It's easier said than done," he stated.

"Oh, I know. It's taken me a long time to forgive what my ex did to me, landing me in that courtroom. I had to forgive to get my power back." Rayne looked over at him. "Why are you looking at me like that?"

"You have no idea how special you are to me," Taylor said.

"I happen to think that you're pretty special yourself."

Taylor had to tear himself away from her gaze. The mere touch of Rayne's hand against his own sent a warming shiver through him, which he tried to ignore. Taylor moved his hand away from hers. "You're definitely not making this easy on me."

"What are you talking about?"

"I don't want things to be uncomfortable between us."

"We're fine, Taylor."

"You sure?"

Rayne nodded. "If you're serious about trying to make this marriage work, then we need to at least act like a real couple."

"The friendship is there," he responded. "I don't want to ruin what we already have."

Taylor was in a private battle. He couldn't imagine waking up and not seeing her smile first thing in the morning. The truth of the matter was that he was in love with Rayne, and he didn't want to lose her. He didn't have any idea when it happened, but it didn't really matter. Rayne was the only woman he wanted to spend the rest of his life with.

I'm in love with my best friend, but I can't

tell her. Taylor just didn't think it was a good idea to put their friendship at risk.

After slipping on a pair of pajama bottoms and a T-shirt, he slid into bed.

Rayne was so quiet, he assumed she'd already fallen asleep.

He settled back against the pillows and closed his eyes.

Sleep didn't come easy.

Taylor was troubled by the look of disappointment on Rayne's face earlier. No doubt she felt he was sending out mixed signals. He was going to have to keep his distance because things between them were too fragile to put their friendship at risk.

RAYNE BIT HER bottom lip and pushed away her fantasies of a life with Taylor. He was determined to keep their relationship platonic, much to her disappointment.

She glanced over to her right, where he lay sleeping.

At least one of us is getting some rest.

Maybe she was wasting her time where Taylor was concerned. He seemed to be able to turn his feelings on and off, but it was not a talent she possessed. Perhaps it was time that she faced reality and let go of any dreams of being with Taylor.

Rayne wasn't sure when her feelings morphed from friendship into something more. No man had ever made her feel the way Taylor did.

Rayne had just nodded off when she heard her name.

She bolted upright. "What's wrong?"

"Nothing," Taylor said, "but I thought you'd want to see this."

He was standing over the crib.

Rayne got out of bed and joined him.

Ian had Ivy's hand in his as they slept.

"Oh, my goodness," she murmured. "Did you get a picture?"

"Yes," he responded. "I'll send it to you."

"What were you doing up?" Rayne asked. "I didn't hear them crying."

"I got up to check on them. I debated whether to wake you."

She smiled. "I'm glad you did. Thanks."

"I guess we should try to go back to sleep. There's no telling when they'll wake up."

Rayne picked up a plush blanket and placed it over them. "It feels a bit chilly to me."

"It's cold, but they seem pretty comfortable. Their bodies were warm."

"You really are a good father, Taylor."

"Go get in bed," he told her. "I'll grab another blanket for us, too."

She smiled in gratitude.

Once Taylor joined her in bed, she turned to face him, his features barely discernible in the moonlight that filtered in through the window.

"Are you still cold?" he asked.

"No, I'm fine." What Rayne really wanted to say was *It would help if you moved a little closer.* Instead, she closed her eyes, pretending to fall asleep.

CHAPTER FIFTEEN

CAROL CALLED HER a few minutes after seven the next morning.

"You must really hate me."

Shocked, Rayne sat up in bed. "Mama, what are you talking about? You know I don't hate you." She kept her voice low to keep from waking the twins.

"You failed to mention that Daniel was also going to be in town. I learned that you were the one who asked them to come in the first place. How could you not mention this to me?"

"Mama, I was only trying to get my family back together. It's been too long."

"You shouldn't have interfered in things you know nothing about," Carol responded.

"I was there, remember? Besides, I had no idea you were coming to the island until after I'd asked them to come," Rayne stated. "I didn't say anything to you because I didn't want you to leave. I wanted you to be here for the twins."

"Just the twins?" Carol asked.

"No. I want you here with me, too. You need

to talk to your siblings. This has gone on way too long."

"I didn't call to fight with you. I just really don't know what to do. I want to just pack my things and leave, but I also want to spend the holidays with you and the twins."

"Please don't leave, Mama. I regret the time we lost with our family. I want to make up for that now, don't you? Especially when they want the opportunity to finally settle things with you."

"You sound like Ella. She's been saying the same thing. I just don't want her getting upset over this."

"Then please just hear them out. It's not going to happen overnight, but I believe things will work out between y'all."

"I guess I can at least do that," Carol said. "I'll hear what Maggie and Daniel have to say."

"Thank you, Mama."

"But I need you to understand that I'm not making any promises."

"I understand," Rayne said. "I really do."

When she hung up, Taylor asked, "Everything okay?"

"She says that she's willing to hear what my aunt and uncle have to say. I just hope my mom means it."

"Have faith," Taylor responded. "I believe

Carol wants this as much as everyone else. She's a Rothchild, and I'm learning you're all stubborn...and family-minded."

"I hope you're right." Rayne got out of bed.

"I am."

"You seem pretty sure about this."

Swinging his legs out of bed, he said, "Let's just say that I have a really good feeling about this."

She broke into a grin. "And it's a good day to get in some exercise. Do you want to go to the gym with me?"

"Sure."

"I'll get dressed. I'm sure Mama would love to watch the twins while we're there. I'll call her back and ask."

Rayne left the bedroom.

She returned twenty minutes later fully dressed. "Mama agreed to watch them... Why are you looking at me like that?"

"You look beautiful," Taylor stated.

"What brought that on? All I did was comb my hair. I don't have on a stitch of makeup."

"You don't need all that stuff."

She was entranced by the silent sadness of his face. Rayne had seen this look a few times and knew he was thinking of the past. She reached over and gave his hand a reassuring squeeze. "Go get dressed before I change my mind."

CAROL WAS DELIGHTED to spend quality time with her grandchildren. But first, she had to contend with her siblings. She knew they were all downstairs waiting for her. She didn't want to have this conversation, but it was necessary. There were things she wanted to say to Maggie and Daniel.

She took a deep cleansing breath before leaving the bedroom.

When Carol descended the stairs, she found Eleanor standing at the bottom waiting for her.

"C'mon, suga…it's time the past is finally laid to rest."

Daniel and Maggie sat together in the living room.

"Before either of you say anything, I want you to hear me out," Carol said. "Daniel, you and Maggie really hurt me. You judged me without knowing all the details. You were home for a visit. You didn't know everything that happened. I was young, and I needed your support."

"You're right," he responded. "I made a lot of assumptions."

"And you didn't ask me about anything. You believed every word that came from that woman's mouth. So did you, Maggie."

"I listened to her back then because I was dealing with something similar," her sister responded. "I'd just found out that my husband had been cheating on me. That woman's pain resonated with my own, and I took it out on you, Carol."

"I didn't know."

Maggie nodded. "I know that you didn't. I hadn't told anyone. I was embarrassed, and it was so fresh… I didn't have a face to pin my anger on. When I heard the things that woman said about you, I raged at you because I couldn't attack the person who truly deserved it. From the way she was going on, I thought you were still involved with her husband. Ella told us that you didn't have any knowledge that he was married."

"I told you the same thing, but neither of you would listen to me."

"Carol, I am sorry, and I ask for your forgiveness," Daniel said. "I wanted to reach out to you over the years, but I knew… I felt terrible."

"I'm sorry, too," Maggie said. "My life hasn't been the same without you in it. Daniel and I were wrong. We realize that. My biggest fear was that I'd never see you again, Carol. I grieved our relationship. You're my little sister, and I love you."

Carol's eyes watered. "Don't make me cry."

"Can you ever forgive us?" Daniel asked.

"For so many years, I believed that it just wasn't possible, but now…in this moment…yes,

I forgive you, Daniel. I forgive you, Maggie." She wiped her eyes. "Can you forgive me for walking around in judgment of you? For being so angry and staying in that space? I should have reached out before now, but I was prideful and stubborn."

"The price of being a Rothchild," Daniel said. "Dad used to always say that we should never let the sun go down on our anger. If we do, we are walking in pride. The Rothchilds are a proud family—we have to practice humility."

"My stubbornness has hurt my relationship with Rayne. I see that now," Carol said. "I hope we'll be able to rebuild what we lost."

"That girl loves you to pieces," Maggie responded. "You and Rayne will find a way to navigate your relationship."

"I had to learn how to do that with my son," Daniel stated. "We have to let go and let our grown children be adults."

Carol nodded in agreement. "It's not that easy for me. From the moment she was born, I knew I had to protect her. But she doesn't want that from me. It's really hard letting go. Rayne is all I have. She's my life."

"It's time for you to make a life for yourself, Carol."

She eyed Daniel. "I think it's too late for me."

He hugged her. "It's never too late. You

weren't meant to be alone, and you're still young. Trust me on that."

"I used to believe that, but not anymore." Carol swiped at her eyes. "I never thought I'd say this, but I'm really happy to see all of you."

She stood up. "Now, I need to get out of here. I'm spending the day with my grandbabies. Can you believe that I'm a grandmother?"

"It's a wonderful feeling, isn't it?" Maggie responded. "There's nothing like it."

"I have to do whatever it takes to keep them in my life," Carol murmured.

TAYLOR HANDED RAYNE a bottle of water. "I'm proud of you. You did great in class."

"I'm...never...doing anything like that again." She could barely catch her breath. "You make this class look so effortless."

"I've been at it for months now. I'm used to it."

She grimaced. "I don't know why I let you talk me into taking this class. I don't have a belt in anything, Taylor."

"You hung in there, though. I was impressed."

"My whole body hurts. I just want to go back to the house and soak in the tub."

On the way out of the gym, Taylor asked, "How do you think your mom's doing with the twins?"

"Having them all to herself…she's in heaven, I'm sure."

He held the passenger-side door open for her. "It's nice your wishes are coming true. It doesn't happen like that for most people."

"I don't believe that," Rayne responded.

"It's true."

"It's almost Christmas, Taylor. I need you to *try* to enjoy this time with my family. I realize that I'm asking a lot from you."

He strode around to the driver's side and slid behind the steering wheel. "Your family is great. I'll try to get more into the holiday spirit, okay?"

She reached over and gave his arm a light squeeze. "It's much appreciated."

"I think you should take your mother to lunch or dinner tomorrow. I know she'd love having some one-on-one time with you."

"That's a great idea," she responded.

When they walked into the house thirty minutes later, Carol and Misty were seated in the dining room. Ivy was in Carol's lap.

"Where's Ian?" Rayne asked.

"He's sleeping. This little girl wanted to join us for some girl talk."

"Looks like everything went fine."

"Did you expect otherwise?" her mother questioned.

"Not at all, Mama." Pointing toward the hall-way, Rayne said, "I'm going to jump into the shower."

She returned twenty minutes later. Ivy was sleeping in Carol's arms.

"Thank you for watching them."

Her mother smiled. "It was my pleasure. I didn't realize just how much I'd missed them, Rayne. That sweet baby scent…"

"I wasn't trying to keep them from you," she said. "I hope you know that. I just got scared imagining they wouldn't have support outside of the two of us, and you were so closed off about my coming to the island…"

"I know that you'd rather I keep my opinions to myself."

"At times," Rayne admitted. "Mama, I'd like for us to have lunch tomorrow. Just the two of us."

Carol broke into a grin. "Really?"

"Yes, ma'am. We haven't done that in a while."

"I'd really love that, Rayne."

She smiled. "I'll meet you tomorrow around one. We'll eat at the café."

RAYNE DIDN'T MEET her mother for lunch until shortly after two in the afternoon, which was late for her, but she had to take care of some last-minute tasks for the festival.

She walked into the café, her gaze landing on her mother. "Mama, I'm sorry about all the last-minute changes. I got caught up with my meeting."

"Hey, sweetie." Carol looked her up and down. "My goodness, you definitely don't look like you gave birth to twins. You're looking better every time I see you."

"Thank you," Rayne responded. "How are things going with your siblings?"

"Better than I could've hoped. I didn't tell you yesterday, but Maggie shared that her reaction was based on what she was dealing with in her own marriage. I had no idea that her husband had cheated on her."

"Oh, wow…"

Rayne didn't miss the shimmer of sadness that shone in her mother's eyes. "At least you're all together again. You've forgiven each other. Mama, we're going to have a wonderful Christmas."

Carol nodded. "I've missed them all. I hadn't let myself realize just how much. For the most part, I was the holdup. They wanted to have this conversation a long time ago, but I kept refusing."

"That's all over now, Mama. We should just look forward from now on."

"Rayne, I'm sorry for what went wrong in our relationship."

"Mama, you didn't do anything wrong, exactly. You were trying to protect me when you cut off contact with the family. I've been angrier than I knew about losing them."

"I thought I was protecting you, Rayne."

She picked up her menu. "I'm beginning to understand this. When I look at the twins…all I want to do is keep them safe. I get why you feel the way you do, but I also want to give them the chance to navigate on their own, Mama. I want them to be able to make mistakes and learn from them. And I want them to grow up with a bundle of cousins."

"Some mistakes you can't come back from," Carol responded.

"That's how you learn. I learned a lot about myself from the mistakes I've made, Mama."

Her mother glanced down at her menu. When she looked up, she asked, "What happened, Rayne? I know there's something you aren't telling me."

Keeping her expression blank, she stated, "Nothing I want to talk about right now."

Carol met her gaze. "You always do that. You hold back certain areas of your life from me. I'm your mother. You can tell me anything. I should be a safe place for you."

"You are," she said. "There are just some things I'm not ready to share yet. Please respect that."

"I don't have much of a choice."

She was glad when the server walked over to the booth. Rayne wanted to have a nice lunch with her mother. In time, she would tell Carol everything, but today was not the day to do so.

THE NEXT EVENING, Taylor wanted to dine out, so they decided to try an Italian eatery in Charleston.

Rayne glanced around the upscale restaurant as they waited for their food to arrive, observing couples engaged in intimate conversations. She glanced over at Taylor. "I was sitting here trying to remember the last time I was on a real date. Isn't that terrible that I can't even recall something like that?"

"Sounds like it wasn't memorable," he responded.

She laughed. "You're probably right. What about you? When was the last time you went on a real date?"

"It's been a while. In fact, you and I have hung out more than I've dated in the past three years."

Rayne took a sip of her iced tea. "C'mon, I find that hard to believe."

"It's mostly on my part," he admitted. "I've been focused on work."

"If I'd known that, I would've told you to get out more and just have some fun. I just thought you didn't like talking about your women with me."

"Maybe you should take your own advice," he suggested.

"I enjoying hanging out with you because we have a good time together."

"And I'm safe for you."

"I hadn't thought of it in that way, but yeah… I do feel safe with you, Taylor."

"And look what happened. We both turned out to be workaholics," he said with a chuckle.

Rayne nodded in agreement. "That just means that we have to play hard to balance it all out."

"Only you would say something like that."

She broke into a grin. "Life is short. We only get one, so we might as well enjoy it every chance we get. Leon reminded me of this exact thing earlier. He was saying that you and I have been so involved in parenting—he said that we need to have a life outside of that. And he's right."

"I guess I always saw them as one and the same," he responded. "You were either a parent or a single person. A parent or a husband, but there's room for both, I guess."

"I suppose it is perspective. I was really worried about becoming a mother," Rayne said. "I was terrified."

"Really? I'm actually surprised to hear this. You're not telling me this to try to make me feel better?"

"No, it's true. I still have moments of doubt when I just don't feel like I'm equipped to be a mom. But then I remind myself that there is no manual. It's trial and error."

He smiled. "You're doing a fantastic job, Rayne."

"So are you," she responded.

"Are you still excited about the festival this weekend? You've done a lot in a short amount of time."

"I am very excited, but I'm also a little nervous," she responded. "I wish I had been a part of the committee from the beginning, but I've done the best I could to help. It should be a wonderful event. They've certainly pulled it off well before I came back… I would just love to bring in some new activities and attractions."

"I understand. You're a perfectionist. Remember, I've worked with you for eight years."

"You make it sound like a bad thing."

"Not at all," Taylor responded. "I appreciate this about you."

Their meals arrived.

"You really plan on staying here, don't you?"

Rayne looked up from her plate. "I really want to raise Ian and Ivy on the island."

"Why?" he asked. "Is it because you're afraid you can't do it without your family?"

"That's not it at all. I felt loved and safe when we lived here, Taylor. I want that for Ian and Ivy."

TAYLOR WASN'T SURE how to respond to what she'd just said. He fully understood what she was saying. "Rayne, I want that for them as well."

"Do you have a problem with them being raised here?"

He shook his head. "No, but I have to say that while this is a nice place for the twins—*I* don't live here. I'll be on the West Coast. We're supposed to be trying to make this a workable marriage. I'm just not sure we're being realistic about this."

"Are you ready to give up before we get started?" Rayne asked.

"No. I'm not seeing how this is going to work, but I haven't lost hope."

"I'm glad to hear that." She wiped her mouth

on the edge of her napkin. "Because I happen to think that we're better together, Taylor."

"I've always thought that," he responded. "We're friends, and we're a team."

"What would happen if the twins and I were to move back to Los Angeles?" Rayne asked.

"We could make a home together for the twins. You could come back to work with me— that's if you wanted to do that. Or you could just stay home with Ian and Ivy. I happen to prefer the latter."

She gave him a sidelong glance. "You think I should be an at-home mom?"

"At least while the twins are young."

"Oh, okay. I can see that, but once they start school, I'd want to work."

Taylor eyed Rayne but didn't respond. He felt the twins should be their priority until they were much older, but now wasn't the time to have that discussion. He decided to put it off until after the holidays.

CHAPTER SIXTEEN

"Wow, THIS FESTIVAL is really something," Taylor exclaimed. "Everybody is going to have a ball—young and old."

"That's the idea," said Rayne. "We have more than a hundred creative and interactive activities, storytelling, arts and crafts, costumed characters and more."

He secured balloons to the double stroller.

Rayne divided her time between making sure everything was running as it should and checking on Taylor and the twins. When Carol arrived, she knew her mother wouldn't leave his side. When her mother pulled out a third blanket and placed it over the babies, she gave him a sympathetic smile.

He gave her a thumbs-up.

"Looks like everything is going well," she said when she spotted Gia with her mother near the information booth.

"Yes," Patricia agreed. "A few people have already told me how much they're enjoying the festival."

"I'm going to check out the lines for the rides," Rayne said.

She ran into Misty near the reindeer merry-go-round.

"Are the kids having a good time?"

"They are," Misty responded. "Talei and Leo are very excited about the candy cane hunt. I love the idea of hiding the mini ones for the older kids and the larger ones for the young ones."

"And we'll be giving away a really large candy cane as a grand prize," Rayne announced.

"I have a feeling that this activity is going to be a huge hit and a festival favorite."

"I hope so. A friend of mine used to host a candy cane hunt at her church every year, and the kids loved it."

Rayne had spent the morning hiding candy canes on outdoor Christmas trees, on window-sills and in the grass. The younger children would have as much time as they needed to find all the candy canes, while the older ones would have a five-minute time limit. The grand prize would be awarded to the one who found the most. The participants would, of course, get to keep all the candy canes they found during the hunt.

The committee had worked really hard to make this year's Christmas festival a perfect holiday experience. There would be free photos with Santa, toy giveaways, ornament decoration, vendors and lots of entertainment.

She moved on to the next ride.

"Everything is so nice," Maggie said.

"Thanks, Auntie." Rayne checked her watch. "It's almost one thirty—time for the first candy cane hunt. I need to gather all the five-and-under children together."

"Is there anything I can do to help?" her aunt asked.

"No, but I appreciate you offering. Actually, could you give Taylor a break? He's with Mama."

"Say no more. I'm on it."

Rayne laughed as she rushed over to the area where they were holding the candy cane hunt. There would be another hunt at two thirty for ages six to nine and another at three thirty for the older children. However, she only had to be present for the first one.

Next on Rayne's task list was to make sure everything was set up at the coloring and face-painting stations.

She saw Talei with some of her friends participating in kiddie limbo with a pole decorated like a candy cane. Smiling, Rayne watched her for a moment before moving on.

Taylor caught up with her. "Hey, why don't

you take a minute and have lunch with us?" he suggested. "You've been all over the place, but I bet you haven't eaten anything. You need to eat something."

Rayne checked her watch. "Sure, we can have lunch if you're ready to eat now." She looked him in the face. Her heart skipped a beat at the worry she saw there. "Taylor, I'm pacing myself."

"This is a huge undertaking," he responded. "You and the committee did a great job. It's well put together. I'm really impressed. It's actually how I'd picture Santa's village if I'd ever thought about it before."

"What would you like to eat, Mr. Grinch?"

He chuckled. "I'll take a chili dog and fries."

She ordered the same.

They made small talk while they ate.

People had come out in large numbers to attend the festival, much to Rayne's delight. She was tired, but she'd enjoyed every minute of the event. The mishaps were minor and went unnoticed. Rayne had considered purchasing one of the slushy drinks that practically every child and teen had been buying all afternoon to keep up her energy.

Taylor checked on her a second time. He brought her a couple bottles of water and made sure she ate more food.

Talei stayed with Maggie and Carol, while Taylor and Misty left with the children right after the puppet show, which ended at four o'clock.

That evening, after the festival was over and she'd taken care of some housekeeping duties, she and Talei were on their way to the house.

"Did you have a good time?"

"I had the best time," Talei responded.

"I'm so glad to hear it. I thought the festival turned out really nice."

"I already can't wait until next year's festival. I'm already excited about it."

Rayne laughed. "Me, too."

The first thing she wanted to do when she walked into the house was take a shower.

Taylor met her at the door.

"I know you're tired," he said, embracing her. "As soon as I heard you pull into the driveway, I started a bath for you."

She gave him a grateful smile.

Taylor was always so caring and considerate. He was truly a sweetheart, always so thoughtful, which she appreciated. It was one of the qualities she loved about him.

Rayne took her bath, then went into the bedroom.

WHEN TAYLOR WENT to check on Rayne, he found her on the middle of the bed fast asleep.

He planted a gentle kiss on her forehead and covered her with a blanket before easing out of the room.

"She's knocked out," Taylor said when he joined Misty and Leon in the family room.

"Rayne wore herself out."

"Does she always put so much energy into her projects like this?" Leon asked.

He nodded. "All the time. I kept checking on her to make sure she ate. Rayne will forget about eating when she's working."

"I hope she stayed hydrated."

"Yeah, I made sure she had water. I was able to get her to sit down and have lunch with me."

"The festival was a huge success," Misty said. "When we were leaving, I heard people saying it's the best one so far."

"I keep telling Rayne that she should consider starting her own event-planning company," Taylor stated. "She has a gift for it."

"Gia and her mom pretty much said the same thing," Misty responded. "How does she feel about the idea?"

"She likes it, but I think she's afraid to just jump out there." He shifted his position. "Right now, the focus should be on the twins."

"Is that her plan or yours?" Leon asked.

"I believe Rayne and I are on the same page with this."

Studying Leon's expression, Taylor inquired, "Why? Did she say something different?"

"No, I just thought I'd ask."

Misty changed the subject, but Taylor's mind was still on the previous conversation. He planned to make sure that he and Rayne were on the same page when it came to the twins. Taylor didn't want Ian and Ivy growing up with babysitters or in day care. Rayne didn't have to work right now—he'd make sure she was financially stable enough to stay home with them until they were older.

RAYNE STROLLED OUT of the bedroom clad in a pair of sweatpants and a long-sleeved T-shirt. She found Taylor in the family room with Misty and Leon watching television. She glanced around. "Where's Ian and Ivy?"

"We put them in our room," Leon said. "We didn't want you to be disturbed."

"Oh, thank you. I can't believe I was that exhausted."

"How are you feeling now?" Misty asked. "Are you hungry? We made pizza, and there's some left."

Rayne's eyes lit up. "Like homemade pizza?"

"Yes."

"Pepperoni?"

Leon laughed. "Pepperoni and veggies. Taylor told us that's how you like yours."

"Warning…he made that one."

She smiled at him. "I trust you, babe."

"You know I got you," he responded. "I'm always looking out for you."

"Yeah…you are."

Rayne went to the kitchen, put a couple slices of pizza on a plate and warmed them in the microwave.

She joined them with plate in hand.

"Taylor, you did a great job. It's delicious."

Leon laughed. "All he did was throw some pepperoni, onions, mushrooms and peppers on top of some flatbread. Misty had already put the sauce on it. Oh, yeah, and he added some cheese."

"Why you over there hating?" Rayne asked with a chuckle. "They didn't let you make one?"

"No, but that's not the point. There wasn't any creativity."

"That's why Leon is banned from making pizzas in this house," Misty said. "The last time he made one, he put some type of meat we couldn't identify on top—"

"It was bologna," he interjected.

Misty frowned in disgust. "Then he put Gouda cheese and something else… Leon couldn't even eat his own creation. The kids didn't even want to try it."

"I think I put too much sage on top."

Rayne burst into laughter. "Oh, wow... I guess you were being creative. A little too creative."

"It's what one would call a gourmet pizza."

"Uh huh," Misty responded. "We're not ready."

Leon chuckled. "Neither was I."

Later, as they readied for bed, Rayne said, "Gia's mom invited me to be on the planning committee for next year."

"I hope you said yes."

"I did," Rayne responded. It warmed her heart that Taylor was encouraging this—her being here next year at this time. "It was a very positive experience for me. I see the way Leon and Trey are contributing to this community, and I just want to do my share."

Taylor sat down in the rocker. "Leon's a funny man. I feel like he's opening up more to me now."

"Leon really likes you," Rayne said. "He told me."

"That seems to really matter to you?"

"Yes, it does. Don't you think it's natural for a person to want their family to accept the person they're married to?"

"I guess. I just think our situation is different."

"About that, Taylor. When you initially proposed the idea of us staying married and raising the twins together, you made it sound more like a corporate merger."

He seemed surprised by her words. "I didn't mean for it to sound that way."

"Then how did you intend it to sound?"

"I…"

"I don't expect you to pretend to be in love with me. I know we get along and we've been friends for a long time, but I thought there would be a little more romance…just a little."

He reached over, taking her hand in his own. He pulled Rayne down onto his lap. "You know that I care for you. I'm very attracted to you, but I think it's best that we move slowly."

"I've been thinking about the picture we're painting for Ian and Ivy," Rayne stated.

"What about it?"

"If we're living together as a married couple, but we're not really a couple, what does that say to them?"

"You're really serious about this, aren't you?" he asked. "The twins are babies. They don't know anything about relationships."

"What do you think of marriage?" Rayne questioned.

"I think it works for other people."

Frowning, she said, "I'm not sure I understand what you mean."

"Marriage isn't a bad thing. All I'm saying is that the reason a lot of marriages don't work is because people bring all sorts of baggage with them. They are often not ready for marriage or parenting. I know that I'm not necessarily a suitable candidate for matrimony. That's why I'm proposing that we proceed slowly and with caution. I'm still trying to work out my issues."

"Wow... You're really not ready for marriage."

"I'm just being honest with you."

"We're friends, and we get along well," he said. "We want the best for Ian and Ivy. If anything ever happened to me—you and the twins would be well taken care of."

"I never really thought about marriage, but if I were going to get married, I'd want to be married to someone who loves me and who I love."

He met her gaze. "You don't think we can learn to love each other?"

Rayne cared for Taylor, of course she did. But a marriage in name only—she was not sure this was the route to take. She released a long sigh. Deep down, she wanted love, romance, all of it. The reality was that they had two little babies depending on them. Having parents who were married would provide a better sense of security, even if it came without love.

But she wasn't ready to give up just yet. Rayne still believed in the magic of Christmas.

HE HELD HIS breath as he awaited her response. Taylor wanted to kick himself for posing the question in the first place.

"I can't believe we're having this discussion right now," Rayne said. "It must be because it's late and we're tired."

Taylor shook his head no. "That's not it at all." He was a bit relieved that she hadn't answered, but there was something in her eyes, intense and undefinable.

She rose to her feet. "We can discuss this another time."

He decided to take a chance.

Taylor stood up and gently grabbed her by the arms. He kissed her cheek. He longed to kiss her lips again, but he knew they needed to talk this through more, not just act on their attraction. "We're not finished with this conversation."

"I know," she said. "Right now, I can't do this. I'm tired, and I'm going to bed."

"I'm going to be up awhile longer," he said. "I'll go to the family room so that I don't disturb you."

"Taylor, we will have that conversation. Just not tonight."

He gave her a tight smile.

Taylor sat alone in the family room, his mind filled with thoughts running all over the place.

MARRIAGE WAS A lifetime commitment.

At least that was what Taylor believed it was supposed to be. It was not something he could casually approach, despite the way that he and Rayne got married. He'd never intended to marry at all, believing himself to be too damaged to be a husband or a father. But now that the deed was done, Taylor had been giving his situation a lot of thought.

He would have preferred to marry for love, although he didn't really believe there was a happily-ever-after written for him. However, he would settle for someone he cherished and honored and with whom he could build a friendship. He had all of this with Rayne.

She didn't need to know that he was in love with her, after all.

Suddenly she was standing right in front of him, bringing her scent and her clear, beautiful face close to his.

Taylor leaned back and looked up at her. He had been so consumed with his thoughts that he didn't notice she was up and about. "I thought you were sleeping."

"I missed you," she responded with a bright smile. "I've gotten used to sleeping beside you. The bed felt really cold without you in it."

He elected to ignore the twitch of her luscious lips. Instead, he placed a kiss on her cheek before saying, "Let's go to bed."

CHAPTER SEVENTEEN

"WANT ANYTHING SPECIAL for breakfast?" Rayne asked when they got up six hours later.

"Why don't you surprise me?"

Her eyes closed briefly, and when she met his gaze again, she replied, "If you don't tell me what you want to eat, I'll just throw something together. Like cereal."

Taylor laughed. "How about a sausage, tomato and avocado omelet?"

"Hmm... I think I'll have one of those, too."

"You know how to make an omelet?" he asked, surprised.

"Kinda," Rayne responded. "Misty's been giving me some tips, so I'm going to give it a try."

He had forgotten. "That's right."

Taylor followed her to the kitchen. He stood in the entrance, watching her.

Rayne was focused on preparing the ingredients for the omelets and seemed to have forgotten he was there. Taylor delighted in the way she pursed her lips whenever she was concentrating on something. She had come a long way from the girl he first met. Rayne always had been good at her job, but filled with anger and bitterness. Once she got her ex-boyfriend out of her system, Rayne had come into her own. Over the years, she'd blossomed into womanhood.

It hit him that she possessed every quality he sought in a woman. Her pull was inexorable and something Taylor was suddenly tired of fighting.

RAYNE MET UP with Leon at the fire house.

"Thanks for inviting me to lunch," she said.

"I wanted some *cousin* time."

She glanced around. "Uncle Walter used to bring me here. It looks just the way I remember it."

They decided to walk to the café.

Misty waved when they walked in.

Rayne followed Leon to a booth and slid inside.

"How are things between you and Taylor?" Leon asked after they placed their order.

She peered into his eyes. "Is this why you invited me to lunch? To talk about my relationship with Taylor?"

"I'm not trying to be nosy. I really just want to make sure you're okay."

"Things are not as strained as it was before," she said, "but we're still not completely back to what I'd consider normal for us."

"You've been through a lot in a short period of time."

"I know, I know," Rayne said. "We got married and had a family before we even had a first date."

"It's not too late," Leon interjected. "For that first date. Maybe that's what the two of you need. It's time y'all shifted things into gear. You're so used to being in the platonic space. Y'all need to shift forward—you can't stay in neutral."

"I'm not sure Taylor is ready for all this."

"What about you?" Leon inquired. "Are you ready to settle down?"

Rayne gave a slight nod. "I don't have much of a choice. I have two babies depending on me now."

He took a sip of water. "Your friendship is a solid foundation for marriage. I believe you should be friends first before you take a step like that. You and Taylor need to try dating. Like, each other. See how you like being in that space."

"I'll probably have to ask him out." Rayne said with a smile.

"There's nothing wrong with that," Leon responded. "You and Taylor aren't the most conventional married couple around here."

"Ha…ha…"

"If you want Taylor to make the first move, I can give him a little nudge in that direction."

Her eyes registered her surprise. "You'd do that for me?"

Leon considered it. "I'd be doing it for Ian and Ivy. Obviously, their parents need a push in the right direction."

"You were always the smart one."

Misty walked over with a tray of food. "Here you go…two chicken-salad croissants with a side of fruit."

Leon slid over so his wife could sit beside him.

"When are you and Taylor going on your date?" Misty asked. "That's what you need. A romantic night out. And don't worry about Ian and Ivy. We have them covered if we can get them out of Aunt Carol's clutches."

"My mama is in love with her grandbabies," Rayne said. "Aunt Eleanor says that she and Aunt Maggie have to practically beg to hold them."

"I'm just glad that everyone is getting along," Leon said. "This Christmas is already turning out to be very special. It can only get better from this point forward."

Nodding in agreement, Rayne bit into her sandwich.

"TAYLOR, I'VE BEEN thinking that you and Rayne need to focus on yourselves for a day. Misty and I are home today, so we'll stay with the twins."

"I don't know how Rayne would feel about that, Leon."

"Trust me," he said. "You need this. You both do."

"Maybe for a couple of hours," Taylor responded.

"Misty has scheduled a couple's massage for y'all. Then you'll have lunch at Paradis."

"Isn't that Aubrie and Terian's new restaurant here on the island?" Rayne asked when she joined them. "What's going on?"

Leon nodded. "I was just telling Taylor that the two of you deserve a day to focus on yourselves."

"Misty scheduled massages for us," Taylor said. "And lunch at Paradis. I heard the food there is excellent. What do you think?"

"I think it's a great idea," she responded. "It's been a while for me."

Taylor looked at Leon. "Then that's what we'll do. Thanks for this."

"It's my pleasure."

Rayne waited until she and Leon were alone. "This isn't exactly the date I had in mind. You and Misty set this up."

"This is a precursor. You have to take it from

here, Rayne. Just be your lovable self, and before the end of the night…he'll ask you out."

"It will take a Christmas miracle," she responded.

THEY STROLLED THROUGH the doors of the Island Princess Spa.

Taylor and Rayne were taken to a private room and treated with tea and a complimentary cheese and fruit plate.

"Are we going to stay in the same room?" he inquired. Taylor glanced over his shoulder at the side-by-side massage tables. He wasn't sure he'd be entirely comfortable with her in the room with him.

"Yes, but we'll have two different massage therapists," Rayne responded. "I've been told by my married friends that the couple's massage is a special shared experience."

"I can certainly use one."

She rubbed her sore neck. "Me, too."

After using the change rooms to put on their swimsuits, they lay on the massage tables, using sheets to cover themselves.

"This is certainly a new experience for us," Rayne said with a grin.

"Yes, it is. But I think I'm going to enjoy this."

Their gazes met and held, only breaking the

connection when the massage therapists entered the room.

After the session, Taylor looked at Rayne and smiled. "I think we should make this a regular part of our routine. At least every other week."

"Works for me," she responded. "That was the best massage I've had in a long time."

He wrapped an arm around her. "You're glowing."

"It's not just the massage, Taylor."

"You have me curious."

"I'm really enjoying you. I've missed how much fun we used to have."

"I have to admit that I'm glad to have you back in my life," Taylor said. "All those months with no word—I was worried about you. I didn't want to think the worst—that's why I kept looking. I needed to know that you were okay."

"I'm so sorry for worrying you, Taylor. I didn't think about the impact my disappearing would have on you or my mom. Looking back now, I realize I was being extremely selfish about everything. Only thinking of myself."

"That's all in the past. We don't have to keep rehashing it." He kissed her forehead. "I guess we'd better get out of here if we want to make our reservation in time."

When they arrived at Paradis thirty minutes

later, Rayne made the introductions. "Taylor, this is my cousin Aubrie and her husband, Terian LaCroix."

"Very nice to meet you both," he responded.

"I'm looking forward to meeting the newest members of the family," Aubrie said. "Congratulations to you both."

She led them to a table in one of their private rooms.

"If you will permit us, Terian and I would like to prepare a special lunch for the two of you. Consider it our Christmas present to you."

He was blown away by the gesture. "I've heard nothing but great reviews about this place, so I trust you."

Smiling, Rayne said, "Same here."

"You really have an incredible family."

"I'm understanding that now more and more," she responded. "I've missed so much time with them. I always thought they would judge me, but I'm realizing that I've never been so wrong."

"I've always pushed you to work on your relationship with your mother because I didn't have one. I would give anything to have had a real family of my own," Taylor said. "It's all I've ever wanted. I didn't crave material items. I wanted the love of a family and—" he stopped short of saying, *and a place to call home*.

"I wish you'd trust me enough to share your childhood with me."

"Trust me, Rayne. It's not worth talking about," he responded. Taylor hadn't meant to show such vulnerability in her presence.

Their server delivered a plate of antipasto and oysters.

Taylor broke into a grin. "How did they know I love oysters?"

"I didn't tell them," Rayne said as she picked up a small plate. "Everything here looks so good."

He agreed.

When the main entrée was served, they looked at one another and smiled.

She glanced down at the braised short ribs, carrots, pearl onions, mushrooms and marble potatoes. "I don't remember seeing this on the menu."

Aubrie and Terian entered the room. "We hope you find everything to your liking."

"Was this on the menu?" Rayne asked.

"No," Terian responded. "This is a very special meal for us. It tells the story of our journey to love."

Taylor reached over and took Rayne's hand in his. "Thank you for sharing this meal with us because it's outstanding."

Rayne took a sip of water. "One day I'd like to hear that story."

When they arrived home, Rayne immediately checked on the twins. While Rayne changed and fed her daughter, Talei updated Taylor. "When I came home from school, Ivy was crying, but she stopped when she saw me."

He smiled. "She knows who you are."

"Yeah."

He found it hard to resist Talei's infectious laughter.

That evening, Leon and Misty took the children to see a play.

Taylor and Rayne cuddled on the sofa as they watched a movie.

During a commercial break, he leaned down, capturing her lips tenderly. He couldn't help himself. Taylor couldn't deny that their chemistry was electrifying.

"I've been giving a lot of thought to what you said about love and marriage."

Rayne pulled away from him. "And?"

"I still think we should give it a try," Taylor said. "I say we should go slow and try dating."

"Huh?" Rayne uttered. "You want to *date* me?"

"Why is that so hard to believe?"

She eyed him. "I have to ask why the sudden change of heart?"

"Because we get along," Taylor responded. "I just think we have to see where this goes. We're married with children. Why not start dating?"

"Sure," Rayne responded. "When you put it that way. You have perfect timing because Aubrie mentioned that the family is hosting a Christmas party on Friday night. You can be my date. Jordin's lined up sitters to watch the children. It's formal, Taylor, so you need a tux, and I have to find something to wear. I'll check with Renee on that."

"I'll shop for one tomorrow," Taylor said. "I should've guessed that our first date would be a Christmas party."

Rayne burst into laughter. "He's a mean one..."

Taylor found himself strangely excited about their first date. It was his chance to prove to Rayne that he could learn to be her partner. They were already a team—this seemed to be the logical next step.

"RENEE, I'M GLAD I caught you before you left. I really need your help," Rayne said when she entered the boutique the next day.

"Hey, cousin. What's up?"

"I need something nice to wear for the party on Friday."

"I'm glad you and Taylor are coming. Du-

Grandpre parties are the best. The talk of Charleston."

Rayne nodded. "I don't have anything suitable to wear to such a formal affair. I'm hoping you have something on sale?"

"Do you have time to go with me to the house? We'll find you something there."

Rayne glanced down at her watch. "Sure."

She walked around the shop while Renee had a conversation with her staff.

"I'm so proud of you," Rayne said when they headed out.

"Thank you," Renee responded. "It's been a journey, but I've enjoyed every minute—even the rough parts."

"Nice house," she said. "I can't wait to start looking after the holidays. Of course, it won't be anything like this."

"Trey and I lived together until he married Gia, then I moved into Misty's old condo. Greg actually found this house when he relocated here. I'm sure you and Taylor will find the perfect house."

"I'm sure we will," Rayne said, not bothering to correct her that the house would be just for Rayne and the babies. She followed her cousin to the basement. "Renee, I heard you talk about panic attacks in one of your magazine interviews and how you've learned to manage them.

I think that's so great." Rayne sat down in an oversize chair. "My life has been quite a journey as well—one filled with a lot of regrets."

"I hope you know that you can talk to me about anything," Renee said.

"I'm so ashamed," Rayne blurted.

"Honey, why?"

"I was so angry after we left the island—I was upset with my mom for taking me away from everyone here, mad because my father didn't want me... Anyway, I was rebellious, and I ran with the wrong crowd and was constantly getting in trouble all through school. When I met this guy—I knew he was trafficking drugs, and I didn't care. I just never figured that he'd throw me under the bus. Anyway, we were stopped one night, and they found cocaine and other drugs in the trunk. I ended up in jail for almost three months. If it wasn't for Taylor getting me an attorney... I might still be in prison right now."

"Why didn't you call us? We're your family, Rayne. We would've stood by you."

"I was embarrassed. The last time you saw me, I was twelve years old! What was I going to say, 'Hey, remember me? I'm accused of being a drug dealer?' I didn't want to bring more shame into this family."

"I love you, and I don't think any less of you

than I did before. We all make mistakes and mess up from time to time, but each day that you wake up—it's another chance to learn and grow. You get to write another chapter. And you have… You're a wonderful mother, and from everything Taylor's said about you, you were fantastic at your job. All of the bad stuff is behind you now."

"Thank you for saying that, Renee." She paused for a moment, then said, "Please don't say anything to anyone. You're the only other person besides Taylor who knows."

"I get it. It's your story to tell. You choose when you want to share. Just know that I love you and I'm here if you ever need to talk about anything." Rising to her feet, Renee said, "Now let's find you the perfect gown. You'd look good in a cinnamon or rust color."

"I'm open to whatever you suggest."

Renee selected three dresses that were hanging on a clothes rack. "Try these on."

"Where's Greg?"

"He's with Trey at the museum. He won't be home for another hour or two."

"You look really happy."

Smiling, Renee responded, "I am. I love being married. We haven't really told anyone, but Greg and I are trying to have a baby."

Rayne hugged her cousin. "That's wonderful."

She took the dresses to the bathroom to try them on.

"Oh, Renee…this dress is absolutely gorgeous," Rayne exclaimed. She stood in front of a full-length mirror in the office/studio downstairs.

The dress fell to the floor and was a brilliant rust color. Rayne loved the draping silk fabric, which was well-suited to a formal evening. The long-sleeve, wrap design, which was slightly gathered at the waist and held together with a rose gold, rhinestone belt, was a perfect fit — almost as if it had been made for her.

"It's yours if you want it."

"I love it…but are you sure about this?"

Renee nodded. "It's my gift to you. Consider it an early Christmas present. What size shoes do you wear?"

"An eight, but—"

"I have a pair of rose gold heels that match the dress perfectly," Renee said.

"I couldn't accept—"

"They have a tiny flaw. It's not that noticeable, but I'm not able to sell them."

Rayne swiped at her face as tears filled her eyes and overflowed. "Wow… I can't believe this. Thank you so much."

"You're welcome."

She helped her cousin hang the dress, then store it in a protective dress bag.

"I hope you and Taylor have a wonderful time at the party," Renee said. "I like him, so I really hope the two of you can work things out."

"I think the most we can hope for is to work out some sort of agreement regarding the twins," Rayne said. "We're looking at Friday as a date, but the reality is that he lives in Los Angeles, and I plan to stay here. Right now, it's still hard for me to see things working out between us long term."

"You never know," Renee responded. "One day, I'll have to tell you about my journey to happily-ever-after."

"I've had so many devastating disappointments. I just can't afford to get my hopes up."

"Aunt Eleanor would tell us that in this season celebrating the birth of Christ, it is the time of miracles."

Nodding, Rayne said, "She used to say that all the time."

"Don't underestimate the power of love, cousin."

CHAPTER EIGHTEEN

RAYNE EYED HER reflection in the full-length mirror and smiled. She was finally back at her pre-pregnancy weight. She loved the way the gown gently hugged her curves.

"You look beautiful," Carol said from the doorway.

She turned around, facing her mother. "I can't believe you're not coming to the party."

"I think it's best I stay here to help Ella and Rusty with the twins."

Rayne knew that her mother was determined to have her own way when it came to the twins. "Mom, I told you that Jordin's arranged for sitters."

"I'd just feel better if they were here with me. They are still quite young."

"I appreciate it, but you're going to miss a great party."

Smiling, Carol said, "You can tell me all about it when you get home. You look really beautiful."

"You sure do," Misty said.

"So do you," Rayne responded. "I love the

emerald green color on you. You look very regal."

"Thank you." Misty wore a long-sleeve gown in velvet with gold accents. Her curly hair was piled on top of her head with a few tendrils framing her face.

"I guess we shouldn't keep Taylor and Leon waiting," she said. Rayne did a final check on her makeup and hair.

Rayne was filled with anticipation of what the night had to offer. The last real party she'd attended was the one she'd hosted at the dealership. The night her life had changed unexpectedly.

What would the evening bring this time?

TAYLOR DID A double take when Rayne came downstairs. She looked stunning in the spice-colored gown.

"Wow," he said when she walked up to him. "I didn't think you could look more beautiful, but somehow you managed it."

She smiled. "Thank you."

"Motherhood certainly agrees with you."

"I suppose that's a good thing," Rayne responded. "I do like the curves I've gained, though."

Taylor nodded. "So do I."

"This is where your cousins live?" he asked

when they pulled into the circular driveway of the massive house in an exclusive section of Charleston.

"This is my cousin Eleanor Louise's house," Rayne said. "Her husband and his brother own the DuGrandpre Law Firm. They're Jadin and Jordin's parents."

"Looks like this is going to be quite the party."

Rayne chuckled. "From what I've heard, their Christmas parties are always the talk of Charleston."

They were seated at a table with Jordin and her husband.

"How are you enjoying Polk Island?" Ethan asked Taylor.

He smiled, laid his napkin across his lap and, picking up his knife and fork, sliced into a strip of grilled chicken. "I'm having a blast. I really like the area."

Their conversation turned to business.

"They're bonding, I see," Rayne whispered to Jordin.

She laughed.

While they ate, the couples discussed their favorite music, authors and charity work. They talked and talked about so many things.

Rayne swayed to the music as she sipped a glass of red wine.

She glanced over at Taylor and said, "You look like you're having a good time. I wasn't sure how you'd feel about the party, especially since you don't like Christmas events."

"I'm here because you invited me, and I wanted to spend time with you."

"There's that brutal honesty," she responded. "I hope you'll try to have a good time, Taylor. Just give yourself a chance."

"I can do that," he said. "But don't expect me to get all warm and fuzzy just because it's Christmas."

"Trust me. I know better than to do that."

"Would you like to dance?" Taylor asked her when the deejay began playing dance music.

She nodded. "You know how much I love dancing. I haven't done it in a long time, though." Rayne took his hand.

They walked slowly to the dance floor, and he took her in his arms. Their bodies swayed to the music. "I love this song."

One song ended and another began while they were still on the dance floor.

She and Taylor decided to call it a night shortly after midnight.

Back at the house, Rayne made a pot of green tea with coconut while Taylor changed out of his tux.

He'd had a wonderful time at the party and enjoyed meeting more of Rayne's family.

"I have to admit that I enjoyed myself," he said. "You must have inherited your gift of party planning from your family. You all know how to throw a good party."

She laughed. "We just love to have a good time."

"I enjoyed tonight especially because we were together. It wasn't a work thing, but a real date. I didn't feel guilty for whatever I feel for you. You're no longer my employee. It was freeing...a great feeling."

"I feel the same way," Rayne responded as she took his hand in her own.

SMILING, RAYNE TOOK a deep breath, then sipped her tea, hoping it would stop her heart from hammering.

"You're quiet."

"I was just thinking about my family. They have all been so understanding and so sweet, which only makes me feel worse for the way I treated them. I never should've blocked them out of my life like that."

"I understand better now why you felt you couldn't trust them, Rayne. We all make mistakes. You weren't a horrible person."

"I was arrested and nearly put in prison."

"It wasn't your fault. You were in trouble because of that dude you were dating at the time. He's the one who committed the crimes and then blamed you."

"I will never forget when they arrested me. It was probably the absolute worst moment in my life. I was so nervous when I came to you asking for my job back, but you were so kind. I didn't know what to expect from the other employees. I was embarrassed, but everyone there was so supportive."

"We just left your Charleston relatives who are all lawyers. I'm sure they would've come to your aid in a flash. You might not have spent any time in jail."

"I was too embarrassed to tell them. Taylor, I appreciate you keeping my secret. You could've turned on me after everything I did, but you chose not to—you continue to have my back."

He sighed. "I never had a family, but having spent time around yours—they'd understand."

She shook her head no. "I can't do it, Taylor. I'm already asking so much of them. I can't share this, too."

"I'm not going to pressure you."

"Thank you for that."

"Can I ask another question? How did you feel growing up without your father?"

She shrugged in nonchalance. "He lied about

being married to seduce my mother. Then his wife came to the island and humiliated us in front of everyone. He put the blame on my mom… It broke my heart to hear such nasty things about her. Aunt Eleanor came to her defense, but I could tell—they all seemed to believe that woman."

"And that's why your mom left."

Rayne nodded. "I was angry with him and his wife. I blamed him for not giving me his name. He's the reason my mother never married. She never trusted another man with her heart after that. There was this one guy…he really cared about her, but Mom just stopped talking to him. Myles was the closest I'd ever come to having a father."

She glanced up at him. "Taylor, I'm starting to think that I've made a huge mess of things. I was only thinking of myself."

"You were thinking of the twins," he responded. "But the thought wasn't fully fleshed out."

Rayne gave him a tiny smile. "I appreciate you trying to clean this up for me."

"You've always been too hard on yourself."

"I'm a realist, Taylor. I made a lot of mistakes."

"We all have. You're not the only one."

"You always seem to make the right choices."

"Maybe it's because I watched my parents

mess up their lives, and I was determined not to follow down that same path," Taylor said. "I still made some stupid mistakes."

"I think this is the first time you've really talked about your mom and dad. What were they like?"

"They are two people who never should've had a child. At least they had the good sense not to have any more. They weren't married, by the way."

"Were they abusive?"

Taylor didn't respond.

Rayne took his hand in hers. "You can tell me. I'm a safe space for you."

He suddenly found himself wanting to open up to her about everything, but to feel her pity was much more than Taylor could bear. Still, he felt compelled to bare his soul to her about that awful period in his life.

He wouldn't look at her as he talked. "My dad...he was a mean drunk. He'd beat my mom...and he'd beat me. He broke my arm when I was ten."

She gasped loudly. "Taylor..."

"I was taken away after that and put in a group home." Taylor met her teary gaze. "Kline Group Home."

"That's why you're their biggest sponsor."

He nodded. "I met Deacon my first day there.

We became like brothers. He got adopted when I was twelve. Even though he had a family now, we remained close."

"I had no idea that you'd grown up in that group home," she murmured.

Shrugging as if it wasn't such a hard subject, Taylor responded, "I never intended to share this part of my life with anyone."

"What happened wasn't your fault."

"I know that," he said. "But it still messed me up. That's why I've kept my pain close to the vest. I don't want people pitying me. I don't want to see it in their eyes or hear it in their voices. I'm not a victim, Rayne."

"No, you're not," she replied. "You're a survivor. You're a really great guy, Taylor."

Rayne glanced down at her empty cup. "I've finished my tea. Maybe sleep will come now."

She stood up, picking up both cups.

When Rayne walked past him, Taylor reached out, taking the cups from her and placing them on the end table before wrapping a strong arm around her waist and pulling her to him.

His head lowered to hers. Rayne kissed him back, her arms around his neck. But she reluctantly broke off the kiss, taking in a deep breath and smiling sheepishly at him.

"Self-control, girl," Rayne whispered as she hurried down the hall. She knew they were battling the chemistry they'd ignored for years. But she also knew that he didn't really love her, he only wanted to ensure they would still be close after all this. "You can't afford to make another mistake."

CHAPTER NINETEEN

TAYLOR PUNCHED HIS pillow with his fist. He was having a tough time sleeping. Although Rayne was trying to play it cool, he knew their connection was still very much alive. He caught a glimpse of it in her eyes right before she walked away.

He wanted to believe that a small part of her heart belonged to him, but he was a realist. Taylor wasn't sure he was the right man for Rayne. He wanted to be because she was his wife and the mother of his children. Lately, he'd begun to think of her as his soulmate.

There is no me without her.

The thought sent shock waves through him. He'd never felt like that about any woman.

Taylor lay on his side, listening to the heavy silence and wondering if Rayne was having as tough a time sleeping, too.

An hour later, he gave up completely on sleeping and got out of bed.

When he peeked into the crib, Taylor was surprised to see that Ivy was awake.

He picked her up, cradling her in his arms. "What are you doing up?" he whispered.

She yawned in response, but didn't cry.

Taylor checked to see if she was wet.

"Are you hungry?"

Ivy met his gaze, then smiled at him.

He felt like he'd won the lottery.

"You just made my night so much better," he whispered, kissing her cheek.

She grabbed his chin.

There was no way he'd ever abandon Ivy and her brother. They were the very best parts of him and Rayne.

When she awarded him another smile, he said, "I love you, Ivy. You and your brother are my reason for living."

WHEN RAYNE WOKE up around two in the morning, she found Taylor sitting in the rocker fast asleep with Ivy on his chest buried under a blanket.

She eased out of bed and rescued her daughter, putting her back in the crib with Ian.

Taylor woke up with a start. "Ivy…"

"I just placed her back in the crib. She's fine."

"I couldn't sleep, and I didn't want to disturb you, so I got up. She was awake and just lying there—she didn't make a sound. We sat up and talked."

"Did you have a good conversation?" Rayne asked.

"We did," Taylor responded.

"We're supposed to go shopping. We need to pick up our pajamas."

"You were serious about that?"

"Yeah. We want to do it as a family, Taylor. Don't be a Grinch."

"I'd feel really stupid walking around in matchy pajamas. Christmas pajamas at that."

"It's all in fun and family."

He grimaced. "How many times have you tried to get me to dress up for Halloween—it's not going to happen." Taylor shook his head.

She smiled at him. "Okay. I hear you."

He couldn't believe she'd actually expected him to put on a pair of pajamas with Christmas trees or worse…tiny little Santa Claus people all over them. Taylor shuddered at the mere thought.

Nope, not doing it.

"CAROL, I'M GLAD you're home, suga," Eleanor said. "It's wonderful having my sisters and my brother here with me."

Carol glanced over at her brother and gave him a tiny smile. It was hard on all of them to witness their sister's inability to remember. She regretted staying away for so long.

"We're happy to be here," Daniel said. "I'm going to make it my business to get home more often."

"Is Barbara here?" Eleanor asked.

"No, she isn't," he responded. "My wife passed away two years ago. You and Rusty came to the funeral."

"Oh, I'm so sorry."

"It's okay. I'm taking it day by day."

"They told me I have Alzheimer's..." Eleanor said with a sigh. "There ain't nothing I can do about it, so I just take it one day at a time myself. Sometimes it's minute by minute. What I don't like is when people treat me like I can't take care of myself."

"I can understand that," Carol said. "But it's only because we love you, Ella."

"I know that, but I'm not dead," she said in a huff. "There's still a lot of life in me."

"And we know that."

"Carol's right. Ella, we promised our parents that we'd always take care of one another," Maggie said. "I fully intend to keep that promise."

"Me, too," Carol and Daniel said in unison.

"I'm so glad to have Rusty in my life, too," Eleanor said. "He's a good man, and he takes such good care of me."

"I can see that. It's clear how much he loves you."

"I love him just as much. You know, I've been blessed to have had two wonderful husbands."

"You're very lucky, Ella," Carol said with a short sigh. "Me… I've never been so fortunate."

Eleanor patted her hand. "Has your heart been open to love?"

"Not really," she replied. "I didn't want to make the same mistake, so I made Rayne my priority. There was this one guy. He seemed really nice, and I started to fall for him."

"What happened?"

"I called him one night, and this woman answered the telephone. He'd told me that he lived alone, but clearly, he was lying. I stopped seeing him."

"You never asked him about the woman?"

"Why? So he could tell me more lies? Been there, Ella. Didn't need to go through it a second time."

"You know that cheater came to the café looking for you after you left," Eleanor said. "He wanted to know where you'd gone. He claimed he wanted to get to know his daughter, but I didn't believe him. He wanted your address. I refused to give it to him. He got so angry with me, but Walter set him straight."

"I was such a fool back then."

"You were human, Carol," Maggie said. "And a young woman in love."

"Ella tried to tell me about him, but I wouldn't listen. I thought I knew better than all of you. I really thought he was going to marry me. Especially after I found out I was pregnant."

Eleanor placed her hand over Carol's hand. "It's the past. Leave it there. If you'd never met him, you wouldn't have Rayne."

"You're right. I wouldn't have my beautiful daughter. I just wish she'd let me in more. I know that something's weighing on her."

"She will in her own time."

TAYLOR CONTINUED TO go back and forth regarding his relationship with Rayne. For so many years, he had trained himself not to act on his attraction to her. That was no longer the issue, but he still questioned whether a relationship other than friendship between them could work. They were from two very different worlds. She grew up wrapped in love while he drowned in a sea of fear and insecurity chained to rejection and low self-worth. Even after she and Carol had left the island, she'd never doubted her mother's love for her.

He'd fought to rise above those feelings, burying them behind a wall of indifference.

Love was not a part of his plans for the future. Taylor focused instead on his company. He'd avoided women who wanted children or a serious future with him. He didn't deviate from the driving force that had been guiding him since leaving the group home.

Taylor tried watching TV, but when he couldn't find anything to his liking, he gave up and reached for the book he'd been reading. When he'd read the same page twice, he put it aside.

He put his hands to his face. *Did I handle this all wrong? Did I set myself up to fail?*

Rayne deserved the love of a good man—not a man incapable of trusting his heart to someone else. Yet, the mere thought of her with someone other than himself struck a jealous chord within Taylor. He could no longer deny the truth. He wanted Rayne for himself. He didn't want the divorce.

They had a long history, he and Rayne. Taylor trusted her with the company. He trusted their friendship, despite her actions in the past eleven months. Outside of Deacon, she was the person he knew he could trust. It made sense for the two of them to end up together, he silently reasoned.

Rayne walked out of the bedroom, putting

an end to his musings. "They're still sleeping. Ivy has Ian's hand in hers—they look so cute."

She sat down beside Taylor.

"Tell me about their birth," he said. "Actually, tell me about the pregnancy, too."

"Well, I found out very early in that we were expecting twins. I'd been trying to figure out how to tell you, but after I found out I was carrying two babies, I couldn't bring myself to. I was sure you'd freak out, and that scared me."

"Were you scared about the babies?" Taylor asked.

"I think I was excited, but terrified and mostly just in shock."

"Was it a good pregnancy?"

"It was," Rayne responded. "There were times I had some anxiety about labor and delivery…fears that kept creeping into my thoughts. Especially whenever I'd think about pushing out two babies instead of just one. Mama was very supportive, though."

She finished off her bottle of water. "I went into labor at thirty-four weeks. I woke up around 3:00 a.m. to use the bathroom. My water broke. Taylor, I remember feeling nothing but peace when I realized what had happened. I guess I was ready to meet my babies. I just wanted to hold them in my arms—I was especially looking forward to having labor be over."

"You're a very brave woman to deal with this all alone."

"Like I mentioned earlier… my mom was super supportive. She tried to convince me to tell you about the pregnancy, too. She thought it was wrong to leave you in the dark."

"Was it a long labor?" he asked, not responding to that.

"By 6:00 a.m. my contractions were strong and coming regularly. At this point, I was still only dilated to around five or six centimeters. I must confess that I asked for an epidural. I couldn't take the pain anymore. Mama was against me getting it, but truthfully, it helped tremendously. An hour later, I was rushed to surgery. One of the babies was in distress. There was suddenly a lot more people in that operating room with me and Mama. Two NICU teams, a lot of nurses and a doctor."

"Were you scared at this point?"

"I think I was completely oblivious to everything else going on. Ian was born at 7:45. He came out so easily, and I remember seeing his little head pop up as they placed him on me for a moment before taking him over to the warmer to make sure he was healthy and breathing okay. Then Ivy was born four minutes after her brother. I didn't see her right away, but I could hear her. Ivy cried before she was completely out."

"How much did they weigh?"

"Ian was 4.4 pounds, and Ivy weighed 4.2 pounds, which was better than my doctor expected. Some oxygen and feeding tubes were needed, but I was able to kiss them before they went to the NICU with my mom while they finished with me. Later that night, I was able to be with them and hold them as long as I wanted. It was a positive experience but also a little sad. I didn't get to share it with you. I know it was my choice, and during that time I did feel some regret."

"I'm sorry you felt you couldn't come to me, Rayne."

"It's that I didn't know how you'd react— that's why I didn't tell you. I have a lot of respect for you, and I thought it might change if you'd asked me to do something like put them up for adoption. You've always been so good to me."

"I know that this sounds surprising coming from me, but I'm glad the twins are here."

"Really?"

Taylor nodded. "I am. I can't imagine life without them."

RAYNE TOOK TAYLOR to High Cotton in Charleston for dinner. Carol wanted to spend time with the twins, so they decided to take advantage of their time alone.

"So, you've never eaten here before?" Taylor asked when she suggested that he try the shrimp and grits.

"Nope. I heard Leon and Misty talking about it, so I thought we'd give it a try." Her eyes bounced around the room, which was draped in rich but soothing jewel tones. For the first time since they got married, Rayne felt like a woman who was enjoying a romantic dinner with her husband.

Taylor looked around the dining area. "It's nice in here."

"I'm glad you like it," she responded. "I think I'm going to order the jumbo lump crab cakes with jalapeño rémoulade for my entrée, and you get the shrimp and grits. We can share."

"Sounds good to me. I know how much you love seafood and spicy foods in general."

The things Taylor remembered about her offered Rayne hope for the future.

Servers began bringing the first course out, arranging the soup and salads attractively on the table. "Crab soup and salads for our first course," he announced.

"Wow," she murmured. "This looks so delicious."

Taylor gestured with his spoon. "Try the soup."

They continued to talk while they enjoyed their meal.

Rayne was blissfully happy. In this moment, her life felt perfect.

"I love seeing you so happy," Taylor said, cutting into her thoughts.

She smiled. "I have two beautiful babies, a wonderful husband who is also my friend. I'm back home where I belong. I have every reason to be happy."

He covered her hand with his own. "This is all I want for you, Rayne. I'm beginning to believe that this is the way it was supposed to be from the very beginning. You and me together."

She looked up at him with an expression of hope. "Do you really mean what you just said?"

"Yes," he responded.

Rayne closed her eyes and smiled. She had gotten her Christmas miracle.

CHAPTER TWENTY

CAROL OPENED THE front door. "You and Taylor looked pretty cozy out here in the cold. I was just watching you two from the window."

Rayne knew her mother was being nosy, but somehow, she appreciated it. "You know that we've always had a friendship, Mama. He's still my best friend."

"He's also your husband."

"This is true," she responded. "I'm hoping we'll always remain close. We want the twins to see that we like each other."

Rayne laughed at the stunned expression on her mother's face. "Mama, I'm just messing with you."

Carol gave a nervous chuckle. "I'm just glad you finally had the good sense to marry the man. I've been telling you for years to snatch him up before someone else caught up to him. I'm happy you listened to me."

"Are you really trying to take credit for Taylor and I being together?" she asked with a laugh.

"All I'm saying is that I've always had this

feeling that you saw him as much more," Carol responded. "That is all."

Rayne looked at her mother. "Uh huh…"

Carol embraced her daughter. "I'm very happy for you, my love."

"And I'm really glad that you're here. It feels so good to be here with you at *home*. Polk Island will always be home to me."

"I have to admit that it does feel like home. I thought that would change after I left," Carol said. "I do regret staying away so long. I should've been here for Eleanor."

"You're here now," Rayne responded. "That's what matters most."

They sat down in front of the fireplace.

"Mama, have you weeded out the thorns in the garden of your heart?"

"What a visual you've given me. It's fitting… I've been trying. I hate admitting this, but I'm lonely. I never thought I'd be alone at this age."

"You're still young, Mama. It's not too late for you to find love. You just have to be open to it."

"Ella says the same thing."

She squeezed her mother's hand. "You don't have to be afraid anymore. Give love another chance."

"As long as you don't allow that handsome husband of yours to get away," Carol said. "You're good together."

AFTER RAYNE AND Taylor left with the twins, Carol walked down to the café to meet her siblings.

She was about to walk inside when someone called her name.

"Carol, is that you?"

She turned around and gave a start. "Myles... oh, my goodness. *What are you doing here?*"

Carol couldn't believe it. After all this time... Myles hadn't changed much over the years, his close-cropped hair was speckled with gray, but he was still in very good shape and still handsome.

"I live here now," he responded. "What about you? What brings you to Polk Island?"

"This is where I'm from," she said.

"Wait, are you related to Polk and Hoss Rothchild?"

Smiling, she nodded. "Polk is my many-great-grandfather. I had no idea that you'd left Texas."

"It's truly a small world. I've been here over five years now," Myles responded. "My job offered me a position in Charleston, not long after...well, whatever it was that happened between us." He blushed. "I found out about the island from my Realtor and decided to settle here."

Carol cleared her throat. She didn't want

to get into what happened between them. He was the only other man she'd ever loved, but things went sour after she called his house and a woman answered. She'd been there before and wasn't about to repeat the same mistake twice. She promptly ended the relationship and decided to give up once and for all on love. Carol was convinced that it just wasn't in the cards for her.

Now Myles was here on the island, by total coincidence. Or by the universe trying to tell her something? She shook that thought from her head.

"How is Rayne doing?"

"She's fine," Carol responded. "My daughter's here on the island, too. She's a mother now. Twins. Can you believe I'm a grandmother?"

"That's wonderful. Please tell her hello for me."

"I will," Carol said.

She heard Maggie's laughter. "I'm having a meal with my family. It was great seeing you, Myles."

"I'd like for us to keep in touch."

Smiling, she responded, "I'd really like that, too."

"Here's my card," he said. "I hope I hear from you soon."

As she walked away, she saw Eleanor watching her, a huge grin on her face.

"How long have you been standing there?" Carol asked.

"Long enough to see that you were held up by a very handsome man," Eleanor replied. "You two sho' looked like old friends."

"He's someone I met a long time ago," she responded. "Myles and I used to date. He just told me that he lives here on the island now."

"Maybe he's come back into your life for a reason," Maggie suggested.

She didn't want to entertain the idea. "Hey, he isn't exactly back in my life. I just happened to run into him on my way here. I hadn't seen Myles for years."

"He seemed pretty happy to see you," Daniel pointed out.

"Not you, too," Carol uttered. "Ella and Maggie both seem to think that I need a man in my life, but I don't." The truth was that she wouldn't mind having someone to spend time with, but she couldn't endure another heartache.

"I didn't say you needed a man," Eleanor stated. "But ain't nothing wrong with knowing that you deserve to love and be loved."

While they ate, Carol thought about her sister's words. Did she dare open her heart to love once again?

Sunday dinner was held at Eleanor's house. Apparently, it was a tradition for her to host a meal the Sunday before Christmas.

Aunt Maggie had done the majority of the cooking tonight. Taylor sat next to Rayne at the dinner table, but he could not read her face as they all passed around bowls and platters, filling plates with fried chicken, macaroni and cheese, potato salad and green beans. It was Southern comfort food at its finest, and he wouldn't mind at all coming to more Sunday dinners like this.

Rusty blessed the food.

Taylor sampled the macaroni and cheese. "This is delicious. I've never had any that had a little kick to it."

"It's my recipe," Maggie said. "I used Colby, cheddar, Monterey Jack and a little cayenne pepper."

"I thought this was Aubrie's recipe," Trey said.

"Uh, no…" his aunt responded. "She learned this little trick in my kitchen."

Rayne and Taylor exchanged a look of amusement.

"Taylor, do you golf?" Daniel asked. He was seated directly across from Rayne. "Rusty and I are going in the morning, if you'd like to join us.

These other guys at the table don't know nothing about the fine art of golfing."

"As a matter of fact, I do. Sure... I'd love to come." Taylor appreciated the effort everyone was making in welcoming him into the family.

That evening, when they returned to the house, he and Rayne settled in the family room while Misty and Leon were upstairs with their children.

Rayne turned her attention to the TV as she drank in his nearness.

Taylor placed an arm around her.

She felt wrapped in warmth. She looked up at him, trying to figure out what he was thinking. He must have been wondering the same thing because he turned to face her and asked, "What are you thinking about right now?"

"How much I missed our friendship all those months." Rayne slowly brought her gaze up once more to his. Her stomach plummeted like a book toppling off a high shelf as his eyes met hers. The feel of his fingers wrapping around her own was like a surge of electricity through her body, one Rayne felt right to her core.

"We had a lot of good times."

She nodded in agreement.

He took a deep breath. "I know right now you may have some reservations about me, but

I intend to prove that I will do anything for our children. And for you."

Taylor gathered her closer as she tried not to be affected by his words, as if he were saying, *I'm going to prove it to you, starting now.*

His fingers loosened a fraction, but he didn't release her. His gray eyes had darkened and were unreadable as they held hers. She thought he was going to kiss her again. She *wanted* that kiss. But instead, he said, "You and I will always be friends, Rayne. And we'll always be there for our babies. If that means staying married, I'm okay with that. I just don't want to lose you again, okay?"

RAYNE HAD WALKED into this with her heart wide-open, and Taylor had unknowingly shattered it like broken glass. Rayne kept replaying the conversation she had with Taylor last night as she left to go visit with her mother after breakfast.

"I need to talk to you, Mama."

"Okay. Would you like some tea?"

Rayne nodded.

They walked down to the kitchen.

"What's going on, hon?"

Tears slowly found their way down her cheeks. "I'm pretty sure that Taylor and I will be getting a divorce after the holidays."

Carol looked stunned by the news. "But why? You looked so happy on Sunday. What's changed?"

Rayne steeled herself. "You know I left without telling him I was pregnant. The only reason he came to the island is because he wanted me to sign the divorce petition, but then he met Ian and Ivy. Until then, I think we both wanted the divorce. But things felt like they were changing since he got here. I thought we were opening up to the possibility of more, but now I know it's not true. He wants to be done with us."

"Oh, dear…"

"I realize how this makes me look."

"You look like a woman who would do anything for her children," Carol said.

"It's clear how much that man loves you, Rayne. And I know that you love him, too. You two should seek counseling or something. I've never been married, but divorce just shouldn't be an option when two people love one another."

"I agree," Rayne said. "But I will not force a man to stay with me when he doesn't want to be there. I want him to choose me. Not stay in this marriage because he feels obligated. And… I think sometimes he feels he has to save me."

At her mother's quizzical look, Rayne knew

it was finally time to tell her the truth. The thing she'd concealed all these years.

"You remember the boyfriend I left Dallas with, when I moved to LA?"

Carol grimaced. "Of course, I do. He was bad news."

"Not too long after moving to Los Angeles, I found myself in the wrong place at the wrong time. We were in my car, and we got stopped by law enforcement. He'd put drugs in the trunk. I had no idea he was using my car for that... Long story short, he threw me under the bus."

"He blamed you?" Carol asked.

She nodded. "I'd only been working with Taylor for a few months at the time. I was at the dealership when the police came to arrest me."

"Honey, why didn't you call me?" Carol asked. "I would've fought tooth and nail to help you."

"Mama, I was embarrassed and so ashamed that I'd gotten myself in a mess like that. I guess I felt I deserved what was happening to me in some way."

"But what does this have to do with staying married now?"

"He paid for my attorney," Rayne said. "I still don't know how Taylor did it, but he was able to get my ex to tell the truth. He told me I still had a job, and he also helped pay for col-

lege. I don't want him to feel like he's just bail-
ing me out all over again. I want him to choose
me and the babies because he wants us…or not
at all."

"All I can tell you is either you two are going
to be married or you're not, but you both need
to be on the same page."

Rayne swallowed hard and bit back tears.
"Mama, I want my marriage. I just don't think
Taylor wants it for the same reason I do."

"Shouldn't you ask him?"

"You think I'm making a rush to judgment?"
Carol nodded. "I do."

"So, what do I do now?"

"Enjoy this time you have with Taylor. Get
through the holidays, then sit down and talk.
Be honest with him, Rayne."

Carol embraced her. "You and Taylor belong together. I knew it the moment I met the
man…and again when I got over my shock that
you'd married him. This is just a bump in the
road, sweetie. I really believe the two of you
can overcome anything."

"I used to think so. Have you thought about
coming back to the island to live?" Rayne
asked.

Carol shook her head no. "My memories are
not pleasant ones."

"Mama, you can't let what happened back

then color all your recollections. I know you miss Aunt Eleanor, and with what she's dealing with—I'd think you'd want to spend as much time with her as possible."

Carol frowned. "I did consider that possibility, but what would I do here?"

"The same thing you do in Dallas," Rayne responded. "Work in the school system. Besides, I'll be here with your grandchildren."

"Are you saying that you want me around?" Carol asked. "We had that big fight about you coming here in the first place. I...I felt like you were choosing the family you barely knew over me. Like you didn't want my help."

"I wanted my babies to have a bigger support network, and I was angry you'd kept me from the family."

"I suppose I understand that."

"And I understand better how hurt you were and how much you were trying to protect me," Rayne said.

"I'm so sorry, sweetie."

"It's fine, Mom. I'm fine."

Rayne stayed for another hour until Taylor called, looking for her.

"I guess I'd better get back over there. I'm sure he's feeling overwhelmed with the twins. Mama, I want you to know that I really appreciate you listening without judgment."

"Thank you for trusting me," Carol said. "To be completely honest with you… I am starting to wonder if I could have a place here. But we'll see what the future holds."

Rayne broke into a grin. "Does Myles have anything to do with this?"

Carol smiled. "A small part, but mostly, maybe I'm ready to come home. It's been wonderful being with Ella and everyone."

"I have a great idea. Why don't you invite Myles to Christmas dinner?" Rayne suggested.

"You really think I should?"

"It can't hurt." Rayne hugged her mother. "I'll call you later."

"Trust your heart…trust Taylor's heart."

"I'll try, Mama."

"CAROL, I WASN'T sure I'd hear from you," Myles said when he answered his phone. "But I'm glad you called."

"I went back and forth with it," she admitted. "I wasn't sure I was ready to reconnect with you after everything."

"I'm glad you said that because I do have one pressing question," Myles stated. "What exactly happened between us? I thought things were going well, and then you abruptly stopped taking my calls."

"I called your house, and a woman answered

the phone. I figured you were involved with someone. I decided it was best for me to bow out before I really got hurt. I don't think I told you everything that happened with Rayne's father, but I was very worried I'd go through something like it again."

He seemed to be searching his memory. "My sister came to stay with me for a while. In fact, I remember it was right around that time because she had to listen to me bellyache about losing the woman I was falling in love with."

She was floored. "I never... I don't know what to say..."

"Truth is, I never really got over you."

Carol heard the sincerity in his voice. "Oh, Myles... I'm sorry. I know I can't really make it up to you, but I'd really like for you to have dinner with us on Christmas. That is, if you don't have any other plans."

"You have no idea how much I appreciate this invitation," Myles said. "I wasn't looking forward to my frozen turkey potpie."

Carol laughed. "Are you still eating those things?"

"Cooking has never been a strength of mine. Anyway, yes, I'd love to join your family for dinner. Thank you."

When Carol walked into the kitchen half an

hour later, Ella asked, "Why are you grinning from ear to ear?"

"I just got off the phone with Myles. I invited him to have dinner with us on Christmas. Myles doesn't know anything about my past," Carol said. "I never told him."

"He doesn't have to know, but I have a feeling that it wouldn't matter to him."

Carol paused in the kitchen entrance. "Ella…"

"Huh?"

"How would you feel if I told you I wanted to stay here…on the island? I'd get my own place, of course."

"Nothing would make me happier," Eleanor responded.

The two women embraced.

"What's going on?" Maggie asked as she entered the room.

"I'm thinking of moving back home," Carol announced.

"That's wonderful news," Maggie said. "I can get in my car and zip down here with no problem. You know I never cared much for flying. Daniel's in Atlanta—we'll be able to see each other more with you being closer."

"I was thinking the same thing," she responded.

Daniel grinned. "I just know Ma's up in heaven

smiling down at us. We've finally come to our senses—that's what she's probably saying."

Eleanor nodded in agreement.

WHILE RAYNE WAS out with her mother, Taylor made a solo trip to Charleston. He was looking for the perfect gift for her.

Deacon called while he was running his errand. He parked his car in an empty space outside of a jewelry store.

"Happy holidays," he said when Taylor answered.

"Ha…ha…funny."

"How's it going with Rayne?"

"I believe it's all good," he responded. "We've been getting along well, and we've been talking about the future. We've even gone on some dates."

"You two belong together."

"You keep saying that."

"Are you saying that you don't believe it, too?"

"I'm not disagreeing with you, Deacon. That's not it at all." He paused a moment, then said, "I know what you want me to say… Look, I'll admit it. I love Rayne. I guess I've always loved her on some level, but over the years… anyway, she and I work. We just do."

"She's your soulmate."

"Rayne is everything I want in a relationship.

She's great. I'm actually out here looking for the perfect gift for her."

"You're buying a Christmas present? Wow, that's huge."

"Blame it on Rayne and her family. Deacon, she has this little cousin named Talei. Man, she's so smart. She helps with the twins. And she's only ten years old. The first time I saw her with the babies—she made me feel incompetent."

"I can't wait to meet your extended family. Sounds like Rayne has an incredible support system."

"They're nothing I've ever seen in my entire life, Deacon. I never thought families like this really existed. They're not perfect by any means, but the love and respect they have for each other…it's real. That's what I want for my children."

They talked for a few minutes more before Taylor said, "I'll give you a call later. I need to get in this place before it closes."

He hung up and got out of the vehicle.

Rayne was truly going to be surprised on Christmas morning.

CHAPTER TWENTY-ONE

RAYNE SAT BY herself in the family room, her hands folded in her lap. She was in love with Taylor. She wasn't sure when it happened, but it didn't really matter.

She made the painful decision not to be selfish. Rayne decided to give Taylor what she felt he truly wanted—a divorce for Christmas.

Her eyes watered as she picked up the petition she'd placed on the table before her.

Taylor was an honorable man, and he wanted to do the right thing by Rayne and the twins—she knew this much. But it would be very selfish on her part to allow him to sacrifice his life for them.

Rayne was willing to work out a generous visitation agreement with him regarding Ian and Ivy. She would never keep them away from their father.

She wiped away the tears running down her face. Her heart was breaking into a million little shards over the thought of signing those papers, but it was the right thing to do.

For Taylor.

She heard his voice as he neared the family room and quickly slipped the documents into a nearby magazine. Rayne swiped at her face once more. She didn't want Taylor to know that she was upset.

"Hey, I thought you were in the bedroom getting dressed for tonight," he said.

She pasted on a smile. "I will in a minute. What about you? Are you changing?"

Taylor eyed her. "I haven't decided just yet."

Rayne shook her head at him. "You can be impossible at times."

"If you remember… I told you that when you first came to work with me."

His words made her chuckle. "You sure did."

"I want you to have fun tonight, so I'm going to do it. I'll wear them…the matchy pajamas," Taylor announced.

"Really?"

Taylor nodded.

Jumping up, she squealed with delight. "Thank you. I want us to just have fun. It's Christmas Eve."

"I guess we'd better get dressed then," he said. "I'll use the bathroom upstairs."

Fifteen minutes later, Rayne grinned as Taylor came back downstairs. "You look snazzy in those Christmas pajamas."

He gave her a sheepish grin in return. "I feel silly."

She straightened his neckline. "Loosen up a little. It's all in fun and family."

"The last time I loosened up, we ended up married, but I have to admit that it hasn't been the worst thing to happen to me."

Her smile vanished. "Thanks, I think."

He embraced her quickly, then stepped back. "All I meant is that I'm married to my best friend."

She paused in her tracks. "You really see me that way? As your best friend?"

Taylor nodded. "I do. I hope you feel the same way about me."

"I never really put a label to it, but yeah… you're my best friend."

Their conversation was interrupted when Leon walked out of the kitchen and handed Rayne a five-dollar bill. "You won the bet."

Taylor looked from one to the other. "Okay, what's going on?"

"I told her that she'd never convince you to wear pajamas," Leon said.

Taylor laughed. "I put up a good fight, but she wasn't having it. Now I know why you were so adamant about me wearing them."

"I don't like to lose when money's involved."

Trey and his family were the first to arrive for the evening festivities.

"You, too?" Taylor said when he handed Rayne a five-dollar bill.

Laughing, Trey responded, "Sorry, man… I really thought you'd stick to your guns on the pajama thing."

"I tried, but your cousin is very persuasive."

Rayne picked up a cup of apple cider. "This is so much fun."

He grinned. "I don't think I've ever seen you this excited about the holidays."

She glanced around. "Maybe it's because I'm home… I'm surrounded by the people I love."

Her mother walked into the house with Eleanor and Rusty five minutes later.

When Carol handed Rayne five dollars, Taylor looked at her. "Did you make this bet with everyone?"

"The only other person is Renee. Oh, and Misty."

"And me," Rusty interjected. "Here's my five."

Talei ran up to them and handed Rayne a dollar. She looked up at Taylor and said, "You let me down. I was sure you weren't going to wear the pajamas."

"Talei… I thought you and I had something special."

"We did until you put those on."

"Give her that dollar back," he told Rayne, who shook her head no.

"How you gonna just take money from a little girl? I didn't know you were so ruthless."

Shrugging, Rayne responded, "I only bet her a dollar."

He snatched a five out of her hand. "Talei, here you go."

She grinned. "Now we have something special."

Taylor placed his arm around Rayne, saying, "You know you're going to have to split the winnings with me."

She laughed. "You just gave your share to Talei."

"Man, don't ever place a bet and think you're not going to have to pay up," Trey said. "You want to see your wife turn into an enforcer? She broke my bank when we were younger and took all my money."

"I was seven," Rayne responded. "And he placed a bet knowing he didn't have the money. You know you still owe me eight dollars on that ten-dollar bet. Since it's Christmas, I'll forgive the interest."

"Wait…" Taylor said. "Babe, that's over twenty years of interest. You might want to rethink that."

"Did he just turn traitor on us?" Trey asked

with a short laugh. "Now we're seeing the real Taylor Carrington, y'all…"

Laughter rang around the room.

Rayne leaned into him. "Glad you got my back."

"Always," he responded.

They dined on salmon, spice-rubbed tenderloin with mustard-cream sauce, skillet roasted carrots and whipped potato casserole.

"I had no idea your mom could cook like this," Taylor said.

"You can't be a Rothchild and not know how to cook," Rayne responded. "Even Trey and Leon cook."

"They sure do," Eleanor stated. "I taught them myself. I wanted to make sure my boys could fend for themselves if they married women who didn't know their way around the kitchen."

Taylor looked at Rayne. "So, you've been holding out on me. I didn't know you were practically a chef."

"What are you talking about?"

"You had me thinking that you only baked muffins and made pasta dishes."

"That's because they were your favorites."

Her words warmed him to the core. Taylor couldn't stop smiling.

Carol chuckled. "Rayne's been cooking since

she was eight years old. She cooked her first turkey when she was fifteen. I gave her a few tips, but she did the work and it was delicious."

"Okay, Mama…"

"I'd like to hear more, actually," Taylor said. "Apparently I don't know you as well as I thought I did."

"Okay, so I can cook. Now you know. Omelets used to give me a fit but Misty taught me a couple tricks with that. I'm about to be the omelet queen."

"What else are you keeping from me?" he asked.

"Nothing. You know everything now."

"I bet Rayne's still keeping a secret from him," Trey said. "A really *plum* secret. Right, sugar? Any takers?"

She sent him a sharp glare. "You know you're wrong for this."

"You have my full attention," Taylor stated.

"Are you going to tell him?"

"Trey…"

Everyone had stopped eating.

"What's the big secret?" Taylor asked.

"It's only a secret to you," Leon interjected. "Everybody at this table knows about this… well except for Misty. I think Gia knows already."

Rayne glanced over at Taylor. "It's really not a big deal."

"Will somebody tell me what my wife is hiding?"

"I'll tell you," she responded. "What Trey is dying for you to know is that I performed in *The Nutcracker* for three years. I was the Sugar Plum Fairy."

"She was the youngest Sugar Plum Fairy in the island's history," Carol said proudly.

"Why would you keep that a secret?" he asked. "That's huge."

"Have you seen *The Nutcracker*?"

Taylor nodded. "When did you stop dancing?"

"When I left the island," she responded.

He smiled. "I'm impressed."

Rayne glanced over at Trey. "Satisfied?"

He laughed, then said, "You're gifted, and I used to enjoy seeing you perform. In fact, I'd like to add the poster of you as the Sugar Plum Fairy to the museum."

She gasped in surprise. "Are you serious?"

Trey nodded. "You're part of the Rothchild legacy."

"Thank you for including me."

Misty served fresh-baked gingerbread with dollops of whip cream on top for dessert.

"You cook and have some real skills when it comes to dancing… Wow."

"It's been a while since I put on a pair of ballet shoes," Rayne said. "As for cooking, it's not that much fun when you're only cooking for yourself. Not for me anyway."

"Now you have a family to cook for," Taylor responded.

She smiled. "Yeah, I do. Time to pull out those cookbooks."

After everyone had finished eating, Carol and Eleanor fed and cared for the twins while Rayne helped Misty and Gia with cleaning the kitchen.

Thirty minutes later, she joined the others, who had gathered in the family room.

Rayne glanced around. "Where's Taylor and the twins?"

"He and Talei took them to the room to put them to bed."

When they returned, Taylor sat down beside Rayne. Talei made herself comfortable on the floor beside him.

Leon brought in a plastic container and sat it beside Eleanor.

"What's that?" Taylor inquired.

"It's our stockings," she responded.

Carol picked up her tote, placing it on her lap. "The first Christmas gift of every baby born in the Rothchild family is a handmade Christmas stocking embroidered with their name," she said. "We keep them for life, these stockings. They were a huge part of our traditions. I'd forgotten about that until Ella pulled out the ones in her garage looking for Christmas decorations. I'd like to get back to our family traditions, so I made stockings for Ivy and Ian."

"Mama...that's so sweet and very thoughtful," Rayne responded, her eyes wet with unshed tears. "Thank you for making their first Christmas special. I only wish we had ours. They got lost when we moved away."

"They didn't get lost," Rusty stated. "They were packed away with Leon's and Trey's. Eleanor and I held on to them until you returned."

This time it was Carol's eyes that filled with tears. "Thank y-you. I was so upset when I thought we'd lost them. It felt like we'd lost a tangible connection to the family."

"I felt the same way," Rayne murmured.

"Taylor, did you have a Christmas stocking or traditions when you were growing up?" Carol inquired.

"I had one when I was taken to a group home, but it wasn't as nice as any of these," he responded. "They would write our names on a piece of paper and pin it to a stocking. They were brightly colored, each of them unique and different, but they really weren't ours. They often changed from year to year." Taylor paused a moment, then continued, "As for any traditions—I guess we had one where we'd pick one of the kids in the group home and each write a story about him. On paper, we could give him families, nice houses and money. On Christmas morning, we'd read them while eating our breakfast."

Carol looked at him. "I didn't know you were in a group home. Is that why you sponsor meals and toys for that group home? Rayne's told me about it."

Taylor gave a slight nod. "Child protective services took me out of the house." He looked around at the concerned, loving faces of the people who were insisting he was part of their family now. He took a breath and shared what he'd told almost no one else, besides Rayne. "After my father beat me pretty badly and broke my arm. I was ten years old at the time. I spent the rest of my childhood living at Kline Group Home."

Rayne reached over and took his hand in hers.

"Well, another Rothchild tradition is that we also give every new member of the family a stocking as well," Carol said, dispelling the tension. Her eyes were shining with tears. "Taylor, I hope you like it."

His eyebrows rose in surprise. "Thank you. It's very nice." His voice broke.

"We are your family, Taylor. Don't you ever forget that."

Taylor cleared his throat noisily, then responded, "I'm speechless right now. I never expected any of you to show me so much love. Rayne is an incredible woman, and I see that she comes from an exceptional family. From the moment I came to this island, everyone has been welcoming and understanding without judgment."

"They are pretty special," Rayne agreed. "I want to take this moment to say that I love all y'all. And I'm sorry I never reached out to you. There's a reason why, and before now I've been too ashamed to tell you. But I don't want to take this secret into the new year. By the time I was old enough to want to make contact with y'all again, I'd made a lot of bad choices."

"You were rebellious," Carol murmured.

"More than that. I was wild, and I didn't think I was the kind of person you'd want to know. I left Dallas with this guy I was crazy about. Mama kept trying to tell me that he wasn't good for me, but I couldn't see it at the time." And she continued and told her family the whole story. The drugs, her car, the arrest at the dealership.

"Rayne wasn't guilty," Taylor said. "I knew

it as well as I knew my own name. I wanted to help clear her."

"*Were* you trafficking drugs?" Trey inquired.

"No, and I didn't know that my ex had put them in my car. I'd been with him when he'd taken trips... I suspected that he was selling marijuana but had no clue it was more than that. I should've known better."

"You have nothing to be embarrassed about," Carol said. To the rest of the family, she said, "And Taylor here not only paid for her attorney and gave her her job back, he helped her through college, too."

"Suga, I'm gon' just say it. You should've called your family," Eleanor stated. "You should never try to go through something like that alone. This family got so many attorneys in it... even if you were guilty—you call on us to support you. We love you, Rayne."

"I know. I know that now."

Carol reached for both Rayne and Taylor, squeezing their hands. "Taylor, thank you so much for believing in my girl. Thank you for giving her a job and just being there for her."

He gave her hand a gentle squeeze. "She didn't deserve what happened to her."

Rayne saw the heartrending tenderness of his gaze, and her heart turned over in response.

She tried to ignore the tingling in the pit of her stomach.

Clearing her throat noisily, she rose to her feet. "I need to check on the twins. I'll be right back."

In the room, she watched her babies sleeping. "I can't believe I'm lucky enough to be your mom," she whispered. "If I was given a chance to choose any man to be your father— I'd choose Taylor. I never realized how much he's been through, but I understand now. He's such a good man. He deserves to be happy. Even if that means he won't be my husband. But he will always be your daddy, and I'll be your mom. We love you both so very much."

Rayne picked up a pen. She felt an acute sense of loss as she grabbed the magazine she'd hidden the documents in and signed them.

She eased the door closed and went back to join the others.

Taylor looked up at her and smiled.

Rayne swallowed the despair in her throat and forced a smile of her own.

"Did they wake up?" he asked.

"No, not at all," she responded, trying to keep her voice lighthearted.

Rayne hung their stockings on the mantle over the fireplace. She ran her fingers over Taylor's name, which had been embroidered on the stocking.

When she was joined by Carol, Rayne said, "These are perfect for Taylor and the twins."

"Honey, are you okay?" Carol asked.

"I'm fine."

"Are you sure?"

Rayne nodded. "It's Christmas Eve, and we're surrounded by the people we love. How can anything be wrong?"

"I want you to know that I'm so very proud of you. You've grown up to be such a beautiful, intelligent woman. I know you're going to be a fantastic mom. You already are a great mother."

Embracing Carol, she said, "I love you, Mama. I learned to be a good mom from you. I'm sorry I blamed you for cutting us off from the family."

Rayne glanced over at Taylor, who was in an animated conversation with Talei, Leo and Fawn. "He's so great with children."

"Yes, he is," her mother said.

"That's why I could never understand why he didn't want any of his own," Rayne said. "I used to watch him with the boys at the group home. Taylor's amazing with them."

He gestured for her to join them.

"What's up?" Rayne asked.

"They want you to tell them a Christmas story," Taylor said. "I don't know any."

"Okay, but I want your help. We'll make one up together." Rayne sat down beside him. "I'll start it off. Once upon a time, there was a little boy who had a wish…"

"He had this one wish," Taylor said. "He wished for a family. Then he met a girl, and she took him to her house for Christmas. See, she had a wish, too. She wanted a brother. The entire family was drawn to the little boy, and they decided to give him a very special gift—the gift of a home and a family. They lived happily ever after."

"I love that story," Talei said. "I'm glad the boy got a family."

"Me, too," Taylor responded.

Later that night, when almost everyone had gone to bed, Leon came into the family room and found Rayne there alone.

"You're still up? Where's Taylor?"

"He's in the bedroom rocking Ian to sleep."

Leon peered intently at her. "Are you okay? You look like you've been crying."

"I signed the divorce petition," Rayne said. "He never asked for any of this—the marriage or the twins, so I'm setting him free."

"He loves them. I believe he loves you, too."

"He only sees me as a friend, Leon. And I have to find a way to be okay with that. As for the twins... I won't keep them from him. I'm willing to work out a visitation agreement."

"Are you sure about this?"

She shook her head. "This is not what I want, but I'm sure this is the right thing to do."

"Rayne, I know you love him."

"Don't you see that it's because I love Taylor that I have to let him go?" A tear rolled down her cheek. "My heart is breaking, but he deserves to be happy."

"Talk to him, Rayne. Maybe you two can be happy together," Leon said. "I've watched you and Taylor—y'all seem to get along great."

"He deserves more than just getting along. He's had so little happiness in his life," she replied in a low, tormented voice. "Despite how harsh his childhood was, he's done so much for me, been so supportive. And the only thing he's ever expected of me was to be a good friend. I can't be selfish any longer by holding him to the marriage."

Another tear rolled down her cheek. Rayne hastily wiped it away, then pressed her hand over her face convulsively.

Leon hugged her. "I'm so sorry. I wish there was something I could do."

Rayne stood up. "I need to wash my face. I can't let Taylor see me like this."

"Go to the bathroom upstairs."

"Thanks for everything, Leon."

TAYLOR WAS STANDING over the crib watching the twins when Rayne walked into the bedroom.

"Hey," she said. "I got to talking to Leon and time slipped by. I didn't realize it was almost midnight."

He peered at her face. "Is everything okay?"

She nodded. "Yeah. I'm fine. Why wouldn't I be? It's almost Christmas. I'm here with you and my family. Everything is great."

Taylor heard her words, but they didn't quite ring true in this moment.

Once they were in bed, Rayne surprised him when she asked, "Taylor, could you please hold me?"

"Sure."

She snuggled close to him.

"I had a good time earlier," he said. "I really like your family."

He could feel her smiling. "I told you that you would."

"Yes, you did, and you were right."

"Merry Christmas, Taylor," Rayne whispered.

"Merry Christmas." He pulled her into a tight hug, wishing he could kiss her again. Wishing she wanted him that way.

They clung to each other as the night wore on.

Taylor wanted all of his nights to end like this one.

"YOU'VE BEEN QUIET all morning," Taylor said. "Are you feeling okay?"

"I'm actually glad we have this moment away from the family," Rayne responded. "I have a gift for you."

He smiled. "I have something for you as well."

She handed him an envelope.

"What's this?" Taylor asked.

"It's our divorce petition. I signed it. I'm setting you free as promised. I want you to know that I won't keep the twins from you. I haven't been a good friend to you lately, but I'm hoping this will help to set things right between us. You're the best friend I ever had, Taylor."

"I, um… I find that I need some air."

"Wait…where are you going?" Rayne questioned. "The family is about to open presents in a few."

He had to get out of there because he didn't want her to see the tears in his eyes. He'd been trying to repair their relationship, but he was too late.

"Taylor…"

"I need a moment, Rayne."

He walked out to his vehicle and sat inside

for a while, gathering his emotions. He couldn't summon the will to drive off and leave his babies. So he buried his heartbreak and got out of the SUV.

Leon and Trey were on the porch.

"You're not leaving, are you?" Leon asked.

"Right now, I'm at a loss as to what to do. My gift to Rayne is a wedding ring," Taylor said. "She just gave me divorce papers…signed. She wants out."

"Did you ask her if *she* wants to end the marriage?" Trey questioned.

"The fact that she signed the papers is self-explanatory."

"Maybe she did it because she thinks it's what you want," Leon said. "If I were you, I'd go back inside to fight for your marriage and children."

"I don't think I can bear her rejecting me again. I'm not going to abandon the twins, though, no matter what. I can't do that to them."

"This can't just be about the children," Trey interjected. "Do you love Rayne?"

"Yes, I do," Taylor responded. "I think I've always loved her—I just never put a name to what I was feeling. She was my employee, and I didn't want to compromise her or myself."

"Have you ever told her how you felt?"

Taylor shook his head no. "Trey, I really didn't want to cross that line."

"What's stopping you now? She doesn't work for you anymore."

"I was going to tell Rayne when I gave her the ring. I don't want the divorce."

"If I were you, I'd tell Rayne how much I love her before presenting the ring."

Taylor shook his head. "She doesn't want to be with me, not like that. She just considers me a friend."

"I don't believe that's true," Leon interjected. "My cousin is in love with you, but she wants you to want the marriage out of love and not obligation. Rayne thinks you're sacrificing yourself for the twins."

"That's not it at all," he responded.

"I'm not the one you have to convince. You need to go back into the house and talk to my cousin."

Trey nodded in agreement. "Man, go talk to your wife. I'm not about to let y'all put a damper on my Christmas."

Leon held open the front door. "Taylor, talk to Rayne and tell her how you really feel."

Taylor squared his shoulders. "You're right. Rayne and I have to talk."

He walked back into the house, checking rooms for her until he came to their bedroom.

He knocked on the door before walking inside to find her seated on the bench at the end of the bed.

"I thought you'd left," she said quietly.

Rayne sounded like she'd been crying.

"I couldn't walk out on you and the twins. Not like this and not on Christmas. I'd never tarnish this day for you."

She looked over at him. "I'm sorry if I ruined it for you. I thought I was giving you what you wanted most. I have to say that I'm really confused right now. I really thought you'd be thrilled to finally put an end to this farce of a marriage."

Just as he was about to respond, they heard Talei say, "It's time to open presents. Yay!"

"I guess we should join everyone before they come to find us," he stated.

She gave a slight nod, and they left the room to join the other members of the family.

As soon as they were seated, Talei walked up to him saying, "This is for you, Taylor. I made it."

He opened his gift and was awestruck. It was a leather pouch with jade beading. "Thank you, sweetie."

"I wanted to make you a wallet, but that's how it turned out."

"I love it, Talei." He blinked back tears. "*Wado*, Precious One."

The look of pure delight on her face when she opened the present from him and Rayne meant everything to Taylor.

He reached over and took her hand. "You did good."

Rayne awarded him a smile. "We make a good team."

"I agree," he responded.

Taylor enjoyed watching the children open their presents. He couldn't wait until Ian and Ivy were old enough to get excited about gifts.

As if she'd read his mind, Rayne said, "Before you know it, the twins will be making lists for Santa."

"Can't we just be honest with them about that?" he whispered, keeping his voice down around the other kids. "Let's just tell them that we're the ones buying the gifts."

"When they're older. While they're young like Fawn and Leo—let them enjoy the magic of Christmas."

"We will definitely talk about this later."

"We can discuss it…"

Taylor laughed. "I can tell from your tone that I'm on the losing end of this particular battle."

"Maybe not. It depends on the conversation."

"I have a gift for you, but I want to give it to you later."

"You didn't have to get me anything, Taylor. I know how you feel about Christmas. I really wasn't expecting a gift. I'm thankful that you're here with us."

He met her gaze. "I wouldn't be anywhere else. Ian and Ivy won't remember their first Christmas, but you and I—we'll have shared memories of this day."

Her eyes widened in her surprise. "Taylor Carrington, are you getting into the holiday spirit?"

"Who me?" he asked. "I'm Mr. Grinch, remember?"

CHAPTER TWENTY-TWO

AFTER THE PRESENTS were opened, Rayne was feeling bruised and tender. She almost started crying again when she overhead her mother and Myles speaking fondly to each other near the fireplace.

"Thank you for allowing me to spend Christmas with your family," Myles said. "I've thought about you over the years. I often wondered if you ever married."

"I wasn't lucky in love," Carol responded, then broke into a smile. "Myles, I never forgot about you. I wanted to because I'd thought you were lying to me. I stopped dating because I didn't trust myself anymore. I thought it better to just be alone. But mostly because deep down I knew that you had taken up permanent residence in my heart. I put all my energy into trying to keep Rayne from making the same mistakes I'd made."

"Now that you're back in my life, I have no intention of letting you get away from me."

"I was just thinking the same exact thing," Carol replied.

Rayne bit her lip and hurried to the dining room, where the family was gathering for brunch. She might have lost the love of her life, but she was so glad that her mother was opening herself to love again.

Rayne didn't have much of an appetite. She nibbled on chicken-and-sage sausages, bacon quiche, fruit and a slice of applesauce coffee cake. She noticed that Taylor didn't eat much, either. Although they made small talk earlier, she knew there was still some tension between them. She was still confused by his reaction to the signed petition. She began to wonder if she'd misread the situation between them, but didn't want to make assumptions. Rayne knew they would have a conversation at some point.

"Taylor, you must be saving your appetite for dinner," Carol said.

He awarded her a polite smile. "Something like that."

Rayne didn't like this uncomfortable silence between them. *He said that I was his best friend.* She knew he cared about her, but Taylor always said that he never saw himself married with a family. She did believe he had fallen in love with the twins. He wanted them in his life—and her, too, as a friend. He didn't know how to make that happen without their marriage. She had to make him see that she would be all right without him.

"Taylor, I've been doing a lot of soul searching, and I realized I was unfair to you," Rayne said when they were in the bedroom changing the babies. She couldn't wait any longer for them to finally have that talk. "I should have told you about the pregnancy right away so we could have made a custody plan together."

Taylor held a hand up. "The truth is that I didn't believe I'd ever want children of my own until I met Ian and Ivy. In fact, I'm not planning to return to Los Angeles just yet. I'd like to continue getting to know them. I want to be in their lives. They deserve the love and presence of both parents."

"I don't have a problem with that," she responded.

Ian began crying, prompting Rayne to scoop him up. "What's wrong, little man?" she asked.

Taylor picked up Ivy when she began whimpering, too. "Hey, beauty."

When the baby met his gaze and her perfect little lips turned upward into a smile, Rayne could see that he could barely contain his joy. He grinned at her, and she laid her head against his chest.

"I promise to protect you to the best of my

ability. I will love you and keep you safe, baby girl."

"I'm beginning to believe that she's a daddy's girl," Rayne said. "Ivy lights up whenever you're around. She only has to hear your voice. Ian does, too. Taylor, I'm really glad that you want to be a part of their lives."

"I have a confession to make," Taylor said. "All I've ever really wanted in life is a family. A real family... I even wrote a letter to Santa when I was ten. The only thing on that list was a family who would love me forever. As you can imagine, that wish never came true. Everything I thought and believed about Christmas was false."

"That's why you don't like celebrating."

He nodded. "There wasn't anything to celebrate. Nothing changed for me. Until now."

"What do you mean?"

"My Christmas wish finally came true when I met my children. I have two babies who look at me with such unconditional love and trust. Ian and Ivy own a huge part of my heart, Rayne. I love them. More than I ever thought possible."

Rayne understood what he was feeling because her very own wish had come true as well. "You have no way of knowing how much this means to me, Taylor. You're such a wonderful man… I always believed that you'd be a good father." She hoped Taylor could the truth in her eyes.

"It was my biggest fear that I'd let down a child the way my parents let me down. Rayne, I never felt safe growing up. I found the best way for me to survive was to bottle up my emotions. I make sure that the boys at Kline Group Home know that someone truly cares about them. Deacon and I are very proactive when it comes to those kids. We make sure they have access to sports, tutors—whatever they need."

"You're a helper," she said. "Taylor, you barely knew me when you stepped up to help me. You have always been so compassionate—not just with me, but with all your employees. This is who you are. What you went through did not shape you—the great man you are today is what you became despite that brokenness."

"You should take your own advice," he responded. "Rayne, your past mistakes don't define you."

It was time to be completely honest with Taylor. It was time to trust her heart and to trust his heart. She took a deep, cleansing breath, then said, "When I left Vegas, I knew that I would never love anybody the way I love you, Taylor. I've never looked for a deep, intense love—I was just looking for someone who would care for me, respect me and be good to me." Her eyes watered, and her voice broke. "Then I met y-you... Taylor, you rescued me. You showed me that I'd been settling. And I didn't have to do that anymore. That's why I signed the papers. You don't have to settle, either. The babies and I will always be here for you."

"Rayne, being with you is never settling. I don't want the divorce," Taylor blurted without preamble. "I'm not sure when it happened, but I love you and my children. *You're my family, and I can't lose you.*"

Tears sparkled in her eyes, overflowed and rolled down her cheeks. "I don't want the divorce, either. I love you, too. The thought of you leaving nearly broke my heart, but I signed the petition because I thought it was what you wanted. I thought all you felt for me was friendship."

"What we share is real, and it's more than friendship, Rayne. I promise that I am committed to our marriage for all of eternity."

"That's a long time," she responded as she wiped her eyes. "Are you sure about this?"

"I am," Taylor responded. "If you will have me, issues and all."

The babies in their crib, he wrapped his arms around her.

Taylor kept Rayne in front of him, his lips blazing a trail against the sensitive skin of her neck.

"I think we should join the rest of the family," she said, pulling away from him. "I'm sure they're wondering where we are."

"Do we really have to?" he asked.

Before she could respond, there was a soft knock on the door.

Rayne opened it.

"Are you coming out soon?" Talei asked.

She glanced over her shoulder at Taylor, who said, "Right now. We're right behind you."

"WHERE DID YOU two disappear to?" Carol asked.

"We were talking," Rayne responded as she headed to the kitchen.

Lowering her voice, her mother said, "If I were you, I'd stay out of there. Ella's trying to take over the kitchen. Misty and her mother, Oma, are both in there, too. If you ask me... way too many cooks in there."

Rayne nodded in agreement. "Oh, yeah. Misty's mom doesn't like anyone in the kitchen when she's cooking."

Taylor surveyed the offerings for the Christmas buffet. "Wow, everything looks delicious. Rib roast, Cajun turkey, roasted potatoes, cream spinach, macaroni and cheese... I don't know where to start."

Rayne chuckled. "We also have seafood gumbo, collards, stuffing, and don't let me get started on the desserts. We have enough food to feed a small army, so I hope you brought your appetite."

Clasping his hands together, Taylor said, "I'll do what I can to help the cause."

In an unexpected move, he pulled her into his arms, kissing her.

"Oh, my," someone behind them exclaimed.

Rayne stepped away from Taylor to find Leon standing in the doorway, grinning from ear to ear. And he wasn't alone. Trey and Gia were with him.

"I know you're not familiar with Christmas traditions, but you're supposed to kiss her under the *mistletoe*," Trey stated. "Now, if you don't know what mistletoe looks like, just ask Talei."

Rayne rolled her eyes heavenward. "That man over there…for your information, we don't need mistletoe to instruct us. You were in the military too long, dude. You still need something to remind you to wake up, get up, kiss…"

Taylor threw back his head and laughed. "That was good, babe."

Trey gave up a full belly laugh as well. "All right, cousin. I see you got your man's back. I like that."

She glanced over at Taylor, then said, "Always."

CANDLES AND CHRISTMAS lights twinkling all around them, Taylor looked around the room. He waited until everyone had finished eating because there was something he needed to say. He wanted the entire family to hear him.

He pushed away from the table and stood up.

The room grew silent.

Rayne looked up at him, a confused expression on her face.

"There aren't enough words to describe what I'm feeling right now," Taylor said. "I've seen what it could look like to have a family over the years. But since I arrived on this island... I was able to *feel* part of a family. I came kicking and screaming..."

"You did," Trey interjected.

Gia put her finger to her lips. "Shh..."

Shrugging, Trey said, "I was just agreeing with the man."

Taylor chuckled. "It's all right, Trey. I'm going to be honest. Y'all...yeah, I said it. Y'all got on my nerves with all this Christmas magic...miracles...Christmas, Christmas, Christmas...but I've finally realized that it was never about the gifts or wishes or magic. It's an opportunity to show love. To honor the people in your lives. It's the joy of family. I've witnessed all of this in all of you, seen how you work on past hurts so you can heal and forgive each other. These are the miracles."

He paused a moment to gather his emotions and his thoughts. "I experienced a miracle in my own life when this beautiful woman… Rayne Rothchild, walked into my life. She married me and made me a father—a position I never felt I deserved. As I've gotten to know all of you, I realized that I robbed you when I did not honor Rayne the way that she deserved."

"What are you talking about?" she asked.

"When we got married, we treated it like a mistake. So much so that when you found out you were pregnant, you felt you couldn't tell me. That's not honor. But I'd like to correct that now. Rayne, I'd like for us to renew our vows." Taylor said. "Have a real wedding."

He read the surprise reflected in her shocked gaze. "You're not serious? Are you?"

"Yes. We don't remember our first one much. I don't even think I proposed properly then."

Taylor dropped down on one knee, a black velvet box in his hand.

Rayne gasped. "Taylor, what are you doing?"

He opened the box to reveal a stunning engagement ring and matching wedding band. "Will you do me the honor of renewing our wedding vows in a larger-than-life wedding?

I'm committing myself to be the best husband and father possible. Now, I just need an answer."

Rayne felt her throat tighten with emotion. "Yes!" she managed between tears.

Taylor slipped the ring on her finger.

"Oh, my goodness." She looked at him. "Did you have this planned all along?"

"I'd planned to propose this morning when everyone was opening their gifts, but you blind-sided me."

Touching his cheek, she whispered, "I'm so sorry."

"Don't be. I think this was the perfect moment."

Trey lightly tapped his glass. "Kiss... Kiss..."

Taylor gave her a chaste kiss on the lips.

Rayne broke into a grin and held up her left hand. *"I'm getting married, y'all."*

"You *are* married," Carol teased.

She chuckled. "I love the offer of a larger-than-life wedding, but I just want a small, intimate ceremony with just family. Is that okay with you, Taylor?"

"Don't have any family outside of y'all and Deacon, so that works for me."

"How about this..." she offered. "We get married at the Praise House, then have a really nice reception at Paradis for family and friends."

"I like that much better."

Trey sighed. "Man… I was looking forward to some serious wedding antics."

Everyone laughed.

"In case you haven't figured it out already… he's the comic in the family," Rayne whispered.

"I love it," Taylor responded. "I love it all."

EPILOGUE

Seven months later

"MY MOTHER WAS a beautiful bride," Rayne said as she and Taylor were preparing the babies for bed in their new house on the island. "It was nice seeing her with all of her siblings, happy and laughing."

"That wedding… It was something."

"She was a first-time bride, and I know that, secretly, she's always wanted a big wedding."

"It was done in excellence. I can't wait to see the photos. Very elegant."

"Did you see the way Daniel broke down as he walked her down the aisle? I started crying, too. I was so mad with him for ruining my makeup. I can only imagine what I'll look like in the wedding photos."

"You looked beautiful as always, sweetheart."

She planted a kiss on his cheek. "Thank you for saying that. Let's hope the camera agrees."

"Myles seems to be a good man. I like him."

She sat down in a rocking chair, watching Taylor on the floor with the twins. She heard a hint of emotion in his voice as he talked to them.

He looked up at her and said, "I finally mastered holding Ivy and Ian at the same time. But now they're getting so independent, crawling everywhere."

She smiled. "You're really good with them."

When he looked down at his daughter, Ivy wiggled her bottom and broke into a grin, her two teeth prominent.

They burst into laughter.

"I spoke with Deacon, and he's interested in buying the dealerships," Taylor announced when they left the nursery.

"So you really do want to sell, then?"

"I really do."

"What will you do?"

"I could open another dealership in Charleston."

"Yeah, but you could do that and still keep the other two," Rayne said. "I don't want you selling your business because of us."

"I don't want to be away from you and the twins too often. While I can work remotely, I still have to travel more than I'd like to check on the West Coast dealerships. I'd rather give my family my full attention."

Smiling, she said, "I'll support whatever you decide, Taylor. You know that."

"I believe it's the right decision for us, here with our extended family. This is what I want for Ian and Ivy. I want them to grow up cushioned in love, surrounded by a strong family unit. I want my babies to always feel safe and secure. We have all of that here on Polk Island."

"I couldn't agree with you more," Rayne responded, holding her husband's hand. "A dream come true."

* * * * *